TUSCAN TIME

LOST IN TIME – TIME TRAVEL SERIES
BOOK 3

BELLE AMI

ARE YOU SIGNED UP FOR DRAGONBLADE'S BLOG?

You'll get the latest news and information on exclusive giveaways, exclusive excerpts, coming releases, sales, free books, cover reveals and more.

Check out our complete list of authors, too!

No spam, no junk. That's a promise!

Sign Up Here

www.dragonbladepublishing.com

Dearest Reader;

Thank you for your support of a small press. At Dragonblade Publishing, we strive to bring you the highest quality Historical Romance from some of the best authors in the business. Without your support, there is no 'us', so we sincerely hope you adore these stories and find some new favorite authors along the way.

Happy Reading!

CEO, Dragonblade Publishing

ADDITIONAL DRAGONBLADE BOOKS BY AUTHOR BELLE AMI

The Lost in Time Series
London Time (Book 1)
Paris Time (Book 2)
Tuscan Time (Book 3)

PROLOGUE

October 19, 1503
Montalcino, Italy

IRIS BELLEROSE CHEWED her bottom lip as she stared out the window. Everywhere she looked, she felt danger closing in. Though the view was unimaginably beautiful, she was aware of the ephemeral quality that was time.

Yesterday, she and Marco had gathered the sunshine-yellow stigma from the purple saffron crocus that bloomed in the garden. The Allegretto family's cook had prepared her favorite dish, a delightful *risotto alla Milanese*, which they enjoyed with the sweet moscadello wine produced at the Allegretto vineyard. Candlelight had played across their faces as they dined at a table set before the hearth where a well-fed fire had burnished their skin in gold.

Over the next few days, they strolled through the vineyard, inhaling the scent of earth and vine. They picnicked and ate crusty Italian bread and cheese beneath the shade of an old, gnarled oak tree and planned a future that was tentative but hopeful. For a few hours each day, they gifted each other time to spend on their creative endeavors. Iris wrote in her journal, and Marco sketched her.

The evenings were reserved for love.

Marco had commissioned a wooden tub to be built based on

Iris's description of bathtubs in the future, and they took candlelit baths together, which inevitably ended with them making love, their limbs entwined together beneath white linen sheets.

Iris knew that tomorrow she might be hurled through time again and snatched away from the arms of the man she loved. She sighed. There was nothing to be done about the inevitable. Soon she would disappear like the colors of fall when the snows of winter dusted the hillsides.

For now, Iris tried to forget the evil woman who coveted Marco and was bent on her destruction to have him. The sorceress, Contessa Catarina di Farnese, would not be dissuaded from her vendetta or her pursuit of Marco's third painting, *Il Letto*, from his *Three Stages of Love* series. Catarina would do anything to get her hands on the painting and its time-travel portal. Having hired bandits to rob Marco of the three paintings *La Sedia*, *Il Divano*, and *Il Letto*, she had found unlimited power falling into her hands. But the magic of the ruby ring given to Marco by the soothsayer had given him the power to cajole two women through his painting's portal to help Iris recover two of the paintings.

Still the contessa was not dissuaded from her goal. She knew that all she needed was possession of *Il Letto*, and the portals would remain open. With time travel at her fingertips, the contessa would amass even more wealth and power, and her minions would cause chaos, death, and sorrow on an unimaginable scale.

For Iris, it would also spell disaster. She would be condemned to being a prisoner of time travel forever—wandering the ages with only short periods of bliss with Marco, or even worse, Caterina would close the portals, forever denying Iris a way back to Marco.

Strong arms encircled Iris's waist, and warm lips pressed to her temple. *"Tesoro, perché sei così triste?"*

"Why do I look so glum?" Iris leaned back against Marco's broad chest and lifted her hand to his cheek. "Because I'm afraid we will never be free of her. Because I don't want to lose you. Because I don't want to disappear from here, not knowing if I will ever return to you. Because I am afraid of the battle ahead and who I will have to fight to win."

They clung to each other, and Iris filled her senses with the beauty of the brightly colored garden and the hillsides adorned with clusters of olive trees and thick-limbed oaks dotting the landscape, breaking the pattern of the row upon row of grapevines that climbed the hills of the Val d'Orcia—where, in the distance, lofty peaks jutted skyward, forming the spinal cord of Italy known as the Apennine Mountain Range. With the vines barren of fruit after the fall harvest, only the brightly hued leaves of red, rust, and gold remained as they prepared for winter slumber.

When the fingers of time tore her away from Marco, like the grapevines, her life would go into hibernation, awaiting the warmth of Marco's love to shine on her again and awaken her.

"We have the upper hand now, *amore mio.*"

His warm breath tickled her ear and kindled the desire she always felt for him. Iris should be the happiest woman in the world, and she might have been content were it not for the worries that plagued her. Marco was her soul mate, and she belonged to him heart, body, and soul, but she worried over the many obstacles that beset them. Besides the obvious problem of being a time traveler, she worried that she would never bear Marco any children. What if being a time traveler had stolen that possibility from her? The thought was crushing, but it was the one fear she never voiced aloud to him, as other threats seemed more pressing.

"That is exactly what troubles me," she said. "We must not let our guard down, and I sense she is not without a plan, a plan to steal our happiness." Iris looked up, admiring the squareness of his jaw and the broad cheekbones that sharply defined his face. After all the horrors she'd experienced, she could never quite believe that he was hers. His love for her defied explanation, but never did she doubt its veracity.

He turned her toward him, and his lips blazed a path down her neck. "She will not succeed, *tesoro*. The fire of our kisses will burn away your doubts."

It was as if he'd read her thoughts. Love was surely a mystery, but was it capable of conquering all the boulders that blocked their path to happiness?

The tingling in her limbs made her cry out. *"Basta!"* It was happening again—she could feel herself fading, and tears flooded her eyes. Marco wrapped his arms tightly around her, trying to hold on to her. If only it would stop—if only he could keep her with him. But she knew he would not win this battle, no matter how hard he tried.

Iris grabbed his face and pressed her lips against his. She would need the scent and taste of him to make it through the days ahead.

"No," he shouted.

"Ti voglio bene, caro. I love you, my darling," she cried, and her heart felt as though it were being torn from her breast.

"Buon Dio, non portarmela via." His fervent plea, *God do not take her from me* rose to the heavens. But it was too late. A flash of lightning blinded them, and she was gone.

The battle ahead had begun.

CHAPTER ONE

New York, New York

G ABRIELLA D'ANGELO TAPPED her foot on the floor in a sharp staccato rhythm, mirroring her impatience. She was annoyed beyond reason and her patience was at an end.

Where are Emily and Jenee?

She loved her girlfriends, but how dare they make her feel like a girl who'd been stood up by a date? She glanced at her cell phone for the umpteenth time, noting the passage of another five minutes. She reviewed in her mind what they'd agreed upon. Maybe she'd misunderstood.

Basta, do not doubt your own sanity. There is nothing wrong with your hearing.

Being a professional chef meant adhering to a strict schedule, and time was something precious, not to be wasted. Gabriella was *always* aware of the fleeting passage of time.

What they'd decided between them was clear in her mind. They'd agreed to do their own thing and meet back at the bench in front of Marco Allegretto's masterpiece series, *The Three Stages of Love*, after an hour, and now it was an hour and forty-five minutes later, and they hadn't shown. It wasn't like them to be late like this. Gabriella was beginning to worry. *Where are they?*

A passing man and woman paused to study the paintings. Gabriella glanced at them and received a withering glare. They stared down at her tapping foot, evidently displeased with her disregard for the respectful, contemplative quiet of the museum. She pinned her foot to the floor, smiled apologetically, and bit her tongue to refrain from telling them to mind their own damn business. Gabriella had a short fuse but was quick to forgive. When had the world become such an intolerant place?

Perhaps that was why she'd sought refuge in a kitchen and become a chef. The less interaction with the outside world, the better. She rarely argued with the pots and pans in her family's Italian restaurant in Chicago. She certainly didn't throw meat cleavers or knives at her staff like she'd heard some chefs were known to do. Sure, she had an Italian temper, but she rarely lost it. Hers was a contained world where she yielded control. Also, she was proud to say she never received complaints from disgruntled patrons about the dishes she gave life to. Her gastronomic creations were a source of great pride to her. Gaby was confident in her cooking skills, even if she doubted herself in other ways. Many of the restaurant's dishes were old family recipes that she'd re-created and rebalanced to suit today's modern cuisine and tastes. Always with a mind to her weight struggles, she'd pared down the unhealthy ingredients and enhanced the more flavorful ones. Italian cooking was best when simplicity ruled the day. Fresh ingredients, tastefully prepared, were the keys to success.

The couple walked away, and Gabriella had to refrain from sticking her tongue out at them. Instead, her foot resumed drumming. *Good riddance.* Another glance at her cell phone put her in mind to leave. She texted her friends again and said she'd wait another fifteen minutes and then head back to Emily's place. She'd make dinner for the three of them—at least that would keep her busy while she waited for Jenee and Emily to return. It had promised to be the perfect girlfriend getaway. Em, a magazine editor, had snagged three tickets to the opening of the Allegretto exhibit and had invited Jen, a successful dermatologist based in L.A., and Gaby for a long-overdue visit.

Gaby blew out a breath, trying not to keep glancing at her watch. Her friends had gone MIA, and she had no idea why. The whole thing was perplexing.

Distracting herself, she opened her purse and took out the book she carried with her everywhere. They'd met in a virtual book club and had bonded over their love of *The Time Traveler's Lover*. The novel had been discovered in a trunk in an attic of a Paris townhouse that was being subdivided, refurbished, and turned into apartments. How often had Gabriella imagined a burly demolition worker sledgehammering a wall and finding the hidden treasure? That the manuscript hadn't been lost or destroyed was a miracle. Thank goodness the worker was prescient enough to realize it was historically significant and had turned it over to the authorities.

Because of the detailed descriptions of World War II and the German occupation of Paris, the unsigned manuscript was thought to have been written by an eyewitness to what had happened. Perhaps a Jewish woman who'd been deported and murdered in a concentration camp, or a member of the French Resistance who'd fought and was tortured to death and forgotten. Was she dead or alive? Time and the passage of years had buried her identity. No one had come forward to claim the book as her own. The mystery was compelling, and when it was published, it gripped the public's imagination, becoming an instant international bestseller.

Gabriella opened the book to one of her favorite sections and began to read, losing herself within the beautiful prose...

The hands of time came for me, with a windy gale so fierce it could have uprooted a tree and carried it away as if it were no more than a single strand of straw. The sound was so deafening that a gunshot whizzing toward me was as silent as snow falling from the heavens. My body felt as if it were held tight within the coils of a boa constrictor, and my scream was a mere grace note that pounded from a keyboard yet was barely heard. I was not myself. Who I was, what I was, or what I would be was lost to me. Where I was going was a conundrum that I had no clue how to resolve. All I could do was surrender to whatever time had in mind for me. I was indeed a creature deprived of any control over my fate. I was a captive of time. And so, I have remained against my will for so long that I've nearly forgotten what came before, but never the moment when it all began and the loss of those I loved.

No one knew if the novel was based on a true story or if the author had written what she knew to have happened. She wrote of Nazi atrocities and what she'd experienced during the horrors of the 1940s in Paris so vividly that Gabriella wondered if that part of the story were true. In the book, she gave vivid testimony of the cruel execution of her parents. What the author described was all too real to have been a fabrication. But that was where reality took flight. In the book, the heroine miraculously survived the bullet of a Nazi officer at point-blank range after watching him murder her parents in cold blood. When he pointed the gun at her with the intent of killing her too, the bullet passed through her and she vanished into the ether of time, appearing and disappearing, from one era to another, until she landed in Renaissance Florence and met one of the most revered artists of all time. In a crowded marketplace their eyes met, and it was love at first sight.

Even though the story didn't have a happily-ever-after ending like most historical romance novels, it still mesmerized, holding readers glued to the pages as they wept with joy and sorrow over every heart-wrenching, beautifully written word.

The three friends had formed their own book club that they referred to as the *I'd Rather Be Alone Book Club*. They met once a month on Zoom to chat about the books they were reading and the absurdity of their dating encounters. And to drink wine, of course. But of all the books they'd read, none meant more to them than *The Time Traveler's Lover*. Maybe because it represented their most fervent wish to find their own soul mates.

Iris Bellerose, the time traveler, and Marco Allegretto, the painter, had found what eluded most people: true love. In the story, Iris and Marco found each other, even though they'd been born hundreds of years apart. Love had triumphed over time. Even when time ripped them apart again, it could never destroy what was meant to be. They were bound to each other and vowed to find each other again, no matter the cost.

Sitting on the bench, Gabriella clutched the book to her chest and stared up at the painting, and a sense of calm came over her.

According to the book, the woman in the paintings was none other than Iris, the time-traveling heroine of the story, and the man who cast adoring eyes on her was Marco Allegretto, the famous Renaissance painter. It didn't hurt that the Renaissance master was positively swoon-worthy, with shoulder-length black hair, intense, dark eyes, and the body of an Adonis. Not to mention he was considered a genius, who stood on equal footing with Leonardo, Michelangelo, and Raphael.

It would take a considerable effort not to give her friends a piece of her mind when they finally did show up. Their abandonment conjured up old feelings of insecurity. It was as if she'd been plunked back to her childhood, and was once again the plump, unpopular, pimply-skinned girl of her teens, yearning to be friends with the popular girls in school. That sad creature was never far below the surface. Her skin had eventually cleared up and, through careful eating habits and regular workouts, the excess pounds had melted away. Em and Jen had often compared her to Sophia Loren, which was truly flattering, even though Gaby had trouble believing it. Maybe it was because of the childhood trauma of being teased and being an outcast. Some days were harder than others.

Was it irrational to feel sorry for herself? Was it way off the mark to get so worked up over their tardiness? All would be forgiven if they would just show up!

Five more minutes, and I'm taking a cab back to the apartment. Gaby glanced at the painting in front of her, *Il Letto,* translation: *The Bed.* She tilted her head, imagining what the woman must have looked like. The woman was nude except for a red scarf draped over her waist that hid her private parts. Allegretto stood nude from the waist up, his muscled back appearing to flex and ripple with excitement in the flickering candlelight where light and shadow danced over his skin.

Emily had explained this was what art historians called chiaroscuro, a dramatic effect of light and shadow used by many Renaissance artists like Leonardo and Caravaggio. Unlike Emily and Jenee, Gaby was not an art aficionado; however, the painting spoke to her with its timeless beauty. And as for the artist himself, what woman could resist him? Gaby could not help but be mesmerized by the emotions he expressed with paint.

For some reason, art historians and conservators could not explain the reason for the mysterious fading of color that had turned the woman in the paintings into a ghostly image. Everything else in the work was as vivid as the day Marco Allegretto had given life to the painting.

Nevertheless, Allegretto had captured the most profound love Gaby had ever seen. The connection between the woman and the man pulsed with erotic tension that leaped off the canvas. She could only imagine the smoldering union that was about to ensue. Her own sexual unions were laughable in comparison. It was one of the reasons that she, Emily, and Jenee had taken a "timeout" on relationships.

It seemed that all three of them had experienced disappointments and heartache when it came to matters of love. Her response to her well-meaning parents was always the same: was it unrealistic to want to be head-over-heels crazy for someone?

I want to feel passion, and I want someone who makes me feel like I'm the most important thing in the world.

Her parents never failed to remind her that she read too many romance books and that real life wasn't like that.

Why isn't it?

Gaby would rather be alone than settle for less than absolute passion. She wanted more, and if she couldn't have it, she would live alone. Besides, she had a great career, doing something she loved—creating magnificent meals for the restaurant's loyal clientele, who constantly sent messages of praise to the kitchen and showed their appreciation through word-of-mouth both in real life and by flooding social media with snapshots and videos of their meals.

At least I've got that part of my life right.

If spinsterhood was her fate, then so be it.

The thought brought an unbidden tear. She sniffled, wiping it away before it encouraged more and flooded her senses with unfulfilled wishes.

Gabriella watched the man and woman who'd given her a dirty look leave, and she realized she was alone in the gallery. An eeriness skittered up her spine, causing the hair on her arms to stand on end. Something moved in the periphery of her vision, drawing her gaze back to the painting.

She shook her head and rubbed her eyes. *I must be hallucinating.* She could have sworn on a stack of Bibles that she'd seen the figures in the painting move. Of course, it was ridiculous. *This is what comes when I dredge up old insecurities that I should have laid to rest long ago. It must be the chiaroscuro, or maybe last night's drinking binge.*

She'd never gone through therapy—her parents had no use for it. They were old school and old country, and believed that you toughened up and solved what ailed you with the help of your family.

If it were a hallucination, it would certainly stop—but instead, she saw candlelight flickering on the bed's headboard in the painting. She drew in a breath, mesmerized by what she was seeing...

An invisible brush worked its magic, bringing vivid color to the faded image of the woman in the painting. Her cheeks grew rosy, her red hair became brighter and more vibrant, and, most disconcertingly, her colorless eyes turned an emerald green. Gaby could not look away as the woman's chest rose and fell with each breath.

It must be her state of mind. It was playing tricks on her.

Gabriella shivered as though someone had opened a door and a cold rush of air had blown in. Her eyes darted around, searching for an explanation for the sudden drop in temperature. There were no windows, and except for a shaft of light that poured from a skylight, everything was hermetically sealed and temperature controlled for the sake of the precious art. She should have brought a jacket or a sweater, but it was summer, and New York was in the grips of a heatwave. Maybe that had something to do with the museum turning up the air conditioning.

But that wasn't the only odd thing occurring.

The floor had begun to vibrate. She jumped up, intending to leave the gallery, but was immobilized by an invisible pressure that pushed her back down onto the bench. Panic seized her, she became dizzy, and a ringing echoed in her ears. The vibration became stronger, making the bench shake. Gaby gripped the edge as if her life depended on it.

I must be having a panic attack.

Her stomach churned, her vision blurred, and her throat constricted—but oddly, her sense of smell and taste, which were highly developed, grew stronger. Of all things, in the middle of Manhattan, she caught the scent and taste of salty air one would encounter only at the seashore.

She glanced longingly at the exit. If only Emily and Jenee would show up, everything would be set right, and the world would return to normal. But her friends were nowhere in sight. Gaby would have to rely on her own inner strength, such as it was, to get her through this.

Just close your eyes, breathe deeply, and focus.

But just as she thought she had reclaimed her grip on reality, a voice whispered in her ear, *"Devi aiutarci."*

Gabriella's eyes flew open, and she whipped her head around, seeking the source of the plea. No one was in the gallery, yet she heard the words again.

"Devi aiutarci."

She covered her ears, but the whisper continued to echo in her ears, more intense, beseeching her.

"Please, help us."

What in God's name is going on? Help who? How? Again, Gabriella looked around, searching for the source of this crazy request.

The emptiness of the gallery carried its own message. She must be having a mental breakdown. There was no other plausible explanation.

The whisper became louder, and she realized it was coming from the painting.

She gasped as the man in the picture came to life, turned, and cast an angry gaze at her. She screamed, but no sound emerged. The artist picked up the wine glass on the table in the painting and hurled it at her. His anger and frustration were palpable. It was impossible, but the glass broke through the painting, shattering into a million pieces around her, like glittering diamonds in the light.

The room began to spin around her, and the artist reached out from the painting and grabbed her wrist. Gabriella tried to pull her hand from his grasp, but he held her in a steely vise. The red-headed woman in the painting also stood, her green, catlike eyes glittering. She smiled, and Gabriella heard what could only be the woman's voice in her head: *Don't be afraid. We will not hurt you. Only you can stop the madness once and for all. But you must help us. You are our last hope...*

Overcome by faintness, Gabriella lifted her free hand to her forehead, and the man in the painting grabbed it and pulled her toward the canvas. Her eyes widened as she moved through the painting as though she were stepping through a thick fog on a dark night. She was keenly aware of every cell in her body humming as though on a different frequency. And then she felt a force pushing her and knew she was falling through the dark void, tumbling head over heels. She screamed but could hear nothing other than the sound of a strong wind whistling past her.

Where she'd end up, she had no idea, but the soothing voice of the woman reached out to her once more. *No harm will come to you. Trust in your destiny. A new world is opening to you. You are the link that will end this once and for all. We need you, Gabriella.*

Maybe this is what death is. Maybe I'm dying and this is some strange sort of afterlife. Despite the soothing voice of the woman in her head, Gabriella wanted this crazy house-of-horrors ride to end.

Just when thought she was really going to lose it, the wind eased up and the scent of the sea tingled her nostrils.

Oh God, I really am dying. I'm falling into some deep abyss.

Her life was over, and all the dreams she had would end with her as she plummeted to a watery grave, beneath tumultuous swells of freezing black water.

She was a lapsed Catholic, but even the most agnostic could not help but turn to prayer in the face of such a paralyzing unknown. Gaby closed her eyes and whispered the Lord's Prayer, and then the Ave Maria just to be on the safe side.

In that instant caught between fear and overwhelming anticipation, she knew that nothing would ever be the same…

CHAPTER TWO

Tuscany, Italy
October 16, 1902

G ABRIELLA OPENED HER eyes. She was lying on the grass. The scent of the sea filled her nostrils, and the sound of waves crashing on the shore seemed only a few feet away. A misty fog floated around her. Either she was dreaming or she'd died and ascended to heaven, because this was not Manhattan. The cells in her body were still vibrating from being hurled through the dark tunnel.

She turned onto her side and sat up, looking around her to get her bearings. She was on a stretch of grass, but in the distance, she could make out the edge of a cliff.

Things could be worse. I could have landed at the edge of the cliff.

Gaby eased up onto her knees and stood. Her legs felt a bit wobbly, but nothing seemed to be sprained or broken.

A pounding sound resonated in the distance. She turned in a circle, trying to ascertain where it was coming from, and more importantly, where she was. It sounded like the thundering of hooves. Her heart began to hammer in her chest, matching the rhythm of the horse or horses. At least, she *thought* they were horses. Whatever the source, it was getting louder and therefore closer.

Adrenaline raced through her veins, and she squinted into the fog that had enveloped her, trying to see. She whipped her head around, looking for somewhere she might hide from whoever or whatever was coming toward her.

Too late!

From the mist emerged a black-cloaked figure astride a black stallion. Frightened out of her wits, she froze. At the last second, the horse reared, and Gabriella saw the beast's eyes widen to the size of saucers. He was as frightened as she was. The horse's hooves clawed the air, and the madman who rode it yelled at her to get out of the way.

Reclaiming her senses, she stumbled back, but her heel caught on something, and she lost her footing. She tumbled over the side of the bluff, her screams echoed in the wind that roared around her, and she felt herself fly. Gabriella flailed her hands, trying to find something to hold on to. She heard the rip of her blouse as it caught and felt a searing pain slice across her abdomen. It was all she could do to hold on to consciousness. Angry curses assaulted her ears, and if she'd had the wherewithal, she'd have hurled back her own set of colorful expletives, but given that she was trying not to die, she focused on grabbing something to hang on to.

There! Her hand latched on to some sort of root growing out from the side of the bluff. Gaby held on for dear life. She dared not look down, but the sound of waves crashing on rocks told her that if she let go, she was doomed.

"Give me your hand, damn it!" a harsh voice demanded from above her.

She looked up and saw the man in the black cloak leaning down toward her, his hand outstretched.

"Why should I trust you? You almost ran me down with your horse. You might take my hand and then let go of me."

He gave a brief chuckle. "Given the situation, I daresay you have no choice in the matter."

Whoever he was, he had an English accent, which brought her an infinitesimal bit of comfort. Emily was English, and despite the abandonment by her friends at the museum, Gabriella still trusted her friends and hoped she could somehow get back home from wherever this place was. Given his accent, she assumed she was in England.

The mist had begun to turn into rain and the sky had darkened. Her fingers had gone numb, and she would not be able to hold on to the branch much longer. She tried to see his face, but given the situation, she could barely see anything. If she could only see his eyes, she would know whether to trust him.

"Your hand, signorina." She could make out a gritted set of gleaming white teeth, as if patience did not come easy. He had switched to Italian, and she had no idea why he would switch to a language other than English. Did he somehow know she was of Italian background and was trying to get her to trust him?

The rain made her grip on the branch slip, and she gasped as she tried to hang on.

She was going to die, and no one would ever know. *That is, except for this exasperating man.*

"*Maledetto!* This is your fault!" she cursed at him.

"I can assure you it isn't," he rasped out. "Now, will you let me save your life?"

She couldn't see his face, but she could hear the anger in his voice, which seemed more threatening than the sea.

"I can't. I'm too scared to let go." She had a ridiculous thought. Thank God her personal trainer had made her do all those push-ups and pull-ups at the gym. Then she had another outrageous thought: *What if I'm too heavy for him to pull up? But what other chance do I have?* "Okay, okay. Please help me."

She heard a deep exhalation of breath, followed by more grunting and cursing in both English and Italian. A moment later, a large hand clamped around her wrist, and she felt herself hurtling through the air once more—but this time she was going up, not down. She screamed in shock and fear and scrunched her eyes closed. "Don't let go! Please don't let go!"

And then everything stopped. She'd landed on something hard. Not the ground. She instinctively wrapped her arms around the hardness and held on tight.

"Am I dead?"

"No."

She realized she was lying on top of *him*. Her rescuer. Well, technically it was his fault that she needed rescuing in the first place.

A rush of heat coursed through her body at the intimacy of their positions. She could feel every sinew of his muscular frame.

She opened her eyes. *Blue.* She blinked a few times because she'd never seen that shade of blue before. His eyes were beyond blue. They were aquamarine, like the Mediterranean, made even more striking by his golden tan. She couldn't tell what color his hair was, as it was wet and plastered to his beautifully shaped head.

Oh, God! He's gorgeous. He must be a male model. Or an actor. Or both.

"May we get up now?" he asked.

"Oh! I'm sorry." She rolled off him and gasped at the sudden sharp pain in her abdomen. She closed her eyes, trying to gather enough strength to stand.

"Here, let me help you," he said.

She nodded and reached out her hand to him. He pulled her up as though she were a rag doll. Her feet touched solid ground, and his arms steadied her.

"What in God's name were you thinking standing on the edge of this bluff? As a matter of fact, who in God's name are you, and what are you doing here? This is private property, and you're trespassing."

"I-I…" Gabriella could scarcely catch her breath, and she trembled at his withering gaze. Answering his questions was more than she could do until she figured out a story about how she got there.

Something about his appearance didn't fit. Where was *here*? She was having trouble thinking of a plausible story, and the pain in her abdomen was making things worse.

It was all too much. Gabriella was no shrinking violet, but her current travails had taken a toll, and she felt herself sway. A haze darkened her vision, and her legs buckled. She was vaguely aware of being caught and lifted by muscled arms and pressed against a broad chest. She pressed her face against his chest, and she could hear his heart beating wildly. Once again, that rush of heat pervaded her senses.

She opened her eyes again and saw his expression. Anger. Frustration. And something else. Humor? Seeing that flicker of laughter lurking in his beautiful blue eyes made her smile.

"Thank you for saving me," she whispered. She didn't know what else to say, so she reached up and pressed her lips against his, and then the dark haze overcame her, and she closed her eyes once more.

"Vixen, what a bother you are," he muttered. "Come, Xanthus." The horse whinnied, following behind. Her savior's long strides carried them away from the bluff's edge. She opened her eyes just enough to peek at this man who was unlike any other she had known before. In what little light there was, she could see long tendrils of wet, wavy hair touching his shoulders and a face so angled that his cheekbones seemed chiseled from stone. Naturally, his stony face was set in a grimace. Even as she felt his wrath, she was tempted to sink her finger into the dimpled cleft in his chin. He was a curmudgeon and completely unmannerly, but he had saved her life and was now carrying her to safety. Somewhere.

She was completely without rational thought and hadn't even noticed her own appearance. *I doubt I look even half as good as this guy.* Her eyes flickered open, and she noted his gaze had dropped to her chest and that his breaths became ever shorter and more labored with every step. He stumbled but recovered himself. "Blast it, cover yourself before we both take a tumble."

His words roused her from her dreamlike state. She looked down and could see her blouse had torn open and her chest was in full view. Luckily, she was wearing a bra. She tugged at what was left of her blouse, trying to cover her breasts, but it was near impossible, as the delicate fabric was completely shredded. "I can't cover up—my blouse is completely torn. Maybe you can just stop looking at them."

He muttered another curse and averted his eyes, focusing on the path ahead, but his lips twitched in amusement.

What is it with this guy? He's cursing one second and smiling the next.

Gabriella hadn't been paying attention to where they were going, and she was surprised when he kicked open a massive wooden door and bellowed up the stairs, "Aunt Kitty, your person is required."

He shook his head like a dog, and beads of moisture took flight. A minute later, a beguiling woman dressed head to toe in black widow's weeds made her way down an imposing red-carpeted staircase. The older woman's gown reminded Gabriella of a picture of her great-grandmother after her great-grandfather died.

Strange. Why is she dressed like that?

"What can be the matter, Jack? You are forever up to some-thing." The woman's eyes widened at Gabriella. "Who—? Oh, dear me, what have you done now?"

If this Jack person had cast a critical gaze at her earlier, it was nothing compared to the vexation on his face when he answered his aunt. "I saved this demented woman's life, that's what I did. She was about to jump from our bluffs. I considered allowing it to unfold but decided better of it. It would have caused an annoying investigation from the local authorities, which would have interfered with your upcoming soirée. So, against my better judgment, I intervened. Something it seems I may live to regret."

Even though he was glaring at her, Gaby couldn't help but notice how unbearably handsome he was. "You can put me down now. I think I can stand on my own," she said.

"Are you sure you won't faint on me?"

"I'm quite sure," she replied. "Fingers crossed," she added.

His lips twitched again as he set her down gently. He still held her arms to steady her.

"Thank you." She took a step back, and pain ripped through her body. She looked down at her wet, muddy midriff, and for the first time saw that she was injured. Blood seeped from an open wound on her stomach. The world spun around her and a wave of nausea took hold, and she stumbled and would have tumbled to the floor had he not pulled her into his chest.

"Good Lord, she's going to faint again."

As if from a distance, Gabriella registered Aunt Kitty's reply. "The poor girl. Can't you see, Jack? She's hurt. Bleeding. Take her to your bedroom, and I'll send Mrs. Livingstone to attend to her."

"For Christ's sake, Kitty, why on earth my bedroom?"

"Because, my dear nephew, every other room in the house is spoken for. The guests will begin arriving tomorrow. If you weren't so busy scrounging the hills for Etruscan treasure, you'd have remembered a full house of guests will demand our attention, and everything must be made ready. The simplest solution is to put her in your bedroom until other accommodations can be arranged."

"But it's inappropriate for her to occupy my rooms. I may have lost my earldom because of my snake cousin, but I will not lose my good name."

"Oh, bother, Jack, your good name is not at risk. You saw its demise long ago, what with your rogue behavior and wandering the world without a care for your father and the estate. What did you expect would happen? The girl needs tending to, and now is not the time to worry over a scandal long since realized."

"But look at her." He sized Gaby up from head to toe. "For all we know, she could have orchestrated this entire debacle."

"Don't be ridiculous. I did not raise you to be cold-hearted and without compassion. You can see the poor girl is injured. And since she fell into your hands, literally, it seems, you must rise to the occasion and see to her needs. Don't make me scold you into doing your duty."

Jack shook his head, scooped Gaby up, and carried her up the staircase. He cursed under his breath, "God's blood, had I known what trouble you would be, I would have left you to the sea and the fate you well deserved."

The whole situation had taken its toll, and although Gabriella hated being discussed as if she wasn't there, she didn't have the wherewithal to protest. She considered slapping the arrogant man's face, but being dropped on the stairs might result in even more injuries.

She tried to hold back, but enough was enough—the dam burst and tears poured from her eyes. No less embarrassing, her nose dripped, and she sniffled like a child. His harsh words had quashed her anger and replaced it with insecurity and guilt. "I'm sorry to trouble you, and I'll be gone as soon as possible."

Their eyes met, and she glimpsed what looked like a shred of compassion and maybe even a guilty conscience. "Good Lord, no tears. I can't abide a woman's tears."

"I'm s-sorry," she said, taking small breaths, hoping to stanch the flow. "If I could stop them, I would."

He expelled a deep breath. "Are you from Piombino?"

"Where?"

"God's blood. The village and port of Piombino are very near here."

Gabriella trembled. "Wh-where am I?"

Jack's impatience returned, and he didn't attempt to disguise it. "Allow me to enlighten you about what you seem to be having difficulty comprehending. You are in Maremma, southern Tuscany, to be exact. That's in Italy, in case you didn't know."

"I know where Tuscany is," she said through gritted teeth. *This guy is too much!* "What year is it?"

His eyes widened at that. "You must have hit your head."

"Please, just tell me." Panic was beginning to grip her once more.

"It is the calendar year 1902, the month of October in the year of King Edward VII's coronation. And an admirably good day it was to see my fine friend take the throne. Bertie is a delightful chap, and I warrant he'll make an upstanding monarch. Although, for now, he, like everyone else back home, isn't speaking to me."

"But that's impossible." Gaby covered her mouth, gripped by sudden nausea, and she feared she might upchuck all over the pompous man.

"What is impossible?" He arched a brow. "Are you suggesting I don't know what year it is or where my aunt's villa resides?" He smirked. "Or perhaps you are insinuating that I don't know who rules over the British Isles."

She sucked in a breath, hoping to quiet her anxiety. "No, no, of course not, but…" And then everything rushed back to her. *1902? How is that even possible?* Wasn't it just an hour ago that she was staring up at Marco Allegretto's painting in the Metropolitan Museum of Art in New York, an ocean away? *More than one hundred years away!*

Gaby closed her eyes and made herself breathe deeply. There was no way she could tell this Jack person who she was and where she came from. He'd probably call the police on her and have her arrested.

She'd read about what they did to women in this era who were declared insane: ice baths and electric shock treatments. Women suffered this fate more than men, as it was a tidy way for men to rid themselves of an unwanted wife.

"But what?" he asked, his eyes narrowed. "Your delay in answering me makes me think you're hiding something."

Damn him! Gaby's temper flared, and she snapped back, "Hiding something? You and your horse almost killed me! Why should I confide anything in you?"

"Perhaps you're a spy sent by my traitorous cousin."

"I have no idea what you're talking about, and you, sir, are paranoid!"

"Quite a big word for a peasant."

"How dare you insult my intelligence. I'd rather be a peasant than some pompous English la-di-da who has his head up his a—"

Gaby bit her lip just in time. Nevertheless, she'd clearly hit a nerve, because Jack kicked open the door to his bedroom, nearly knocking it off its hinges. He strode to the bed and dumped her on it like a sack of potatoes.

She gasped at the pain in her midriff. "Do you know something? You're a bully." Fresh tears stung her eyes as she saw the anger flash in his. She covered her face, worried he might hit her.

"Rest assured, under no circumstances would I ever raise my hand to a woman," he said in a stiff tone. "I am a gentleman, and I am respectful of the opposite sex, no matter her station. What is your name, wench?"

"Gabriella." *Wench?*

"Your surname."

"Gabriella D'Angelo." She wanted to ask him why he was so angry at her. His anger seemed so misplaced, as if he was taking out on her what was meant for another. He'd mentioned his traitorous cousin, but she dared not ask him. Everything about him was formidable, from his towering height to his broad shoulders, to his brawny arms and thighs. And those huge hands! When he looked at her, it made her quiver like a leaf caught in the bluster of an October wind. She'd never had such an emotional reaction to anyone, let alone a man, and it was wreaking havoc with her ability to think clearly. Her attraction to him mystified her. Yes, he was gorgeous, but she'd never allowed herself to fall for a handsome man in the past. *What does it say about me?*

"I will make inquiries as to who your people are. Hopefully, we can find your relatives so that they can collect you."

Gaby rolled over and bit her lip, trying to control the torrent of tears that was threatening to burst, but she couldn't keep her shoulders from shaking.

"Damn and blast!" he said.

Gaby refused to turn around. Refused to say anything more. She heard Jack's footsteps recede and then the door close with a thud.

Good riddance, you jerk!

How had she gotten here, and why was she here? And more importantly, where could she go? It seemed her time in this house was limited. All she wanted was to go home, but if Jack was correct, she'd landed in Italy in the early 1900s. There was no going home from here. At least not by boat or airplane.

She eased onto her back and scrunched her eyes closed as the pain from her midriff took her breath away. *I need to get up. Find something to treat this wound.*

Oh my God! What if it gets infected? Did they have antibiotics in 1902? Okay, calm down, Gaby! Get a grip on yourself.

"I told you, I cannot abide a woman's tears."

Gaby's eyes flew open in surprise at his return. A jolt of pain made her flinch, and the sudden motion elicited a cry as a sharp stab tore through her.

Jack hastened to her side and sat on the edge of the bed. There was contrition in his face. "Now, now, it's not that bad. Let me have a look." His nearness made her heart thunder in her chest, and she feared he could hear it. Her keen sense of smell drank up his masculine scent that overrode the salty brine of the sea. An exotic, spicy, woodsy aroma emanated from his skin and tickled her olfactory senses.

Gently he raised the shredded blouse and frowned as he examined her wound. "It's not too bad, just a surface cut. Mrs. Livingstone will clean and bandage you up, and you'll be good as new in no time. And, of course, you will remain here until you are recovered. I will not risk you wandering the bluffs and taking flight."

"Thank you," she murmured. Perhaps there was some kindness in Jack after all. "I'm truly sorry to have put you through this."

"Never mind, although I'd like to know what you were doing standing near the edge of a cliff."

"I—I don't remember," she lied. "If I did, I would tell you, but I assure you, I'm not suicidal. I think the traumatic experience robbed me of my memory."

"I daresay you've had a shock and need rest. Hopefully, your memory will come back to you after you've had a decent sleep."

"Yes." She nodded. "I hope so."

"Well then, I should leave you to Mrs. Livingstone—she should be here any moment."

"Thank you for your kindness."

He chuckled. "I would say kindness is the least of what I've been to you." He stood. "Feel better, Signorina D'Angelo."

"What should I call you—surely not Jack?"

"Where are my manners? I am Lord John Henry Langsford, Earl of Whitton, Marquess of Bainbridge, although, for the moment, my cousin Beauford has usurped my title and my lands. But he will not prevail, not if it costs me my last breath."

"I am very sorry you have to deal with this nasty cousin. I hope you recover what is rightly yours."

His gaze softened. "Thank you. My friends call me Jack, and when not in public, I'd like you to do the same. I believe the intimacy of our meeting warrants such an address."

Gaby's cheeks flushed at the mention of intimacy between them. Although, in truth, no such intimacy existed. "Thank you, Jack. You may call me Gaby if you'd like."

"I'd like that very much, Gaby." Her name rolled off his tongue like a caress, and she couldn't help but imagine his lips pressed to her ear, repeating her name in the heat of passion.

Holy crap! Get a hold of yourself, Gaby. Like that is ever going to happen.

"You know the Chinese say that once you save someone's life, you're responsible for it forever."

"I've never heard that before." She didn't understand why the thought of belonging to him didn't make her uncomfortable or want to run to the ends of the earth. Instead, warmth lit inside her. "You needn't worry. We're not Chinese, and you owe me nothing."

Why her words brought a frown to his face, she couldn't imagine. He grumbled, "I will leave you to Mrs. Livingstone's good care." Yet he lingered, studying her for a long moment. She thought he would say more, but instead he gave her a brief nod and spun on his heel. His long stride carried him from the room, and his larger-than-life presence was gone.

CHAPTER THREE

Maremma, Italy
October 16, 1902

T HE DOWNPOUR HAD dwindled to a drizzle, and Jack took the opportunity to clear his head. He couldn't get the vision of the vixen's breasts out of his mind. The temptation of those honey orbs had nearly blinded him, and it took all his forbearance not to bury his face against them when he'd carried her. He couldn't help but smile as he recalled the shocked look on her face and her mad scramble to cover herself. Of course, that was impossible, given the tattered state of her clothes.

Those luscious breasts and that bold mouth of hers drew him like a magnet. What was it about her that stirred his imagination and wouldn't let go? Maybe it was that curious mix of bravado and vulnerability. Yet her bluster and fluster didn't stop him from sneaking a peek at the smooth olive skin of her stomach, the only part of her not splattered in mud. It certainly hadn't stopped him from wanting to plant kisses on every inch of her, or to slowly meander along those beautiful curves he'd felt.

He'd feared she'd slip and fall to her death. His heart had drummed in his ears as he reached down to pull her to safety. He'd lost his footing and tumbled back, and she'd landed right on top of him. Thankfully, she'd been so flustered and frightened by her ordeal that she hadn't noticed his almost immediate physical response to her soft, luscious curves.

And then, when he'd carried her upstairs to his room and dumped her on his bed, it was all he could do to stop himself from diving on top of her. He regretted not laying her down gently. But, God's blood, just looking at her made his cock stand at attention.

It was maddening, but his heart thundered against his chest when he held her. It was uncontrollable, reminiscent of how his body had reacted to his first kiss or the first time he'd lain with a woman.

His instinct told him that Gabriella D'Angelo was a danger to his peace of mind and to the life he'd planned for himself.

It was as if she'd cast a spell on him, and he was powerless to break it—and even more upsetting, nor did he wish to. What he wanted—forget that, what he *needed*, was to bed her and then be done with her. He needed to quash this impossible attraction, and then he could move forward with his courtship of Cynthia Maxwell and her immeasurable fortune. A fortune that would give him the wherewithal to reclaim his lands and title. Then he would be assured the revenge he so desperately sought against that bastard Beauford.

Even as he tried to convince himself of what he needed to do, he couldn't stop the rush of desire for Gabriella that infiltrated his body like an enemy army quartering in his loins. With no other option, he walked the grounds of the Villa Nido dell' Aquila and cursed under his breath, determined to crush his craving, even if he had to walk all night. The last thing he needed was a complication to interfere with his plans, and that minx was a definite distraction.

A common local girl—what was he thinking? No, she wasn't local. And she was anything but common. Her beauty and those glorious curves were definitely Italian, but her accent and her entire demeanor was American, which raised the questions, who was she and what was she doing in Maremma? Yes, he itched to satisfy his curiosity about who she was and what she was doing here, almost as much as his aroused cock wanted to explore her depths while his fingers, tongue, and mouth brought her to satisfaction.

His imagination conjured images of Gabriella lying beneath him and melting from his amorous embrace—yes, he had no doubt that she was a woman capable of deep passion, nothing like the lily-white swans of his class and the games of seduction they practiced. Twittering, giggling women without a head for anything but landing a husband.

A fleeting thought crossed his mind that even if he married Cynthia, who did not stir his loins in the least, there was nothing to stop him from keeping a mistress. Why not satisfy his physical desire with this exotic flower who'd literally landed in his lap? Once he'd reclaimed his title and lands, there was nothing to prevent him from spending as much time away from England as he chose. The mere thought of lying between Gaby's legs made every muscle in his body grow taut.

But for the time being, he could do nothing about his physical needs except walk the hills.

He shook his head. "Damn, woman." His imaginings were having a reverse effect on him, and his shaft was harder than ever. *Such a waste!* To pour his seed in her would feel like heaven. He was sure of it.

Jack did not consider himself a womanizer by any means. In fact, at most times, he avoided entanglements with the fairer sex—but there was something about Gabriella D'Angelo that had hit him like a thunderbolt.

His primary focus had always been archaeology. He'd spent four years in Luxor, Egypt working with his friend, the prominent archaeologist and Egyptologist Howard Carter. Carter was the inspector of monuments of Upper Egypt. Jack would have stayed there, where he knew great discoveries would be made in the Valley of the Kings in the next few years, but his father's unexpected death had taken him back to Staffordshire and the thousand-acre family estate, Singly Park.

After his long, arduous journey home, Jack's life had turned completely upside down when he found out his cousin, Beauford Bastion Broome, had usurped his title and inheritance by convincing Jack's father to submit a patent for a special remainder to amend the line of succession. How Beauford had achieved such a devious and despicable goal was beyond Jack's imaginings. The letters patent had somehow been accepted and sealed, denying Jack anything other than the modest inheritance his late mother had bequeathed him.

Jack, who was at least a foot taller than Beauford, could have killed his cousin with his bare hands on the spot, but the weasel had surrounded himself with a small army of mercenary bodyguards who promptly tossed Jack from the estate. Returning to London, Jack had become persona non grata among the *beau monde*. He had been away so long that Beauford had had plenty of time to execute his nefarious scheme and perfect his vile lies—to the point that even Jack's closest friends from Oxford had believed the deceit.

Wretched and alone, Jack had had no choice but to abandon England and seek out the one person who would never jump ship—his father's sister, Lady Katherine Darling. He sought solace with Aunt Kitty, who'd long ago been tainted by her own scandal, and had fled society to a villa near Piombino, Italy. There, the eccentric butterfly who'd followed her heart, and paid the price, had established her new life. She'd turned the villa she'd inherited into an exclusive hotel where she welcomed well-heeled clientele who sought luxurious accommodations, the finest Italian cuisine, and a home-away-from-home atmosphere as they escaped the dreary, coal-sodden air of London. With only six luxury suites, the villa was always in demand.

Kitty had welcomed him with open arms and an open heart and told him he could stay with her for as long as he needed. Jack would be forever grateful to Aunt Kitty for giving him the time he needed to regroup and plan his strategy to reclaim his patrimony.

His long strides took him to the cliff's edge where he'd first seen Gabriella. The storm had moved on, and rays of moonlight sparkled iridescently on the Gulf of Baratti. He peered over the edge and could see the tree that Gabriella had grabbed that grew out of the cliff face. It was more than miraculous that she hadn't fallen to her death.

Gabriella. Even the curl of her name on his tongue created an inexplicable longing. He'd gotten off on the wrong foot with her, but he would amend the situation tomorrow and find out more about her. After all, he could be quite charming when he wanted to be, and he needed to be in this instance. Aside from wanting to find out who she was and what she was doing there, his desire for her was all-consuming, and he would know no peace until he buried himself inside her.

CHAPTER FOUR

Maremma, Italy
October 17, 1902

G ABRIELLA OPENED HER eyes. For a second, she thought she was safe at home in her own bed. But as she looked about the room, yesterday's events returned to her. The room's heavily carved bed and matching armoire and the brown, black, and gold colors reflected male ownership. The room was as dark and forbidding as the man who dwelt in it.

Jack, or Lord John Henry Langsford, or Earl of Whitton, or marquess—whatever, he was bad news! Arrogant. Entitled. Conceited.

And utterly irresistible. Which means I need to stay away from him.

She'd never met a man like him. Virile, confident to the point of arrogance, Jack radiated a powerful aura that captivated her. He was not a man to be trifled with. Truly they were like oil and water! But for some inexplicable reason, she couldn't stop thinking about him.

Get a grip, Gaby! He saved your life and is a gorgeous hunk of a man, and that's why you're thinking about him.

She blew out a deep breath. She needed to stop thinking about Jack and start thinking about how she was going to get back home! Not just back to Chicago, but to the modern day and her beloved family.

Her life had been turned inside out when she was dragged back in time to 1902. She had no idea how she would ever find her way back. Could it be only two days ago that she'd been hanging out with Em and Jen as they stuffed themselves with lasagna, drank wine until they were tipsy, and giggled like teenagers who'd ditched school? She'd give anything to be able to return to her friends, her family, and the world she belonged in. But no amount of wishing would make it so.

She looked around the room, searching for anything that might spark a thought, idea, or reason for why she'd been brought here, and by whom. Well, she kind of knew by whom— the Renaissance painter Marco Allegretto and his red-headed muse and lover. That, alone, was mind-blowing. But what they'd wanted from her was even more inexplicable. Over and over, she'd heard them say the word: *Devi aiutarci!* As though only she had the power to help them. But help them with what? And why? *Why me?*

A silly giggle bubbled up inside her. *Maybe I should look under the bed for a pair of ruby-red slippers!* Then she could close her eyes and click her heels together while repeating, *There's no place like home.*

Instead, she got out of the large bed, crept to the window, and pulled open the heavy, burgundy-colored velvet drapes. Blindingly bright sunlight poured into the room, and she blinked rapidly. The view was breathtaking. Well-tended lawns and gardens stretched to the bluff's edge, which likely was where she'd nearly met her demise last night before…

Jack.

The man now held a primary place in her thoughts, which annoyed her. She sighed, relegating her thoughts of him to what she hoped were the farthest reaches of her mind. Titled men like him looked down on women like her. They used them and tossed them away.

Gaby sighed. Nothing was to be done; it was best to put her attraction to him under lock and key.

Beyond the lush, verdant landscaping, the bluest waters she'd ever seen met the distant horizon. The day was so clear that she could make out Elba's sinuous curves and granite promontories. The largest island in the Tuscan archipelago lay between the Ligurian and the Tyrrhenian Seas. It held the distinction of being Napoleon's last home.

At least she was back home. Well, her grandparents' homeland, anyway. Even if it was the wrong century. Gaby had been to Italy several times, and the view reminded her of her last visit to the Tuscan coastline. She'd taken a ferry to Elba with her roommate and friend from cooking school. They had rented mopeds and ridden from Marina di Campo, from one end of the island to the other. They'd visited the Villa San Martino and Villa Dei Mulini in Portoferraio, where the deposed emperor Napoleon had lived in exile.

Gaby had been enchanted by the hearty islanders, the seafood cuisine, and the wines that had been locally produced since Roman times. She'd found out that those delicious wines were favored by Lorenzo de' Medici during the Renaissance. At the time, she wished she could have stayed, maybe opened a cute little trattoria that served up Italian-American-international fusion dishes. But reality prevailed, and she'd returned to Chicago to work in her parents' restaurant. Still, it had been an eye-opening trip that brought her closer to her Tuscan roots, and if she'd *had* to turn up in some distant time and place, this was better than most. And bonus, she spoke fluent Italian. Although, given that Jack and Aunt Kitty were both English, communication wasn't the most pressing issue.

Gaby opened the window and inhaled the sea breeze. Even though her past travels might help her navigate the situation she'd been thrust into, she took no comfort in that. She fretted it wouldn't be enough. After all, what did she know about how to behave in the early twentieth century? It dawned on her that neither World War I nor World War II had been fought yet and that nearly everyone alive in 1902 would be affected by the coming conflagrations. She took it to heart, realizing that at least

Jack would be too old to fight in the war to end all wars.

But not too old to be a commanding officer—

Okay, stop that! What was she thinking? His fate had nothing to do with her. But she couldn't stop her stomach from churning at the thought of Jack being wounded or worse.

A gentle knock at the door interrupted her musings. Mrs. Livingstone poked her head in, and her smile calmed the nervous flutter of Gaby's belly.

"*Buongiorno,* signorina, I hope your rest was pleasant. My mistress desires you to be properly attired, and I brought you a dress, shoes, and stockings. It is a glorious day, is it not?"

"Thank you, Mrs. Livingstone—paradise indeed. Let me help you." Gaby hurried to Lady Katherine Darling's lady's maid and relieved her of the items that filled her arms. Mrs. Livingstone carried her short, diminutive body with grace and elegance and had a most delightful demeanor. She spoke highly of Lady Darling, keeping up a pleasant chatter about how she'd been her lady's maid since Kitty was a young woman. The motherly, gray-haired woman had been most kind last night, tending Gabriella's wound with care and making chamomile tea to help her sleep.

Mrs. Livingstone puffed out a breath from her exertion. "Thank you. I will change your bandage and help you dress. Lady Darling also insists you should be treated as a guest and afforded deference and kindness. She is a grand lady with a heart of gold."

"She is a most gracious lady indeed, unlike her nephew," Gaby let slip, and then covered her mouth, mortified. But she couldn't help but notice the differences between aunt and nephew.

Mrs. Livingstone gave a slight chuckle. "Do not fear; your comment shall never leave this room."

"Thank you. I apologize for my rudeness."

"It is true—the earl is a difficult man to figure out, to be sure, but the titled live by their own rules, and they are not for you or me to understand."

"I didn't mean to be critical," Gaby added, but Mrs. Livingstone was correct. Even in the twentieth century, those blessed with a noble birth didn't answer to the same powers as the rest of the common folk.

At least Lady Darling appeared to be of a different ilk. She was a woman who deserved admiration. Unlike her nephew, who displayed an arrogant demeanor and a short temper, she seemed thoughtful and generous. Yet, for an instant last night, Gaby had spied a glimmer of something more hidden beneath the carapace that enclosed Jack, but it was so fleeting that she now doubted she'd even seen it. It was probably the fact that she'd been exhausted and in pain. Not to mention her attraction to the moody man. Why she found his bad-boy persona magnetizing, she had no idea.

She'd never been the type of woman who was attracted to "bad boys" or "rich boys"—or "gorgeous boys," for that matter. Her awkward years as a chubby teen with lousy skin had seen to that. Working in the restaurant, she was always back of the house, in the kitchen. Rarely did she mingle with the patrons.

And that was how she liked it. She'd always preferred being in the background. Her dating life had been rather dismal, with only one significant relationship that went on for too many years, probably because he wasn't around a lot. Ian was a sommelier and wine salesman. She should have known that a man who lived on the road was seeing other women. For Ian, "a girl in every port" or in his case "a girl in every glass of port" had proven apropos. In the end, Ian dumped her for a so-called celebrity chef.

It wasn't until Gaby met Jen and Em, both gorgeous and confident, that her own confidence was boosted a bit. Still, it was hard to undo a lifetime of low self-esteem. She'd studied hospitality in university, and, still suffering from the Ian experience, had taken a big chance and enrolled at the Florence Culinary Arts School. That had been a stroke of genius and honed her true chef talent.

Now she was back in Tuscany—granted, a hundred years earlier than the last time she'd been here. But of all things, to be attracted to a man who, even if her attraction was reciprocated, would likely break her heart even worse than Ian? That would be a disaster.

She considered her weakness a defect and something she needed to remedy. Yes, Jack was handsome and had a body like an Adonis, but he was moody, irritable, and not very nice! The last thing she wanted was to be involved with a man like that!

What am I thinking? I have no idea how I got here and no idea how long I'll be staying. My primary goal should be figuring out how to get the heck out of Dodge, not mooning over that arrogant, conceited oaf!

She had always hoped for a warm and passionate man who worshipped her like Marco Allegretto worshipped his muse Iris in *The Three Stages of Love*. Her parents, whom she missed terribly— and she fretted she might never see again—had tried to fix her up with a nice Italian boy, but she hadn't liked him at all. Pat was just another spoiled son of an over-doting Italian mama that thought he was God's gift to womanhood. Nope, that had not gone well.

Mrs. Livingstone helped her with her ablutions and assisted her with the gown Kitty had chosen. When Gaby saw the s-bend corset that the older woman held up for her, she backed away, shaking her head. "Oh, no, that's out of the question. I don't think I can survive wearing that straitjacket."

"But, miss, it would be unseemly to do otherwise, and it looks far more forbidding than it really is. You will not feel restricted. In fact, given your comely curves, it will only enhance your lovely figure."

Gaby's arched brow expressed her suspicions that Mrs. Livingstone was probably saying whatever it took to get her into the torture contraption. She was being sold a bill of goods, and it brought to mind the story of the infamous swindler who'd coined the phrase *if you believe that, I have a bridge to sell you. The Brooklyn Bridge, that is.*

"Please, I promise you will be comfortable."

"But what of my wound?" The wound did not hurt her, but perhaps it would dissuade Mrs. Livingstone from placing her in a boned cage.

"We will not lace it too tight."

Gaby sighed, realizing that she should graciously comply rather than argue with the woman, who was simply following her mistress's directions. She held up her arms, allowing the lady's maid to do her worst.

Turning before the mirror, Gaby couldn't quite believe her transformation. The outfit was simple, a blouse of white voile with a ruffle and a dark navy skirt that hugged her hips and thighs before flaring to the ground in a ruffled flounce. Mrs. Livingstone was correct—she'd never felt so attractive. The outfit complemented her figure by accenting her narrow waist and boosting her full bosom. She felt utterly feminine without the overt sexuality intended by the styles of the modern world she'd come from. With Gaby's thanks and a profuse apology, Mrs. Livingstone left the room smiling.

The lady's maid had suggested that Gaby head down to the dining room, where breakfast was served. She also indicated that Gaby might like to eat in the garden, given the lovely day. As Mrs. Livingstone had explained, several guests were arriving today, and the household staff would be busy preparing. Lady Darling had instructed that Gaby should make herself at home and enjoy herself like any other guest at the villa.

Given what she'd been through in the past twenty-four hours, Gaby thanked her lucky stars for ending up where she had. Lady Darling was beyond kind, even if her nephew wasn't. And now that Gaby was here, she had to make the best of it. At least she could recuperate in these lovely surroundings while she figured out what to do next.

After a last look in the mirror, Gaby stepped into the hallway. Her ears perked as she heard music emanating from somewhere in the house. The rapturous melody was so beguiling that she felt compelled to find out where it was coming from. Following the notes as if following a scent, she descended the stairway.

The beautiful sound of piano and cello echoed through the house and led her to a pair of double doors. She hesitated a minute, afraid to interrupt—but, unable to contain her curiosity, she quietly opened the door. Lady Darling was at the piano, her brow damp from exertion, her fingers flying across the keyboard with dexterity and ease. Before her, seated on a chair facing the piano at a three-quarter angle, was Jack, his imposing figure deep in concentration. His back muscles strained beneath his white shirt, and Gaby found herself mesmerized.

Lady Darling darted her eyes to Gaby for a second, a hint of a smile tilting her lips, and then, with not a word, she returned her gaze to the sheet music and continued to play. Jack, intent on the complexity of what he was playing, seemingly had no idea Gaby was there. His broad shoulders swayed with his efforts as his bow caressed the strings. His long fingers were powerful yet delicate as he coaxed the most miraculous notes from the instrument. She tried not to imagine what it would feel like to feel those fingers dancing on her skin. The music had a dark, spellbinding power, yet with a poignancy that was enough to elicit tears. Even with her limited knowledge of classical music, Gaby sensed the musical storytelling that captured her senses was of the highest order.

She held her breath as the two instruments blended harmoniously. First, the piano took the lead while the cello offered support in a melodious flow, then the piano yielded to the cello, whose sonorous tones were so beautiful, they took her breath away. It seemed incongruous to her that the imposing man, within whose arms the cello rested, could play with such delicacy and emotion. Given his stature, the cello seemed but a toy.

His hair. Gaby could finally see its color now that it wasn't wet and plastered to his head. The long locks that caught the light from the window reminded her of rays of sunlight. Caught in a golden nimbus, they only enhanced his masculine beauty as he poured his heart and soul into the music.

Lady Darling and her nephew were accomplished musicians, and their perfect synergy could only come from years of playing together. It was apparent they both shared a deep passion for music, and Gaby found herself quite taken aback by how she had misread him. Anyone who could play so beautifully and be so emotionally connected to the music couldn't be all that bad.

He hadn't shown this side to her yesterday. He'd been arrogant, gruff, and insinuated she was some sort of "loose woman" who'd shown up to cause trouble. Clearly, there was another side to Jack. And that revelation shook Gabriella to the core.

In fact, she recognized an affinity in their natures. He clearly had a passion for music, just as she had a passion for cooking. Was he a good guy beneath his arrogant exterior? It awoke a curiosity in Gaby to delve deeper into the makeup of the man, and an impromptu vision of lying beneath him stole her breath. Her thighs pressed together as she tried to control the sudden arousal that grabbed hold of her.

Madonna! Get a grip, Gaby!

Her physical reaction to Jack was quite unlike her. She'd never had this issue in the past with men. She hated being set up on dates by well-meaning friends and relatives, and loathed dating apps. She preferred to spend most of her time in the kitchen developing recipes and trying new dishes, or at the gym. Other than the waiters and male kitchen staff, who were more like brothers to her, she had little to do with men and had next to no social life. Maybe that was why her reaction to Jack was so strong? She had to tread carefully regardless of her physical attraction and her curiosity about him.

The piano and cello chased each other in a series of repetitive crescendos, filling every corner of the room, and then it was over. The last notes hung in the air as if disappointed that the instruments would dare not continue, allowing them to disappear into nothingness. Silence descended.

More than anything, Gaby wished she could hear more of the magical music. She felt lightheaded, as if she'd had a climax and her body, having reached its ultimate contentment, now relaxed, wanting to do nothing more than reflect on what just happened.

Without thinking, immersed in a blissfulness she'd rarely ever felt, Gaby applauded.

The formidable giant who held the cello jumped up and turned his steely gaze on her. Gaby's heart thundered in her chest, and she leaped up from the seat she'd taken in the back of the room.

But rather than acknowledge her with a gracious bow, Jack speared her with an angry gaze. "What are you doing here? Do you always intrude where you are not wanted?"

"Oh, Jack, stop acting like an ogre," Aunt Kitty scolded. "The young lady is merely showing her appreciation." With a flick of her wrist, she dismissed her nephew and turned to Gaby with a warm smile. "How do you feel today, my dear?"

Gaby tried not to wither from the intensity of Jack's scornful glare. His mouth clamped shut after his aunt's reprimand. "I'm sorry to disturb you, but the music was so beautiful. I had no intention of causing trouble by intruding. Please forgive me." An errant tear slipped from her eye, and she hastily brushed it away, hoping the ogre didn't notice it. Trying to gather her composure, she straightened her shoulders and avoided looking at Jack.

He might look like a golden god, but he acted like a sullen schoolboy.

"Don't be silly; music needs an audience. I am happy you enjoyed our practice," said Lady Darling. "We will be playing a short recital on Saturday for our guests after what will no doubt be a stimulating dinner party. As long as you are a guest in this household, you are welcome to partake in whatever activity you choose. I do hope you will join us."

"Thank you, your ladyship. I would love to hear that piece again. May I ask the composer?"

"It is Brahms's Cello Sonata No. 1 in E minor, Op. 38," Jack said in a less blustery tone. "Er, my aunt is right." He cleared his throat. "Music without an audience does not fulfill its purpose." He offered nothing more, no apology, simply stared at her.

Why is he looking at me like that? Like he's blaming me for something. She'd done nothing wrong and had arrived here through no fault of her own. Of course, she couldn't admit that to Jack or Lady Darling, especially without telling them the truth. The old adage, *the truth shall set you free*, sure as heck didn't apply here.

"Jack, since you insist on presenting your least appealing self to Signorina D'Angelo, I believe you should keep her company while she breaks her fast," Lady Darling said. "Perhaps your mood will improve with a hearty breakfast. Come, my dear—the music has awakened my appetite."

She disarmed Jack of his cello and bow and placed them on their stand. Taking Gaby's hand, she called over her shoulder, "Come along, Jack. I have no idea what has been going through your mind recently. Signorina D'Angelo is deserving of our hospitality and welcome."

Jack snorted. "Aunty, you are ever mindful of the feelings of others. I may not always agree with your assessment of their character, but I will acquiesce to your judgment until such a time as I find your kindness ill-used."

Gaby glanced back and found his penetrating gaze on her. He did nothing to hide his suspicions that perhaps Gaby might be one of those nebulous "ill users." Though clearly reluctant and dour, he followed Gaby and Lady Darling from the music room.

CHAPTER FIVE

Maremma, Italy
October 17, 1902

L ADY DARLING CHATTED amiably about the dinner party she
was planning and the guests soon to arrive. Gaby didn't
understand why, but the gracious lady treated her like an equal
and a friend. Perhaps she lacked friends in this remote area of
Italy, or she was simply one of the kindest people Gabriella had
ever met.

Jack trailed behind them, offering nothing to the conversation, and when Gaby glanced back at him, their eyes met. Before
he looked away, she sensed he'd been watching her, which
triggered a blast of heat that climbed her neck and filled her
cheeks.

"Constance Shipley is an American, like you. She's from
Boston, I believe," Lady Darling said. "She will be arriving today
with her companion Blossom Rosalind. According to the art
dealer Stefano Bardino, who will also be joining us from Florence,
Constance is a major collector of Renaissance art and is here on a
buying expedition."

Gabriella's ears perked up when Kitty mentioned Renaissance
art, and she forgot her discomfort. The words of Marco Allegretto
and his muse echoed in her mind: *Devi aiutarci! You have to help us.*
Trust in your destiny. Whatever strange supernatural forces had

brought her here, perhaps it had something to do with the upcoming dinner and, more importantly, the dinner guests. This wealthy American woman and the art dealer from Florence were possibly linked to Allegretto's artwork.

But why me? How was she meant to help Allegretto and his muse, and to what end? Gaby felt like some sort of newbie undercover agent who'd been parachuted into a mysterious case she had no idea how to solve. And the stakes couldn't be higher.

But this was not a James Bond movie. Even if she somehow figured out how to help Allegretto, which was a very big if, how would she find her way back to her life in the future? Would Allegretto come for her? *Otherwise, how else am I supposed to get home?*

Her chest constricted. Thinking about her family back in Chicago and how worried they must be gave her heartburn. Gaby always checked in with her mom, every day. And it had been more than twenty-four hours since she'd been hurtled back in time. Her mom must have called Em and Jen to find out what was happening by now.

If only Em and Jen had gotten back to the bench in time. Gaby wouldn't have been there for Marco Allegretto to hurl back in time. She could only imagine how guilty they must be feeling, which only made Gaby feel worse. They must have been beside themselves when they realized that Gaby was gone. Not gone back to Em's or gone back to Chicago, but *gone gone.* They must have contacted the police by now. Surely an investigation was underway.

Oh, what a mess!

Gaby's instincts told her that her presence there at Lady Darling's must be connected to Allegretto. Nor could it be a coincidence that an American art collector would be one of the guests at Lady Darling's party. If she could figure out what Allegretto needed her to do, she might find a way back to her friends and family, and everything would be all right. She had to believe that it would.

Gaby noticed that the villa had quite a few paintings on the walls, but none she'd seen so far was an Allegretto. She hadn't seen the entire house, but a painting of such import would be prominently displayed. It could be hanging in Lady Darling's bedroom. After all, Allegretto had been known for his sensual boudoir paintings. Gaby would have to sneak a peek into the bedroom. She would have considered Jack a better candidate for hanging a sexy portrait over his bed—but alas, the painting above his bed was a landscape.

"Who else will be visiting?" Gaby asked, her curiosity now thoroughly piqued.

"The Marquess of Danbury and his wife are meeting friends from Paris, Chief Inspector Xavier Doumaz and his wife. I can't recall her name, but the wife was born in Paris and once lived in America. They are all friends and planned a vacation and reunion together here in Maremma. You might share similar experiences with the marchioness. Perhaps being in the company of several Americans will return your memory. That would be wonderful, wouldn't it?"

Gaby almost teared up at the hopeful expression on Lady Darling's face. "Yes, it would be wonderful," she replied in a husky voice.

"I forgot to mention that Sir Albert Findley's widow, Donatella Falaguera, is scheduled to arrive today. The baron's beautiful niece Cynthia is accompanying them. Cynthia recently lost her father too. The baron was an old friend of my dear, deceased husband Stewart, but I haven't seen dear Bertie in three years… Not since Stewart's passing—and now, poor dear, he's gone too. It's too much to bear." Lady Darling wiped a tear from her cheek.

"I'm truly sorry about your late husband," Gaby said.

"Thank you, my dear," Lady Darling said, patting her hand. "It is difficult to lose a loved one, but life is not without risk. And love is the greatest risk of all. But oh, so worth it."

Gaby heard Jack mutter something behind them and was tempted to sneak a peek over her shoulder again, but she didn't dare.

"Now, where was I?"

"You were telling us about dear Bertie," Jack dryly said from behind.

Gaby did turn around at that, and her eyes met his once more. She was surprised to see his gaze no longer held anger. In fact, there was a notable softening of his expression, although he was as unreadable as ever.

Gaby averted her eyes to not encourage her cheeks to redden and her pulse to quicken whenever she met eyes with Jack.

"He recently married Donatella Falaguera, who I've heard is an Italian countess," Lady Darling continued. "Bertie died within months of their marriage, as did Cynthia's father. We are hopeful that Cynthia might accept Jack's suit and become his future countess, since he desperately needs a wife. Cynthia's dowry is no less than what a king's daughter might provide," she added in a teasing tone, throwing a wink over her shoulder at her nephew.

Gaby felt her heart wrench. Of course Jack would be spoken for. Money went to money. Or, in this case, Jack's desire for money.

Gaby had once read about how some aristocrats were poor and had to marry wealthy non-aristocrats to keep their fancy estates. Even if Jack was a moody jerk, he was gorgeous and accomplished, from what Gaby had seen of him. She could picture her nonna shrugging her shoulder in that typical, fatalistic Italian fashion. *Meglio soli che male accompagati.* That was what her nonna would say. *Better to be alone than in bad company.* And so far, Jack was the very definition of bad company.

Well, it's nothing to do with me. I was sent here to help Allegretto, not to find a husband. She needed to hold that thought, or she'd never get back home. And being stuck here to possibly see Jack marry this Cynthia heiress was not part of the plan. If only she could figure out her purpose here, she'd be home free.

"I believe it is somewhat premature to announce nuptials, Aunt Kitty," Jack said in a dry tone.

"Well, we'll see what happens this weekend, shall we?" Lady

Darling replied in an equally dry tone.

Gaby felt a cramp grip her stomach, and it had nothing to do with her wound. She pressed her hands against the sharp stab. So much for it having nothing to do with her. Why it would bother her that Jack intended to marry this woman, she couldn't explain. Perhaps it was just the shock of hearing that the man she was dangerously attracted to was promised to another. She had no claim to him. She wasn't titled, or possessed anything beyond the clothes on her back, which were not even hers. It was ridiculous. They shared nothing in common. Yet it was all she could do to hold back the tears.

"Are you all right, my dear?" Lady Darling said. "Is your injury bothering you? Jack, do something."

Jack grabbed Gaby's elbow, and she looked up and found what she would never have expected from him—tenderness. He looked as if he cared about her, as if her suffering had caused him pain too. It was impossible to read what he was thinking exactly, but she could see he worried for her, and it stole her breath.

"You really should be in bed," he said in a husky voice. "You need to recover from your wound and near-fatal fall off that cliff. Allow me to be of assistance."

Before she knew what was happening, he'd lifted her in his arms as though he were carrying a basket of feathers.

"Oh!" she said in surprise as her eyes met his. Those Mediter-ranean baby blues were regarding her intently. Not that look of tenderness she'd glimpsed before, but something else— something that made her want to close her eyes and lean into him.

Oh God, I'm in deep trouble. The more time she spent with him, the more she wanted to be near him. She needed to be careful. She needed to stay in control. And in no way could she allow her physical desire for Jack to override her common sense.

"Thank you for your assistance. I-I was feeling lightheaded for a moment. It must be from yesterday's ordeal." A lie, of course. She was sore, but the only thing making her lightheaded was being in Jack's arms.

"Jack will carry you into the dining room so you can have something to eat," Lady Darling said, patting Gaby's shoulder. "Come along, Jack, hop to it!"

Jack flashed his aunt a grin, and Gaby nearly did faint.

Madon! *When he smiles, he's even more gorgeous. If that's even possible.*

Jack set her down on one of the comfortable chairs in the dining room. The remnants of a smile still hovered on his lips.

"Thank you," Gaby said, her eyes meeting his again. She felt the same intense heat she'd felt last night; an almost overwhelming desire to ask him to carry her upstairs and make mad, passionate love to her for the rest of the day.

She looked away, wondering if the roguish gleam in his eyes meant he could read her thoughts. *What is wrong with me? I better get a grip on my unruly crush on Jack, or I'll never get back home.*

"Now, let's get you something to eat," Lady Darling said as she sat beside Gaby.

The sound of breaking china startled them, and they all turned toward the butler's door that led to the kitchen.

"What the devil?" Jack said.

Another crash was followed by a barrage of curses shouted in Italian.

"Stay here," Jack ordered them. "A thief may have stolen in through the kitchen."

He strode toward the door, but before he reached it, it swung open, and Mrs. Livingstone came running out, clutching a bottle of amber liquid to her breast.

Someone inside the kitchen screamed in a voice that sounded demonic to Gaby's ears. Something like the girl in the *Exorcist* movie. "Give that back to me, you witch!"

Someone else yelled, "Duck!"

An object hurtled through the swinging door, barely missing Mrs. Livingstone and Jack. It smashed against the wall, shattering into a thousand pieces.

Jack steadied the lady's maid. "What in God's name is going

on in there?"

"Signora Fratelli has been swizzling, and I'm afraid she's quite blootered," Mrs. Livingstone said, catching her breath. "She refuses to cook and is hurling dishes at anyone who dares defy her. I managed to grab the bottle she was hiding, but now she's threatening to kill me." Her words were almost drowned out by another crash of crockery.

Lady Darling turned to Gaby. "I'm terribly sorry that you have to witness this, my dear. Signora Fratelli is a talented cook, but given to a temperamental nature when she indulges in the drink." She looked at Jack. "Oh, my dear, whatever will we do?"

"What complete and utter nonsense!" Jack shouted over the fracas. "I'll tell you what we'll do."

Gaby jumped up from her chair. She'd known Jack less than twenty-four hours, but she knew he had a short fuse, and the thought of his killing the cook had her racing to the door to avoid disaster. She beat him to the butler's door, determined to stop further damage. Diplomacy would invariably be better than violence. Besides, she'd encountered enough temperamental chefs in her training and learned how to deal with them.

But Jack was not to be dissuaded. "Oh, no, you don't." He grabbed her around the waist just as Gaby swung open the door. She gasped, and Jack growled. "God's blood!"

A heavyset woman wielding a meat cleaver stomped toward them.

"Stand down, woman, or I'll be forced—"

"Jack, don't!" Gaby shouted, unthinkingly calling him by his first name. "She'll kill you."

His reaction was instantaneous. "I think not, my daring lass." He wrapped his arms around Gaby and turned with his back toward the door, effectively keeping it from swinging open.

Another crash was followed by more cursing and a tremendous thud as something heavy smacked the door, and a clatter as it landed on the floor.

"That sounds like a pot," Gaby whispered. "And a hefty one at that." She turned in his arms to face him. "Please let me go. I think I can calm her down."

"I think not, my sweet. Not until I know it's safe."

It seemed forever, but it couldn't have been more than a few minutes when the cursing and crashing of crockery stopped, and he let her go. "Get behind me." She nodded, and he eased open the butler's door. Gaby snuck in under his arm and peeked in.

The cook was slumped on a chair, snoring, her hair and clothing covered in flour. Littering the floor were broken plates, cutlery, pots, and pans. The counters and walls were smeared with smashed tomatoes, and upturned bowls of lemons and various other fruits and vegetables were scattered over the large wooden island in the middle of the kitchen.

Gaby was filled with anger and dismay at the destruction. The woman was a menace to herself and the entire household. Not to mention the waste of good food and all the damage she'd done.

"Please see Signora Fratelli is returned to her family, where she can sleep off her overindulgence of the devil's brew," Jack said to Thomas and the footmen who'd entered the kitchen from the side door leading out to the herb garden. His voice was calm, but Gaby saw the frustration in his eyes and something else—sadness as he watched the men pick up the still-snoring cook and carry her out.

Gaby had thought him a jerk when she first encountered him, but then she saw how sweet he was with his aunt and the passion he conveyed playing the cello. And now she could see how much he cared about his aunt's home and everyone who worked here.

It was sad to see the self-destruction that alcohol could wreak on someone's life. Gaby hoped the cook's family would be able to help her. At least to keep her from drinking. Gaby's nonna had been only six years old when her parents brought her and her brother Salvatore to the United States to start a new life after World War Two. Growing up, her nonna had heard all the stories of the desolation and collapse of people's lives because of the war.

Two serving girls hesitantly stepped into the kitchen. Both looked to be in their early teens, and Gaby's heart went out to them. They must have been frightened out of their wits. She smiled at them, nodding in encouragement. They gave her shy smiles and began to clear up the debris.

"Oh dear," Lady Darling said from behind them. "I daresay breakfast will be late this morning."

Gaby's gaze met Jack's in a moment of surprise at Lady Darling's bland statement, and they both burst into laughter.

Lady Darling looked at them as if they were inmates of an asylum. "You may find humor in this situation, but losing Cook now is a catastrophe. Whatever will we do? How will we feed everyone?"

Gabriella took a deep breath, her hand on her chest as she regained her composure. "I will take care of feeding everyone."

Jack and Lady Darling looked at her as if she, too, had been dipping her cup into the scotch.

"Surely you jest," said Jack.

"I am not jesting," Gabriella said calmly. "I am a professional chef and run"—she cleared her throat—"ran a kitchen. I'm used to serving a hundred meals in a single sitting. It would be my pleasure to help you, to thank you for your hospitality."

Jack regarded her with an arched brow, his arms crossed over his chest. "You are full of surprises, Signorina D'Angelo. I wonder what other skills you might be hiding from us."

Gaby ignored the innuendo in his statement, but the gleam in those blue eyes made her knees weak. "Give me a chance, and I will not disappoint you. The way I see it, you have no other options. After dinner, you can decide based on your satisfaction with what I prepare. That way, you will still have enough time to find someone, should you not be pleased with my cooking."

She could see by Jack's lifted brow that he was considering her challenge.

"But what of your injury? Is this not too much for you after your ordeal?" asked Lady Darling.

"The best thing for my recovery is to keep busy. Cooking has the same effect on me as I'm sure playing the cello has on you, my lord, or the piano has on you, Lady Darling."

"It's against my better judgment," said Jack.

"Mine also," Lady Darling added, "but your offer is welcome, given our choices and what is at stake. The guests will arrive, and we will have to feed them, not to mention ourselves. You have my blessing—but first, I need a good, strong cup of tea and some toast and preserves."

"I think I can manage that." Gaby smiled.

"Come, Jack—let us leave our chef to her important work," Lady Darling said with a wink at Gaby.

Jack threw her a peculiar look over his shoulder as he escorted his aunt back to the dining room, as though he were trying to unravel a mystery.

He can muse all he wants but will only figure out the truth if I tell him. And there's no way I can do that. At least working in the kitchen would enable her to stay away from him and give her time to think about Allegretto, the painting, and what she would make for dinner.

CHAPTER SIX

Maremma, Italy
October 17, 1902

JACK RODE XANTHUS at a gallop to Piombino, where he was determined to find answers to the myriad questions plaguing him. The mystery of Signorina Gabriella D'Angelo topped the list. Where did she come from? How had an American woman appeared suddenly out of nowhere?

He recalled the heart-stopping moment when she toppled over the side of the cliff, and how he had to coax her to take his hand, to trust him to help her. And then how she clung to him after he pulled her up and fell to the ground. All he'd wanted to do was wrap his arms around her, make love to her, and never let her go.

He'd experienced several narrow escapes in his travels and encountered more than his share of dangerous bandits and killers. But something had happened to Gabriella before the cliff fall, something that haunted her beautiful hazel eyes that changed color like a chameleon, and he wanted to know what that was.

The revelation of her being a chef and running her own establishment was a surprise. Did she work at some trattoria in Piombino? Or perhaps she was from Florence and had escaped to Piombino to escape a violent lover? The thought that some brute might have abused her made Jack's blood boil. If that were the case, he'd find the beast and make sure he never bothered her or anyone else again.

Jack expelled a deep breath. Losing his temper would get him nowhere, and he'd have to be careful as he made his way through town. He didn't want to arouse suspicions about Gabriella's presence at his aunt's home if she were in danger. But he needed to do something, and someone in the seaside town might have some answers.

"Good boy!" Jack said after his horse jumped a high fence, a shortcut to get to town via a farmer's field. He patted the animal's neck as he slowed their pace. "You'll get two apples for that."

Xanthus neighed in response and shook his head from side to side.

"Okay, three apples," Jack said with a chuckle.

Named after Achilles's immortal talking horse, Xanthus had been a gift from Jack's father, given in better days and happier times. His father was gone, but not so the magnificent beast. The pain of losing his father, of not having the chance to say goodbye, was a regret that would haunt Jack for the rest of his life. But his grief had been muddied by anger and shock at what his father had done. The finality of his father's last act of disinheritance had hardened Jack and made him suspicious of everyone's intentions.

Most days, he was able to push his anger away so that he could focus on regaining his inheritance. A wave of guilt washed over him as he thought about Cynthia Maxwell. Marrying the heiress meant gaining the funds he would need to challenge his cousin in a court of law. But he didn't like the thought of using a woman's wealth to do it. What choice did he have? His birthright had been stolen from him. Aunt Kitty had offered to mortgage her home so he wouldn't have to marry for money, but he couldn't do that to her. Her estate was more than a home. It was her life.

Ironically, Jack had never been one to think about money, nor had he ever been inclined to avariciousness. The possible discovery of treasure on an archeological dig had always fascinated him. But not for the money. It was more about a need to uncover the past and share it with the world. To gain a deeper understanding of civilization and humanity.

Now, he had no choice but to give up his work and try to make the best of the tattered remnants of his life.

His ability to trust had been sorely damaged, and it was no wonder his imagination wreaked havoc on his emotions. He realized that was likely why he suspected Gabriella of ulterior motives. Until he discovered who she truly was, he would treat Signorina D'Angelo with the meticulous attention he used when investigating the origins of an artifact or approaching an archeological dig. Though his body had other ideas he must resist, he would need to control himself and keep his distance from her.

At least, that was what he'd intended, but the morning's events had only enhanced his growing fascination with her. Her offer to step in and help Aunt Kitty after the cook's drunken tantrum was as kind as it was surprising. He recalled their shared laughter at Aunt Kitty's banal comment about breakfast being late. The way Gabriella's face glowed with humor made her even more beautiful. He'd never seen a woman laugh like that so naturally and without artifice. *She's no tittering miss, that's for sure.*

Nor could he help but notice Gabriella's reaction to Aunt Kitty's announcement of his possible engagement to Cynthia. The flash of dismay that flickered in her eyes before she hastily looked away had more than intrigued him, and it made his heart skip a beat.

He had had his share of paramours over the years, usually widows still young enough and eager for bed sport, but sometimes married women bored with their lives and in search of a bit of sensual diversion. He didn't give a thought to his actions other than taking his enjoyment wherever he found it. But sensing Gabriella's passionate nature had sparked something in him. Something he'd never felt before.

The thought of making love to the voluptuous beauty made him rock hard. Not a comfortable feeling while sitting astride a horse along bumpy terrain. Jack shifted in his saddle to ease his discomfort.

He feared he would want more of her. What if he fell under her spell and a few romps beneath the sheets weren't enough? What if he wanted all of her every day for the rest of their lives?

Damn! What if I'm falling in love? A ridiculous notion.

That would have disastrous consequences. There was no room in his life for love, and certainly not with a mysterious woman who had just dropped into his life yesterday.

But he couldn't forget each time he'd held her in his arms, how perfect she felt, and the thundering of his heart when he touched her. The look on her face in the music room had turned his world upside down. Every cell in his body had longed for her at that moment. And he didn't give a rat's arse that she wasn't wealthy or from an aristocratic family. Besides, the world was changing, and even members of the English aristocracy needed to acknowledge that.

Double damn! He needed to tread carefully, to think very hard about this. He couldn't afford to be distracted from his mission of regaining his inheritance.

Don't be a fool, Jack. Think with your head and not your cock. He was confusing sexual attraction with love. Yes, that was it. It had to be. He would find out who Gabriella was and satisfy his curiosity, and perhaps his smoldering need for her, and be done with it.

GABY TIED THE apron around her waist. She'd lined up everyone who worked in the kitchen. There would be no second-guessing or questioning of her authority. In the kitchen, there could be only one leader.

She was relieved to learn Angelina, the older girl, was adept at baking, and her cousin, Maria, usually made the desserts. That took a huge burden off Gaby's shoulders. She could focus on the main meals and oversee the rest with the help of the two girls, who seemed eager to please. They reminded Gaby of herself at that age, how she loved hanging out in the kitchen with her grandmother and mom, absorbing their wisdom like a sponge. Her nonna had instilled in her the importance of respecting every aspect of managing a kitchen. No job was menial, from making sure that plates, glasses, and cutlery were spotless to properly dicing an onion to creating a light and delectable mousse. Everyone in the kitchen did their part to ensure a meal's success.

"I realize I'm a stranger to you, and you are probably still in shock from the cook's inexcusable behavior," Gabriella said in Italian. She thanked her lucky stars that her family had taught her the language from infancy. And her one-year apprenticeship in Florence also refined her fluency. "My name is Gabriella D'Angelo, and I am a professional chef. I do not want to hear gossip about Signora Fratelli. I hope she finds peace in her life, and I wish her well. Nor do I want to know how she managed this kitchen. I have my own way of doing things and what I expect from you. We shall respect each other and work hard together, and we will create unforgettable meals that will bring praise and pleasure. We will all thrive if we work as a team without putting on airs, and your positions will be secure."

Gaby laid out the notes she'd made after they'd finished cleaning up the kitchen. "I've reviewed the menu for tonight's dinner and the dinner party for this weekend and have made some adjustments. I will need your help as I familiarize myself with the sources and the availability of ingredients."

"What do you mean by sources, signorina?" asked Luigi, the boy who managed the livestock and tended the garden.

"I mean things we do not grow or raise here on the property. Surely, things like saffron, fish, and shellfish are bought from vendors in the village or private individuals." It was going to take an adjustment for Gaby, and she had no idea how things were procured in this isolated area, nor the ways of turn-of-the-century Italy. Thank goodness she'd taken a few classes in food history, and her grandmother had told her stories of how they did things by hand "back in the day."

"*Si, si,*" Angelina said, beaming at her. "On Fridays, there is an open farmers' market in Piombino, and Cook would most times provide a list of what was needed for the week."

"I see. Then I take it everything has been ordered for Saturday night."

"*Si*, signorina. What hasn't been delivered should arrive today and tomorrow."

"Then we will use what is provided." Gaby smiled at the three teenagers. "In the future, I would like to go to the market myself, and you can all take turns accompanying me. It will give us a chance to get to know each other. There's a great deal to learn from attending a market, and it's never without excitement."

Angelina, Maria, and Luigi looked at each other as though they'd stepped into another universe. Gaby swallowed the lump in her throat and blinked back sudden tears. She'd been lucky enough to have been taught by patient and gifted women, and she believed that joy in the kitchen brought joy to life. How she missed her family. Would she ever see them again? She had no idea. But for now, she had to make the best of things and carry on until she could figure out what Allegretto wanted her to do.

"I commend you all for your hard work putting this kitchen back in working order. And Luigi, the garden is lovely. I can see it is well cared for, and I look forward to creating delicious dishes from its bounty. Angelina and Maria, I'll need you to show me where everything is stored and what is on hand in the root cellar and pantry." Gaby looked around at the trio of excited faces and smiled. "Now, roll up your sleeves, and let's get to work!"

It felt good to lose herself in cooking and have little time to feel sorry for herself. Gabriella let her passion take over and pushed the Marco Allegretto and Iris Bellerose mystery to the back burner. She'd made a promise to Lady Darling, and she would work her butt off to make sure the dinner party went off without a hitch.

The kitchen was her domain, and just being there restored her confidence. All the ingredients were fresh, and with gentle suggestions to her staff, she implemented a new set of rules on proper food handling, storage, and preparation. She found no resistance from the staff when she put her knowledge from the future into action. Though they looked at her with curiosity, they understood that every *capo* had their own way of doing things.

Gabriella went to the garden, snipped sprigs from the fragrant sage growing there, and added them to her basket. She also dug up several large, bright gourds of butternut squash that she planned to roast in the oven to use as a filling for hand-cut gnocchi dressed in butter and sage for the first course. For the main course, she'd decided on comfort food, a dish for which her nonna and mom were famous. A chicken cacciatore flavored with onions, garlic, red and yellow peppers, carrots, mushrooms, black olives, basil, thyme, parsley, and oregano. It made you want to scoop up the rich, rustic sauce with warm, crusty bread.

She was excited and a little nervous about dinner. She wanted to please Lady Darling, and if she were being completely honest with herself, she wanted to please Jack too. Cooking for friends and family had always brought her joy, but she'd always secretly dreamed of cooking for the man she loved. Perhaps that was a foolish and old-fashioned notion; nevertheless, it was how she felt. She hoped that Jack was as passionate about food as she was. Or at least passionate about eating her cooking.

Gabriella fanned her face at the thought of Jack showing her the depth of passion she'd glimpsed in those smoldering eyes. She'd known him less than a day but felt instant sparks every time he looked at her, not to mention the rush of heat when he'd held her in his arms.

Gabriella looked up, hearing the approach of horses' hooves and coach wheels on gravel. The carriage stopped, and a tall man with white hair brushed back from his high forehead, and a perfectly groomed white mustache, descended. Even from a distance, Gabriella could see he was elegantly dressed in an impeccably tailored three-piece suit, with a white-winged collared shirt and blue silk tie. His eyes twinkled as he watched Lady Darling come down the steps to welcome him, her hands extended in greeting.

The dapper man took her hands and kissed her knuckles. "Katherine, it has been too long since I've seen you." His smile dazzled against the glow of his golden tan.

"Stefano, welcome to Nido dell' Aquila. I am so happy to see you. I've looked forward to your visit."

"Ah, *si*, the gallery has kept me away for too long, but we will make amends. Has Signora Shipley arrived yet?"

"No, but I received a telegram from Constance yesterday, and I expect her and the other guests tomorrow. But tonight, we will share a more intimate dinner, and you can fill me in on everything happening in Florence."

"The steel workers strike that crippled Florence and beyond is over, thank God. It reminds us that we are all beholden to the worker. I am of the opinion that they should be recompensed commensurably for their efforts." Stefano looked around and asked, "And where is Jack?"

Kitty waved her hands dismissively. "I find myself uttering those exact words countless times a day. Where is Jack? Gone to Piombino on some fool errand. I tell you, Stefano, you must have a talk with my nephew. I'm beside myself with worry for him. He promised to return for dinner, so you'll have an opportunity to pound some sense into him. Come inside, and we will have tea while your things are delivered to your rooms."

Stefano patted his stomach. "Refreshments would be welcome. Don't worry; I'll have a heart-to-heart talk with him. If only I could have spoken to his father, may he rest in peace, before he made such a rash and ill-advised decision."

"That is precisely why I'm so glad to have you here—that and my undying affection. My brother was a fool who listened to fools, and now Jack is paying the price. He is not dealing well with the situation, and I'm afraid it has made him bristly and cantankerous." Kitty linked her arm through Stefano's and led him into the villa. "Hopefully, you will help us set things right."

The conversation between Stefano and Kitty lingered in Gaby's mind. She felt guilty at eavesdropping on their conversation, but her curiosity had gotten the better of her. Thank goodness the lush lemon trees and the profusion of vegetables growing in the garden had given her cover.

Gaby sensed Jack's trip to Piombino had something to do with her, because he'd asked her if she was from there. Maybe she was giving herself too much credit, as it wasn't likely she took up much space in Jack's thoughts.

Considering what Lady Darling had said to Stefano Bardino, she couldn't help but be curious about what Jack had done to warrant such punishment from his father. Whatever it was, it had cost him dearly and provoked his courtship of the Cynthia woman.

A shot of jealousy coursed through Gaby at the thought of Jack marrying the heiress, and she tried to shake it off. But she couldn't help wondering why Jack's father had disowned him. What had Jack been accused of that his father would strip him of his title and inheritance? Given how much Lady Darling adored her nephew, it was somewhat perplexing that his own father would believe unfounded accusations.

Gaby shook her head as she gathered the herbs she needed for dinner. She didn't have time to ponder all the questions percolating in her head, as there was too much to do before dinner was served. She slipped the shears into her overflowing basket and headed back to the kitchen.

CHAPTER SEVEN

Maremma, Italy
October 17, 1902

S TEFANO WIPED HIS mouth, sat back in his chair, patted his
stomach, and sighed. "Whoever is cooking in the kitchen has
golden hands. This meal was *squisito*."

Aunt Kitty beamed. "I agree. It was a splendid meal."

Jack stared down at his empty plate, wishing Gaby had joined
them for dinner. Stefano was right—everything had been
delicious. The cacciatore was spectacular, but the soft pillows of
gnocchi had stolen his heart, or rather, the beautiful chef who'd
prepared them had stolen it.

His ride to Piombino had been an utter failure. No one there
had ever heard of her, nor did they know of any dark-haired
woman chef. The only indisputable revelation to be had from
today was that Gabriella D'Angelo was a master in the kitchen,
which only gave rise to more questions.

Tomorrow Cynthia Maxwell would arrive, and he would be
expected to entertain her when all he wanted to do was spend
time with Gaby. His instincts told him that the only way he could
find out about Gaby was from Gaby herself.

Gaby. He didn't know when he'd started thinking of her as
Gaby and not Gabriella, but the nickname had come to mind as
Jack rode back to Aunt Kitty's, and he'd found himself whispering

it aloud, as if his lips were pressed to her ear in a moment of passion. God, he was acting like some lovesick schoolboy. He'd never been ruled by such foolish notions before.

He raised his glass and finished his claret, hoping the conversation would turn elsewhere.

"You will not believe this, Stefano, but the golden hands that prepared this meal only yesterday were rescued from certain death by none other than our Jack."

Stefano's brows lifted. "Surely you jest?"

Aunt Kitty shook her head. "You will meet her tomorrow. Unfortunately, she deigned to remain in the kitchen tonight with the staff. She is a charming girl and pretty as a picture." She turned to her nephew. "Don't you agree, Jack?" Not waiting for his reply, she returned her gaze to Stefano. "Gabriella is American but of Italian heritage, and possesses a lush, exotic beauty and an effervescent spirit that is simply captivating. You, of course, will see it at once. It is an undefinable quality, an irresistibility. Jack, perhaps you can better explain what I mean."

Jack met the knowing gaze of his aunt. He'd never been able to hide his feelings from her, and now he worried about how much he'd revealed of his interest in the cooking goddess. "I think you exaggerate, Aunt Kitty. She is comely, but I see nothing out of the ordinary in her magnetism."

Jack knew his aunt was disappointed in his decision to marry for money, but what was he to do under the circumstances? He'd been denied his birthright. His father's line must not be broken, and his children should not be denied their patrimony. That was the duty of a firstborn son, to perpetuate the family, and he'd failed—or rather, been forced to fail by his deceitful cousin.

Frustration and anger besieged him. If only his cousin hadn't been so duplicitous, he would not be stuck in limbo, biding his time. On the other hand, he might not have met Gaby, either. He would have either been in London or Egypt.

"Oh, I do most certainly disagree," Aunt Kitty said with a lifted brow. "Few men would be able to resist that face and figure. I am in awe of your power to resist her, Jack."

"I suppose there are some men who would find her attractive. Those that are drawn to that earthy quality," he amended, feeling a bit heated under the collar. Now, both Stefano and his aunt were regarding him with knowing looks.

Aunt Kitty turned to Stefano and confided, "Jack has taken a decided dislike of our dear Gabriella. He has trust issues. But she is very much alone in this world and suffers from amnesia from her near-death experience, and I am of a mind to do what I can for her. I am offering her a permanent position as our chef. She is far more than a cook; frankly, I fancy her as a friend."

"I cannot wait to meet the beautiful Gabriella. Be careful, or I might steal her away from you." Stefano winked. "I am certain she would be a great asset in Florence. A woman who can cook like an angel and looks like a goddess." He whistled. "A man could do worse. The joys of bachelorhood are highly exaggerated, *veramente*."

"Bachelorhood may be truly, as you say, exaggerated, but Signorina D'Angelo will not be leaving Nido dell' Aquila," Jack blurted. Again, he felt like that errant schoolboy as Aunt Kitty and Stefano's brows rose in response to his outburst.

"I beg your pardon, Jack, but I don't believe you have any authority over Gabriella or her future," Aunt Kitty reprimanded him. "As much as I would hate to lose her, her future might be brighter in a bustling city than a country estate where she's unlikely to find any suitors or make any friends her own age."

Jack pushed back from the table and stood. "If you will excuse me, I need to stretch my legs and require some fresh air."

"Go, darling. Stefano and I will retire to the library and take our dessert and coffee there. Please join us after you have walked your temper off."

The room felt impossibly stuffy. Jack bowed stiffly and left the room. His aunt knew just how to get his goat. And she and Stefano were clearly in cahoots. Well, they could yabber all they wanted. He needed to think.

>>>><<<<

"EVERYTHING IS IN order." Gaby beamed at her staff. "Thank you for helping make tonight's meal a success. I am more confident than ever that we will become a great team. Get a good night's sleep, as we have not only tomorrow's dinner to prepare, but the dinner party on Saturday will demand our best efforts. I will see you at five in the morning. We have much to accomplish."

Gabriella untied her apron and left it in the laundry basket for tomorrow's wash. Taking a clean cloth, she dipped it in a bowl of fresh water and wiped her face. She needed to decompress, and the coolness of the night called to her.

The moon was nearly full, and the sky was clear of clouds. A star-filled sky greeted her, and for the first time since she'd arrived in Maremma, she began to reclaim her positivity and confidence. Even the possibility of her never finding her way home to the twenty-first century couldn't dampen her belief that she could survive and maybe even prosper here.

But she would not give up. Tomorrow she would explore the house for the Allegretto painting. If she could find it, there might be a way back.

The path she took meandered down to the bluff's edge. A slight breeze blew, and she stopped and unpinned her hair, breathing a sigh of relief as she massaged her sore scalp. The cool air lifted the tendrils of her hair, tickling her shoulders. Moonlight shimmering on the Mediterranean drew her, and she walked to the bluff's edge.

A shiver shimmied up her spine as she saw the shrub she'd clung to. It was so unsubstantial; she couldn't believe it had held her weight. The waves rolling in were deceptively soothing as the frothy water swept over the craggy rocks below. Only the sharp-edged tips poked through the surface as the tide ebbed and surged. Gaby would never have survived, had she fallen.

"I do hope you are not intending to repeat yesterday's performance."

The voice did not frighten or startle her, because she'd recognize that sensual baritone anywhere.

Slowly turning, she stepped away from the edge. "I suppose your sneaking up on me is better than you astride a horse and bearing down on me."

Jack chuckled and took a puff of his cheroot. "I'm glad to find you are not suicidal."

She hadn't seen him since the morning and had never seen him in evening attire. His hair was brushed back off his high forehead and fell in golden waves below his winged collar. His velvet frock coat displayed his broad shoulders and narrowed at the waist.

Self-assured and in command, he was intimidating, and she found herself at a loss for words. The way he stared at her made her heart stampede in her chest. He had such a profound effect on her, and she found it hard to understand why. She was aware of how she must look, tired, in a rumpled dress, her hair loose and untamed.

He took a step closer, and she took a step back.

"Whoa." He held his hands up. "Do not walk backward. I don't think we'll be as lucky as last night. I will not intrude on your space. Please come away from the bluff's edge." He backed up, giving her space to follow.

It was the "please" that got to her. It seemed the most unlikely of words coming from Jack. Joining him, she stood her ground, facing him. "I hope you found the meal satisfactory, my lord."

"The meal, yes…" He paused as he puffed on his cigar.

She held her breath as she waited. She so wanted him to like her cooking, and it surprised her just how much it would mean to her.

"It was extraordinary," he said, turning to look at her. "Truly, I've never had such a delicious meal." There it was again, the tender smile that made her tingle from the top of her head down to her toes. "Wherever did you learn to cook like that?"

"Thank you, my lord." Gaby could barely speak; she was

almost mesmerized by the warmth in his blue-green eyes. "I—um—I don't know…" She hesitated, hating that she was lying to him. "The recipes are clear in my head, but unfortunately, the rest of my life is a blur. I don't remember."

What would you say if I told you my family had one of the most successful restaurants in Chicago? You'd want to find out about it, but you'd find nothing because Trattoria della Vita won't exist for another sixty years, when my great-grandfather Luigi D'Angelo opens it on Canal Street.

It was a shame she couldn't confide in him, because she sensed if he were a friend, he would be a loyal one. She needed a friend and wished he didn't suspect her of malicious intentions.

I wish I could tell you where I come from. I wish I could tell you what brought me here… I wish you would take me in your arms and kiss me.

That was a wish she didn't expect to come true, and one that would only end badly.

His eyes seemed to drill into her. "I see you haven't recovered anything from your earlier life. It's almost as if you magically appeared out of nowhere."

Gaby felt her cheeks warm, and she hoped in the dim moonlight, he couldn't see. Jack had no idea how spot-on he was. "I'm sure I came from somewhere. I wish I could remember."

"So, I'm to believe the only memory that has returned to you is the cookbook in your head."

In the pit of her stomach, she could feel her temper begin to simmer. "No, my lord, but as you may have noticed, I speak English and Italian with an American accent. Certainly, the staff in the kitchen noticed and had some trouble understanding me, which leads me to believe that I was raised in the United States."

"Perhaps the U.S. Department of State can help us. A missing person report may have been filed."

"I wouldn't have a clue how to go about that," she stammered.

"I will look into it. Don't you want to be reunited with your family?" he asked in an abrupt tone.

"Of course I do, more than you know."

"Or perhaps there's a husband who is frantically looking for you."

"I'm not married—"

"How do you know that?" he interrupted, his voice sharp.

"I—I just know. That's all." She held up her left hand. "I don't have a wedding ring, do I?"

"You could have lost it. It could have been stolen. Or you might have taken it off yourself."

"Look, I'm not married; that's that!" She took a deep breath and let it out slowly, trying to calm her nerves. "I appreciate everything that you and Lady Darling have done for me. Cooking for your aunt is my way of thanking her for her generosity. And when all is said and done, and I have to make my way in *this* world, then at least I have a skill that should serve me well. I am sure I could find a suitable position somewhere."

"My aunt would never throw you out; she is far too kind to do that. And besides, you have more than cemented your place after you stepped in and saved the day with your cooking prowess." He took a puff on his cigar and assessed her. "Besides, she's taken a liking to you."

Gaby knew she was playing with fire, but she could not stop herself from asking, "And you, my lord, would you throw me out, or have you also taken a liking to me?"

The rise of his brows showed his bewilderment. "You ask the most impertinent questions, Gaby. What would you have me say? I am as smitten with you as my aunt and wish you to remain within my protection forever? Is that what you are asking?"

Yes. No. "Oh, I would never be so presumptuous to expect anything of the sort from you."

"You are the most exasperating woman I have ever met."

"Well, you are the most arrogant man I've ever met." She'd never held the upper hand in their prior exchanges, and the rush was enough to make her giddy and a little too daring. "But then, I'm sure you're not used to any woman willing to match wits with you or a woman that won't kowtow to your overbearing nature."

Jack dropped his cheroot and ground it beneath his heel. He stared at her, and her pulse quickened. *What is he thinking?* Had she made him angry, he might do something rash, like throw her over the bluff. She'd witnessed both his temper and strength, which were formidable. But for some reason, she couldn't walk away. She was frozen to the spot, her eyes locked with his, desperately wanting him to kiss her…

HE WAS ROOTED to the spot, his eyes locked with hers, wanting desperately to kiss her. The very idea of favoring her set his pulse racing. An internal battle was raging within him, and his entire body answered the call. The bayonet between his legs responded, demanding satisfaction.

The ache was maddening, and as much as he tried, he couldn't suppress it—nor, in truth, did he want to. It had been a long time since he'd bedded a woman, and never had he wanted to more than with Gaby. The way the little minx stood up to him was exhilarating. He had long ago decided he would not saddle himself with a woman who couldn't think for herself. To live like that would be a tedium he could not bear. Yet, due to unforeseen circumstances, that was precisely the kind of woman he was courting. Cynthia would always depend on his judgment and do as he wished, like a compliant servant. The boredom would surely drive him to madness, or at the very least in search of entertainment outside of marriage.

He could see by Gaby's expression that she knew she might have pushed him too far. She was worried, and rightly so. Something was going on with her that he needed to figure out. Her past, most of all.

Amnesia, my arse! If they were playing poker, he'd call her bluff. Maybe that wouldn't be such a bad idea. He could challenge her to a game of strip poker. Now that would be something. His cock swelled at the thought of watching her slowly peel off each layer of clothing. Her long, wild hair brushed over her nipples. Nipples he ached to touch, to draw into his mouth and suck on—nibble, bite, and tug with his teeth, then soothe with his tongue…making her beg for more.

Damn! Damn! Damn! It wasn't often that his saber's need replaced his ability to think, but the vixen drove him mad with desire. He was sure she wanted him, and he wasn't about to let the opportunity pass. He would subdue that cheeky mouth in the best way possible, and who knew where it might go with a bit of luck? If everything went well, he'd have her, and after, he'd hopefully be free of this cursed desire.

He grabbed her and pulled her against him. Naturally, she could feel his hardness press and pulse against her. There could be no denial of the effect she had on him.

Her eyes widened, and a gasp escaped those full, sensuous lips. A low, rich rumble of desire escaped him. "I do favor you, Gaby," he rasped. "More than you know." He held her gaze, watching as the meaning of his words registered in her beguiling hazel eyes. Ever so slowly, he lowered his head, claiming her lips.

Her body relaxed against him as she returned his kiss; by God, it was the most heavenly thing he'd ever tasted. Those ripe breasts, whose vision tormented his sleep, were firm against his chest. Shockingly, she wore no corset, and her protuberant nipples poked against him, the full, round orbs of her femininity pressing against his shirt. How he wanted to touch them. How he was certain that Gabriella D'Angelo would desire more, beg for more, he didn't know, but he felt sure that the kitchen goddess would prove to be a goddess in the bedroom.

Her lips parted, his tongue gained entry, and the thought of another part of her body opening to him brought a low growl from him. In his wildest dreams, he hadn't expected waves of desire to render him vulnerable. It was as if Gaby had taken over his entire being.

He held her face, delivering kisses to her closed eyes, delicious lips, and temple, kissing down the softness of her neck and then back up to the delicate shell of her ear. "Gaby…Gaby…Gaby. My darling girl, I want you desperately."

Her breathless moan nearly undid him. He was close to tugging her down onto the grass when she pushed against his chest. "Jack, I don't think…"

He silenced her protestation with his mouth and pulled her back against him. He'd been right—she was passion personified. Her kisses weren't those of a novice. He hadn't expected her to be. But the way her body fit against his, every inch contouring to fit his muscled frame, his mind was boggled to such a degree that the very possibility of spilling his seed just from the pleasure of kissing and touching her made him tremble as he sought to regain control. To feel such uncontrollable passion was not something to be taken lightly. He could only wonder at what awaited when he possessed her fully.

With concerted effort, he ground against her vulva and deepened the kiss. He swept his hands down her back, tracing the sinuous curves of her delectable bottom. Desire and dissatisfaction were one; he wanted to feel her skin and not the fabric of her dress. He wanted to kiss the smooth skin of her stomach that he'd glimpsed when he rescued her and then delve into her wet warmth and bring her to satisfaction.

Damn, we can't very well make love here in the open on the grass. Though convincing my cock is another matter when my shaft's only goal is to be lost in the perfection of her cunny.

"Come back to my rooms, Gaby."

She pulled from his arms, and he searched her face. "I can't. If I do, I will be lost. We should forget this happened. We would both be doing each other a disservice."

"Are you mad? A disservice? Do you not feel the same powerful attraction to me as I do to you?"

"Jack, even if I do feel attracted, what good is it? It can only bring heartbreak. Cynthia Maxwell will arrive tomorrow, and you will begin your courtship. The worst scenario is I might be left with a child. You will recover your title, lands, and good name, and then you will return to your estate. Where would that leave me?"

Without realizing it, Jack had begun to pace. "What would you have me do, Gaby? How can I make it right so that we may explore this passion we both feel?"

She brushed at the tears beginning to fill her eyes, and his heart wrenched at the sight.

"There is nothing to be done, Jack. You can't make it right. It's best if we forget what just happened. No harm was done, and we will forget it in a few days or surely in a few weeks. I bid you goodnight."

GABY TURNED TO go. She needed to get out of there before the flow of tears overwhelmed her. She'd allowed the kiss, welcomed it, and now she was bereft of it. There was no choice open to her. Their lovemaking would assuredly provide pleasure beyond any she'd ever known, but the rejection that must follow would be impossible to bear. There would be no tomorrow for them. No future.

Jack grabbed her arm and stopped her. "You can disabuse yourself of one thing. I would never abandon you under any circumstance if you were with a child. In truth, I have given this much thought. I've even imagined building a house here in Tuscany, a house for you once I've reclaimed my earldom. I could arrange my life to spend much of the year here with you. That is how I see our future."

Gaby's pulse pounded in her ears, and it wasn't from joy. It was pure, unadulterated anger.

She whirled around to face him, punctuating every word that poured from her with an index finger to his chest. "You smug bastard. Do you think you can buy me like you would a horse? What a pretty picture you've painted. You, married to your countess who will bear you sons to inherit your earldom and carry on your name, and all the while, you will keep me, your *putana*, in the countryside with your bastard offspring? You certainly have conjured up a fairytale future in your mind. I will never be your whore, Jack. Never!" She freed her arm from his grasp and ran down the path from whence she'd come.

Tears streamed down her face, and she whispered curses under her breath as she slowed to a walk. Why could the one man who evoked her passion never be hers? Gaby adored Lady Darling, but the thought of living here at the villa and one day seeing Jack return with his new bride would kill her as surely as a bullet from a gun. She had to find that painting and find a way back to the world she came from.

But even if she found herself stranded here in the past, she would have to find another position. Perhaps once the guests were gone, she could confide in Lady Darling and ask for her help. It occurred to Gaby that Jack would likely leave with Cynthia Maxwell and return to England to prepare for their nuptials.

She glanced back and could see the shadow that was Jack with his back to her. Overcome with a heart-wrenching pain, she lifted her skirt and ran toward the villa.

CHAPTER EIGHT

Maremma, Italy
October 17, 1902

J ACK LIT ANOTHER cheroot and puffed agitatedly, staring out to
sea. His body, taut with frustration and denied satisfaction,
would torment him throughout the night. How Gaby had
managed to tie him up in knots was beyond him. His good sense
and logic were nowhere in sight.

He was reminded of a line from Shakespeare's *Richard III*,
"My kingdom for a horse." Judging by the snarl of his thoughts
and his body's reaction to her, in his case, more apropos would be
"my kingdom for a kiss," or rather "a romp in the hay."

Damn her.

But though in his thoughts he cursed her and tried to make
less of what he was feeling, he couldn't deny there was much
more between them. Something deep and lasting that would not
be denied.

Gabriella D'Angelo had rejected him, and he couldn't believe
it. He offered more than she could ever possibly attain in this
world. By God, he'd build her a palace if it made her happy. His
passion for her was so powerful that he might even be falling in
love with her.

Dare he lay his cards out on the table and tell her? Indeed, if
they had children, he would love and support them as much as

any children born legitimately. Why couldn't she understand that what he offered was not a diminishment of what they felt for each other? It was just the way of the world. In truth, he knew of few society marriages where love was a factor. Marriage among the titled, in most instances, was simply a means to an end. Great love was shared as often as not outside of a marriage. No one would ever admit this to be true, but none would deny that it might be.

Puffs of smoke evaporated in the cool night air, but not so the anger that simmered in Jack. He would find a way to convince her—he must. But how?

A sardonic chuckle escaped him. The tightness of his trousers reminded him that it would be another night of walking until exhaustion claimed him. But it would provide an opportunity and the time needed to find a solution.

He returned to the path that led to the villa but veered off in the direction of the stables. A moonlight ride on Xanthus would wear him out enough to sleep. The horse was sensitive to his moods and would undoubtedly read his anxiety.

If he possessed Gaby, would he rid himself of this insatiable hunger? The few kisses they'd shared had only whetted his desire for her. He was so consumed with her he could think of nothing else.

He shook his head. *What is wrong with you?*

He also knew that Aunt Kitty would not be pleased with the arrangement he envisioned—Cynthia as his wife and Gabriella as his mistress. Though she sometimes vexed him, his aunt's opinion mattered to him. After the death of his mother, it was Kitty who had filled the void. And knowing that she would disapprove of his intentions only made him feel worse than he already did.

He saddled Xanthus and cantered toward the bluffs, riding along the cliff's edge. No matter how far he rode, he could not let go of the fire that Gaby had ignited. The way she molded her body to his bound him to her more than any band of gold. No woman had ever held such power over him, and now he dreaded the arrival of Cynthia tomorrow.

If Gaby was in a huff now, seeing Cynthia would only rile her more. Although she held no appeal to him, Cynthia was beautiful, well-mannered, and had been raised for a society marriage. He could already imagine Gaby comparing herself to the heiress and finding herself wanting. But in his eyes, there was no comparison.

He needed to do something heroic in Gaby's eyes, something that would convince her to trust him and risk everything for him. He had to convince Gaby that his marriage to Cynthia wouldn't interfere with their future. They could have a wonderful life together, if only she would see reason.

The cool night air cleared his head and soothed the tension from his body. Of course, he would need to enlist the help of his aunt. He'd have to convince Aunt Kitty to help in his campaign to win over Gaby. Surely, Gaby would eventually understand that there was no other way, and he had no choice. He needed to marry Cynthia because he needed the funds to fight for his inheritance. He could hire the finest legal minds in England to build a case where Beauford took advantage of Jack's father's weakened state and tampered with his will.

I have to make Gaby understand just what is at stake.

Jack squeezed Xanthus's flanks with his calves, and the fleet stallion extended his stride, flying over the turf toward the comfort of his stall and a well-deserved bucket of carrots. The clever horse knew that obedience to his master meant a tasty reward, and Jack couldn't help but hope that Gabriella would soon learn the same.

He would find a way to conquer whatever obstacles stood in their way, not only for his own satisfaction but hers. He had to get through to that beautiful, stubborn spirit. The sooner she accepted they were meant to be, the sooner he could give her the pleasure he so desperately wanted to give her.

An idea occurred to him. If he bedded Gaby, and God smiled on their union and got her with child, she would have no choice but to acquiesce to his plans. No mother would deny her child the love and protection of a father, especially if that child was a bastard. He hated that word and would kill any man or woman who labeled his child as such. Still, only a father's love and beneficent gifts could keep that child safe and the gossipmongers at bay.

For the first time since Gaby's rejection, he found a glimmer of hope. Now all he needed to do was seduce her into his bed.

With a growl of satisfaction, he spurred Xanthus homeward.

CHAPTER NINE

Maremma, Italy
October 17, 1902

G ABY NEARLY MOWED Mrs. Livingstone down when she
rushed into the kitchen after her encounter with Jack. She
needed to move out of his room and into another. The lady's
maid happily helped her gather her belongings and take them to
the former cook's room. The room was dark, dingy, and sparsely
furnished, but Gaby knew some fresh cut flowers and herb sprigs
would scent the air and spruce the room up a little.

After washing up in the staff's communal lavatory, she lay
down in the narrow bed and blew out the candle. She brushed
her fingers over her lips, still feeling the burn of Jack's kiss, and
closed her eyes.

But sleep would not come, even after such a grueling day.
After tossing and turning for hours, she finally gave up, dressed,
and went to the kitchen, where she had always found solace.

She was beyond pissed off that he would proposition her,
offering her the exalted position of his mistress to be available at
his beck and call while he went off and married a rich woman and
took his place in society.

And yet she couldn't get his kisses out of her head. It was as
though she'd been struck by lightning. Barely two days ago, she
was sitting in the Met looking at a painting, waiting for her

friends, when she was hurtled back in time to 1902 Italy! And now she was working as a chef for an aristocratic yet eccentric British expat. Her entire world could not have been upended more. Even though Lady Darling was indeed a darling, her nephew was not!

How dare he?

Gaby was still shaking from anger, yet she could not forget the feel of his lips on hers and still wished the kiss had never ended.

Why? Why was she falling for a man who was not only utterly wrong for her for so many reasons, but a man who couldn't offer her the future she'd always wanted. He was no different than the men she'd dated in Chicago, only more entitled and more selfish. Also, way more attractive and charming and fascinating…

No! She refused to think of his good qualities. His arrogance far outweighed those. Besides, she had far more important things to occupy her mind and time. She had to figure out how to help Allegretto and his muse, and hopefully, they would help her go home.

And then I won't have to worry about Jack because I'll be more than a hundred years in the future. And that's as far away as you can get.

It turned out Gaby barely had time to think about anything other than work, supervising her kitchen staff, and keeping an eye on the beef stock simmering on the stove. Even though much of the prepping was for tomorrow night's festivities, there was today's breakfast, lunch, and dinner to contend with and bring to table.

Things became frenetic when two hunters arrived at the kitchen door with a cart bearing a freshly killed wild boar for tomorrow night's stew. Gaby instructed Angelina to dice the onions, carrots, and celery for the marinade. At the same time, she enlisted the help of Luigi and the footman Thomas to help her butcher the boar. Of course, Gaby had learned to take apart any bird, animal, or fish from her nonna. Then, in cooking school, she'd enriched those skills by studying the cuisine of other cultures. Every part of the carcass would be preserved for later use.

Still, her first imperative was to get the boar meat marinated. It needed at least twenty-four hours to tenderize, and then it would be browned with the vegetables and simmered for hours. The wild boar stew would be served with creamy polenta and vegetables. To pair with such a heavy main course, she planned a lightly dressed arugula salad, served with shaved parmesan and *pomodorini*, Italian cherry tomatoes known for their exceptional sweetness. She instructed Angelina to bake a thick, rustic Italian bread to sop up the gravy from the wild boar stew and a *torta di mandorle*, a traditional almond cake served with pears poached in buttery syrup.

Having gotten the wild boar marinated and stored in the icebox, Gaby stepped out to the garden to grab a breath of fresh air. She'd been working for hours and needed a break. She untied the kerchief that held her hair back, shook her curls free, broke off a sprig of mint, and nibbled on the leaves. With a basket beside her, she got on her knees and began snipping oregano and thyme for the minestrone she had planned for tonight's main course.

The clip-clop of hooves on limestone announced the arrival of a carriage. It pulled up to the villa's entrance, and two beautifully attired women stepped out. A lady's maid followed them onto the limestone drive. The older woman was tall and statuesque, with raven-black hair, but she drew only a momentary glance from Gabriella. The beautiful younger woman, whose lustrous blonde curls were swept up in a stylish Gibson updo, commanded all of Gaby's attention.

Gabriella stared, her hands unconsciously smoothing her own messy, dark waves. She felt a growing unease that stole her confidence and took her back to her high school days. The fair-skinned beauty could only be Cynthia Maxwell, Jack's future countess.

The tall, slim girl looked about with apprehension, her limpid blue eyes taking in the house. "Aunty, you are sure they are expecting us?"

"What an inane question. Of course they are expecting us. This is the way things are done in my native country. Their relaxed attitude is one of the things I abhor about the Italians." The older woman looked around critically. "Things move at a different pace here in the countryside. Cynthia, show some backbone. You are a desirable commodity. Heads above that detestable young man you made a fuss over."

Cynthia's eyes dropped to the ground, and she bit her lip.

The baroness rested her hand on Cynthia's shoulder. "Let us not speak of him again. He might have ruined you if I had not intervened. Things turned out for the best, and if all goes well, you will be a countess in a few months."

"Yes, aunty."

The front door opened, and Antonio, the butler, emerged. "*Baronessa Blythe Hollow e Signorina Maxwell, benvenuti, all* Nido dell' Aquila. I am Antonio, at your service." The engaging butler, Antonio Jr., was the son of the previous butler who'd retired a few years back and trained his boy to take over the position.

The imperious woman in black flicked her wrist in agitation. "We do not need to listen to your prattle. *Siamo stanco ed affamato.* We require refreshments without delay. See that our trunks are sent to our rooms. Where are Lady Darling and Lord Langsford?"

The startled butler stammered, "*Si*, signora. I will see to everything. They are in the library having tea and have asked that you join them there. Please follow me."

"Come, Cynthia—we will greet our hosts, quench our thirst, and assuage our hunger. After which, I must retire to our rooms and rest."

From her vantage point in the garden, Gabriella watched the elegant women follow Antonio into the house. The determination on the baroness's face was unmistakable. Her purpose was to ensure that her ward, Cynthia, was soon wedded.

Gaby's stomach twisted into knots at the thought of Jack marrying the wealthy blonde heiress. She hadn't paid attention, but now recalled Kitty saying the baroness was Italian. The only tidbits she'd picked up were that the baroness was a recent widow of a British financier and had inherited the guardianship of his heir and niece, Cynthia Maxwell. Gaby found it odd that a young woman who'd inherited such great wealth would find herself under the thumb of such an unlikeable woman. She supposed Cynthia didn't have a choice in the matter if her uncle had named his wife her guardian in his will.

She couldn't make heads nor tails of the strange exchange she'd overheard. Especially the part hinting at Cynthia falling for a man in London that her aunt deemed beneath her. From what Gaby had gleaned, Cynthia had almost compromised herself.

In any case, she imagined the young woman could hardly wait to marry Jack and be free of her dour guardian. Being with him would surely be preferable to being ordered about by this aunt.

A sensuous vision of luxuriating in bed with Jack naked caused her cheeks to warm. *Where do these foolish thoughts come from? You are shameful.* But as hard as she tried, Gaby couldn't stop thinking about what it would be like to make love with him.

Fortunately, her daydream was cut short by the arrival of another carriage. Two beautifully dressed women emerged from the elegant conveyance. The older woman, her gaze drawn to the sea, said, "Blossom, is this not the most beautiful place on earth? I am so delighted to be here. Stefano was right to suggest we spend a few days in this paradise before going to Florence."

"*Oui*, Constance, we will take some lovely walks, and we will have a wonderful reunion with the Marchioness and Marquess of Danbury, and the chief inspector and Madame Doumaz," said the younger woman with a lilting French accent.

A much-harried Antonio bustled back out to greet them. "*Signora Shipley e Signora Rosalind, benvenuti,* I am Antonio the butler. Lady Darling and Lord Langsford await you in the library, where tea is being served."

"Antonio, thank you. Blossom and I will be delighted to join them, if you would please lead the way."

Antonio bowed, smiling. "Come this way. I will see that your things are taken to your rooms."

"That will be much appreciated." Constance and Blossom linked arms and followed a much happier Antonio into the house.

The contrast between these ladies and the previous couldn't be more apparent. The American art collector displayed a happy countenance, a good nature, and a polite bearing, while the baroness was brusque, bossy, and overbearing.

Gabriella picked up her basket and sighed. It was time to get back to the kitchen. She only wished she could see the interaction between Jack and Cynthia. Maybe then she could face reality and banish her yearning for him for good.

It would never have worked anyway. Even if Cynthia wasn't in the picture, even if he didn't have to battle for his birthright, their backgrounds couldn't be more different. And the biggest matzo ball of all was they were from two different centuries. *Talk about a long-distance relationship!* The sooner she accepted that fact, the easier it would be to survive.

⋙✕⋘

JACK GAZED INTO his teacup as if the dregs could conjure up some vision for him to divine. When he'd returned to the house late last night, Mrs. Livingstone had been waiting up for him to give him the news—Gaby had quit his rooms and was now staying in the servants' quarters.

He'd been tempted to go upstairs, flip her over his shoulder, and bring her back to his bed, where she belonged. But he knew how that would end. And so, he'd slept miserably in his lonely bed. Even though Mrs. Livingstone had changed the sheets, Gaby's scent of lemon and freshly tilled garden after rainfall still lingered in his chamber.

His nerves were on edge. He couldn't bear the thought of her living in such meager circumstances, but there was nothing to be done about it, at least not yet. Traveling the world and working on archeological digs had taught him to appreciate how other cultures lived. Luxury was something he enjoyed but could easily live without.

A vision did pop into his head, one of Gaby lying gloriously nude on his bedroll in his tent in Egypt. What a sight, indeed! He'd seen her disheveled, her clothing in wet tatters when he rescued her, but it didn't take much for him to imagine what she'd look like naked with those luscious, dark waves cascading around her shoulders and those pouty nipples playing peekaboo through her curls.

Damn! He needed to calm down, or he'd soon be sporting a raging erection. He almost barked out a laugh as he realized the teacup had given him a vision after all—a vision of a dark-haired Italian-American beauty who haunted his days and nights.

Aunt Kitty raised her teacup to her lips. "You've hardly said a word today, Jack. You have many unaccountable behaviors, but silence is not one of them."

He looked at her as if hearing her for the first time. "I'm simply pondering the importance of Cynthia's arrival and the formality of asking her to marry me."

Aunt Kitty's eyes met his over the rim of her cup, and he saw that familiar gleam of mischief in her gaze. "Yes, I'm sure it preys on your mind. Your rogue bachelor days nearly being at an end must be somewhat startling, and perhaps even terrifying."

He chuckled. "You and I both know that is all rumor and innuendo. Beauford might as well have accused me of stealing the crown jewels or seducing Queen Alexandria."

"Heaven forbid! You have enough troubles without inviting Bertie's wrath. He'd probably see you swinging from the gallows."

Jack held his tongue but thought King Edward would probably be grateful for keeping the queen occupied and her attention off his well-known dalliances.

The door opened, and the baroness and Cynthia swept into the room, making a grand entrance.

Jack rose to his feet, and the baroness held her hand for him to kiss. "We are finally delivered from our wearisome journey. Lord Langsford, Lady Darling, how delightful to see you again."

Jack lightly bussed the proffered hand and then turned to Cynthia, took her hand, and bent to place a chaste kiss on it. "It is nice to see you again, Cynthia." The young woman, as always, reminded him of a pale lily—white, thin, and far too delicate. The contrast between her and Gaby was like the difference between night and day.

He took a deep breath, tamping down his frustration. He was determined to do what was best for the future of the earldom.

"I am pleased to see you, Lord Langsford," Cynthia said in a soft voice, barely meeting his eyes. "The sea view is so lovely, I—"

The sound of laughter and the door opening left Cynthia's comment dangling and unfinished. Stefano strode in with Constance on his arm and her companion close behind. The trio was chatting animatedly and with good humor.

"Ladies, I am delighted we can share this time together before traveling to Florence," Stefano said. "It will give us a wonderful opportunity to strategize how to expand your collection, Constance, especially after that terrible loss of your Allegretto."

"Think nothing of it, Stefano. The important thing is that no one was hurt. Besides, the painting was well insured, and I recovered my investment," said Constance, waving her hand and dismissing the subject.

Stefano approached Kitty with Constance on his arm. "Dear Lady Darling, I found these two lovely ladies wandering around. It seems our gathering is growing." He introduced everyone to each other, adding colorful commentary to each introduction. Everyone agreed to drop the formality of titles and address each other by first names. Kitty invited everyone to sit and partake of the freshly brewed tea and the pastries Antonio had rolled in on a three-tiered cart.

Jack exchanged pleasantries with everyone, but he was particularly intrigued with the American heiress. He'd heard she'd settled in Paris some years ago and frequently traveled throughout Europe, visiting auction houses and galleries or seeking out private sales of paintings and unique pieces to add to her collection. The woman radiated warmth and charm, yet Jack could see a keen awareness and a sharp intelligence in her eyes.

Her companion, the French woman named Blossom, was even more intriguing. Her dark hair was pulled back in a severe bun, and her tinted spectacles made it challenging to discern what she was thinking. Her simple gray dress was modest compared to Constance's elegant blue silk ensemble that included a jaunty jacket with a ruffled neckline and priceless pearls. Blossom dimmed in comparison, yet something was arresting about her, an intensity of purpose that her modest appearance could not diminish. It was as though she were purposely hiding behind a drab costume. Jack's curiosity was piqued.

"Dear Kitty," Constance said, taking the older woman's hand in hers. "Your home is *molto bello*, and its view of the sea makes me yearn for my cottage on the cape back home in America."

"Thank you, my dear Constance," Kitty said. "I hope you'll avail yourself of the enchanting walking paths surrounding Nido dell' Aquila, or perhaps you would like to ride? We have some splendid horses."

"That sounds divine," Constance enthused.

"Yes, I think a lovely walk is in order tomorrow," Blossom added in her lilting French accent. "Do you know when the marquess and marchioness will arrive, and the chief inspector and his wife?"

"Yes, I received a telegram from them this morning stating they will arrive Saturday," Kitty replied. "The foursome enjoyed a few days together in Paris and will travel together here."

"Excuse me if I digress from this quaint exchange," the baroness, whose given name was Donatella, interrupted, "but did I hear correctly, dear Constance? Were you robbed of an Allegretto painting?"

Jack had noticed that the baroness had perked up when she heard mention of the stolen painting. Constance turned to regard the baroness with a bland expression, but Jack glimpsed a gleam in her eyes, easily missed if one weren't paying attention.

"Yes," said Constance with a sigh, "it was a harrowing experience, something I would rather not speak of. To have one's home invaded is quite unsettling. Naturally, we have increased our security measures. One must always be vigilant in these matters." She reached out and patted Blossom's hand. "Blossom can attest to what a difficult time it was for all of us, including my friend and former companion Jenee, who is now married to the chief inspector. You will meet her on Saturday."

"How dreadful for you, not to mention the loss of such a valuable work of art," Donatella tutted before taking a dainty sip of her tea.

Jack noted a tense undercurrent between Constance and Donatella. He wished Gaby was here, as he felt sure she would have noticed it too. Heck, he wished he could slip away to the kitchen and coax her into his arms.

Instead, he bit into one of the cream-filled pastries and almost groaned as he imagined licking the custard off her breasts. He swallowed and took a gulp of tea, trying to control the ever-present urge that had plagued him since he'd set eyes on the luscious, dark-haired siren.

He glanced at Cynthia perched next to the baroness, nibbling on a biscuit. He probably should ask her to go for a walk at some point.

He inwardly sighed at how his life had come to this. How foolish and naïve he'd been to trust his cousin to watch over his father.

Jack shook off his morose thoughts as he focused on the conversation.

"You might know of the fate of another Allegretto," Stefano said. "The third painting in the series, *Il Letto*, is rumored to be hidden somewhere in Tuscany. It was stolen from the Uffizi Gallery in Florence in 1737, shortly after the death of the last Medici, Grand Duke Gian Gastone. He died without heirs, ending the family line. A shame, indeed, but it enhances the mystery surrounding the missing painting and the unfortunate end of such an illustrious family."

"How mysterious," said Kitty. "I do love a good mystery, don't you, Jack, dear?"

"Er, yes, but I have enough to do with the upcoming exploration of the Etruscan tombs at Populonia."

"Oh, I had no idea," Constance said, setting her teacup down. "What a fascinating vocation you have, Jack. I should like to know more about your archeological work."

"Indeed, I would be happy to enlighten you." Jack smiled.

"That gives me a tremendous notion," Kitty piped up. "I'm certain Jack would be happy to arrange an outing. Perhaps a picnic at the excavation site?"

"Yes, that could be arranged," Jack replied.

"And you could show us the tombs. You're always telling me about the necropolis and the city of the dead."

"Dead?" said Cynthia. "Oh, I don't think I'd want to see any dead people."

Jack struggled not to cringe. "I will look into it first thing tomorrow," he said. "I think an excursion is a fine idea." He turned to her. "I can promise you there won't be anything to fear, Cynthia. But if you are uncomfortable, you may remain here and enjoy the sun and fresh air in the garden."

The baroness cast a disparaging gaze at Cynthia. "Don't be ridiculous, Cynthia. You need to take an interest in everything Lord Langsford does. For it is the foundation of a happy relationship."

Cynthia looked down, acquiescing to her aunt's chastisement. "Of course you are right, aunty. I spoke without thinking." She glanced back at Jack, a smile hovering on her mouth. "I'm sure it will be safe with you there."

"Good—then we will plan it for the day after tomorrow," Jack replied. "I think the other guests will find it interesting too."

"Yes," said Aunt Kitty. "I will speak to Gabriella about our plans. She's our new chef and has hands of gold, as Stefano will testify. In fact, I will invite her to join us."

Donatella's eyebrows spiked up to her hairline. "You're going to invite a cook to socialize with us?"

Aunt Kitty cast a frosty look at the baroness. "And why not? This is the twentieth century, after all. Gabriella D'Angelo is an intelligent, charming, and educated young woman. A trained gourmet chef who stepped in, thank heavens, to cook for us due to our cook's recent and unexpected indisposition. Gabriella also hails from America, and I am certain Constance will appreciate a fellow American joining us."

"Oh, I cannot wait to meet her," Constance chimed in with a grin. "I am so pleased with your kind consideration, Kitty."

Jack's lips twitched at Constance's quick support for Kitty's suggestion, although his aunt could hold her own under any circumstances. But Kitty knew full well about his argument with Gaby and her move to the servants' quarters. Yet she'd made a point of talking about Gabriella.

What are you up to, Kitty Darling?

CHAPTER TEN

Maremma, Italy
October 18, 1902

G ABY DRIED HER hands on a kitchen towel and cast a critical eye around her. Sofia, the scullery maid, was finishing scrubbing the counters down with a boar's hairbrush and a soapy pail of water. Gaby patted her on the shoulder. "I can see my reflection in those counters, Sofia." She chuckled. "Excellent work today; now go get some sleep."

Sofia was the youngest on staff, the least recompensed, and worked harder than anyone else. Gaby's heart went out to all the kitchen staff; they were all teenagers. They were all dedicated, willing to take on new tasks, and eager to learn. She planned to ask Lady Darling for a small raise for everyone, but a slightly larger one for Sofia, a sweet girl who cared for her ailing mother.

They reminded her so much of herself at that age. The kitchen had always been her favorite place to be. She was forever hovering around her nonna, mother, and aunts. Absorbing, watching, learning. Listening to their stories, their singing, their arguments, and their laughter.

Oh, how I miss them. Would she ever see them again? Had it only been a few days since she'd arrived? It felt so much longer.

She swallowed the lump in her throat, untied her apron, and dropped it in the hamper with the other soiled linens. The dinner had gone well, with Kitty sending congratulations and praise back to the kitchen. Gaby was exhausted and should have gone upstairs to her room, but the cool night air beckoned her.

On tiptoes, she crept along the hallway to the library's door. She looked around first and, seeing no one, pressed her ear to the door and listened to the conversation and laughter that drifted out to her.

Everyone sounded like they were having a wonderful time. They'd certainly imbibed enough of the delicious Tuscan Chianti to turn even the most taciturn into giddy guests. She heard Jack's rumbling bass voice booming with laughter as Stefano, the art dealer, recounted a recent scandal in Florence, where an errant priest got a Florentine conte's wife pregnant. Even the baroness, whom Antonio had aptly given the sobriquet of *il reclamante*, the complainer, laughed.

Satisfied that Jack would be otherwise occupied, Gaby grabbed a blanket, wrapped it around her shoulders, and left the house to enjoy the cool night air. Keeping a safe distance from the bluffs, she walked a path that led past the stables. She gazed at the night sky. Clouds had rolled in, and she smelled rain in the air. If she'd been back in New York or Chicago, she would have checked the weather app on her phone. Now she only had her senses to rely on.

An occasional neigh floated out to her from the stables. As a child, she had yearned for a pony, but the expense of keeping one wasn't something her parents thought worthwhile. She'd been so upset that she'd cried herself to sleep. But she soon got over her disappointment. Between school and working in the family restaurant, she had plenty enough to occupy her time.

Watching her grandmother in the kitchen preparing the recipes from her upbringing in Tuscany had awakened a passion in Gabriella. Becoming a chef became *una passione*, and Nonna became her teacher. Upon moving to America, her grandmother adapted her family recipes to the ingredients available in a Midwestern city. Still, it was a compromise she never adjusted to fully. She would explain to Gaby the differences, and when they became more readily available, the restaurant imported certain items in bulk from Italy. A stickler for quality, she always complained to the purveyors who supplied the restaurant if something didn't meet her exacting standards.

When Gaby was in college, her grandmother died peacefully in her sleep. While going through her things, her father found a folder with all his mother's recipes written in Italian. On front of the folder was written: *Per la mia cara nipotina, Gabriella. Il cuore della nostra famiglia continua a vivere in queste ricette.*

For my dear granddaughter, Gabriella. The heart of our family continues to live in these recipes.

Her parents gave her the folder at her graduation, which was the best gift she'd ever received.

Gaby, studying for a degree in hospitality management, had never intended to fill her grandmother's shoes. Like the child of many family-owned businesses, she had wanted to forge her own path. But her grandmother's gift changed everything. Gabriella spent the summer in Tuscany, then time at a culinary school in Florence, and became fluent in her grandmother's native language. When she returned to Chicago, she took over the kitchen at Trattoria della Vita and never looked back.

Tears filled her eyes as she walked, reminiscing. Her younger sister, Lisa, had followed her career path and learned to make all the treasured family recipes on the restaurant's menu. Gaby knew Lisa could easily step in to steer the ship along with her parents, who managed the business. She knew they must be suffering, knowing she was missing, believing she might be dead. But there was nothing Gaby could do, no way to send them a message or alleviate their pain, and it cut through her heart like a knife.

Raindrops began to fall, and they blended with her tears, trickling down her cheeks. She pulled the blanket tighter around her shoulders and picked up her pace as she headed back to the villa. The wind whipped her hair across her face, and she brushed it back, gasping as a lightning bolt lit the sky, followed by a booming crack of thunder. The black clouds let loose, and a torrential downpour fell. Gaby was drenched in a matter of seconds, and she ran to the safety of the stable.

JACK GRITTED HIS teeth. He'd had enough. His face ached from the frozen smile he'd been forced to wear. He'd been painfully aware of Aunt Kitty's unwavering scrutiny throughout the evening. She reminded him of the Cheshire Cat, grinning with glee as though she could read his mind.

She probably can.

The minestrone, sausage with polenta, and roasted vegetables were delicious, as was the lemon cake they'd enjoyed for dessert. Jack favored the *cucina povera* style of preparing food, and felt better when he ate it.

Unfortunately, every bite only served to remind him of the lovely chef in the kitchen. He hadn't seen Gabriella all day, and it took all his restraint to hold himself back from running to the kitchen and whisking her into his arms. He'd had too much to drink, but rather than mellowing his mood, the wine had only fueled the fire burning in his loins for the cooking goddess, which was how he'd begun to think of her.

When the discussion turned to art again, he did his best to show interest.

"My savvy patroness Constance and I have our feelers out," Stefano mentioned before he took another sip of his brandy.

"Yes, it would be lovely to find a little gem of a painting tucked away here in the countryside before we leave for Florence," Constance added.

"You mentioned that you believe the Allegretto stolen from the Uffizi might be in this part of Tuscany. Is that the true reason for your visit?"

Jack found it curious that the baroness pinned Blossom with a steely gaze. *Why the companion?*

Blossom was no shrinking violet, and responded without hesitation. "Constance believes in the triumph of love, and

Allegretto's paintings exemplify that belief. He apparently found everlasting love with the woman in the painting, who became the sole focus of his artistic endeavors." There was a challenge in her tone.

Donatella laughed, waving her hand dismissively. "Then why is she completely forgotten? She remains nameless, lost in the cobwebs of time. Perhaps she never existed or was simply a simple peasant who sat for the artist. Allegretto, as I recall, often used people from the lower class as models for his paintings, including prostitutes, much like Caravaggio. The only difference was Caravaggio kept it a secret because it would not do for people to know that the model who sat for the Madonna was a *puttana*. But then again, Allegretto wasn't nearly as talented."

A gasp escaped Cynthia, and she turned to the baroness, her eyes wide with shock. "Aunty, that is truly scandalous. How-how could anyone want to buy paintings of—of those kinds of women?"

"My dear Cynthia," Stefano said before the baroness could respond, "those are often the most sought-after works of art."

"Well, I would never allow a painting of that sort in my home," Cynthia said. Her face had gone even paler, if that were possible.

Jack felt another knot twist in his chest. *Lord, is this to be my future?*

"Allegretto and his muse had a very special bond," Blossom said, her gaze spearing the baroness. "He immortalized her, immortalized their love. His artistry and influence will always live on."

"You are an idealist, Blossom. I am reminded that if wishes were horses, beggars would ride." Donatella gave a mirthless laugh.

"And I am reminded of something Leonardo da Vinci said: 'Beyond a doubt, truth bears the same relation to falsehood as light to darkness.'"

Jack sensed an undercurrent in the exchange between Blossom and Donatella that went beyond a heated debate about art. Blossom also surprised him with her knowledge.

He noticed Constance lay her hand gently on Blossom's arm as though to temper her. It seemed unlikely to him that Blossom and Donatella had met before, but the intensity in the way they eyed each other seemed to indicate otherwise.

Cynthia, too, had grown uncomfortable with the exchange. "Aunty, all of this talk of paintings and long-dead artists and their scandalous lives is most distressing."

Donatella's eyes narrowed, and she glared at her niece. "I forget how simple your mind is, my dear. What would you have us discuss? The latest fashions from Paris, or perhaps those Gothic romances you seem to favor."

Jack felt sorry for Cynthia, who no doubt often felt the sting of Donatella's insults. The poor girl's head seemed to shrink into her shoulders like a turtle into its shell. Again, he was reminded of the difference between her and Gabriella. Gaby was fiercely independent and would have torn into anyone who treated her the way the baroness treated Cynthia. Cynthia, with all her wealth, was dependent on this exasperating woman.

But in what way? Was it emotional control or financial, or both? And what would happen if he and Cynthia married? Would this imperious woman continue to reign over Cynthia's life and fortune? Jack would have to find out what exactly was stipulated in the late baron's will. The thought of living in the same house as the baroness gave him agita.

"Baroness, I will not have you insulting Cynthia in my aunt's home," he said. "Cynthia's interests, whatever they may be, do not warrant such harsh words."

Donatella pinned him with her gaze, and a smile crept across her face. "It warms my heart to hear you show protectiveness toward my niece. I hope it foretells a deeper sentiment and a future alliance."

Jack bit his tongue. He would not fall into the cunning woman's trap. He wasn't ready to commit to a future with Cynthia, and he detested the word *alliance*, implying he was aligning himself with the baroness. "I am a gentleman, and as such, I consider it my duty to defend a lady when she is being maligned, even by her own guardian."

"Ah, well, a gentleman also protects the woman he loves, does he not? Even risking his life to do so," the baroness countered with a sly smile.

"Any gentleman would risk his life to protect a lady," Jack said. He didn't love Cynthia and never would. But Cynthia did not deserve to be used as bait in Donatella's schemes.

Jack felt the burning gaze of Aunt Kitty on him, her disapproval evident. Kitty was a rarity among the upper echelon. She'd stood up to her father and brother and married for love. Sir Stewart Darling had not been chosen by Kitty's family. Moreover, he was rumored to be a pirate and a rogue. When she eloped with him, it sent shock waves through the *ton*. But Kitty had defied the naysayers and her blood relations and married the only man she would ever love. That was enough to ostracize her, and she and Stewart moved to Italy to escape the wagging tongues of the muffin wallopers.

Tragically, Stewart was taken five years ago in a hunting accident, but Kitty never regretted her decision to marry the dashing adventurer. Jack had been lucky to have spent so much time with Aunt Kitty and Uncle Stewart. After Jack's mother passed away when he was ten years old, his father had shipped him every summer to Italy. During those summers, Jack discovered his own thirst for adventure and what would be his lifelong passion for archaeology. The ancient world and the secrets of the past transported him away from the mundane banality of the world he lived in. But, because of his father's premature death and the loss of his estate, he'd been forced to abandon his life's work in Egypt. In a less-than-satisfying way he dabbled in his passion in Populonia.

Frustrated and angry, Jack needed to get away. He needed to think. "You will excuse me. I feel the need for some cool night air."

"Be careful, Jack," said Kitty. "There's a storm brewing."

He suspected she was referring to more than the weather. "I should check on the horses and see to their comfort." Xanthus would soothe his restlessness.

He wished everyone goodnight and strode out the door. Leaves flew in the blustery wind that whipped through the trees. Kitty was right—a storm was coming. He pulled the collar up on his mackintosh and headed to the stable. It bothered him that he hadn't seen Gaby all day. By now, she was likely tucked beneath the covers, exhausted from a long day in the kitchen. He missed her desperately and wished he'd sought her out earlier to apologize for last night and compliment her on the delicious meal. But it was too late now. He'd have to wait until tomorrow.

The stable door had been left open, and the sound of horses, restless in their stalls, was discernible above the howling wind. It wasn't like Luigi to be so careless. Jack would have to speak to the boy tomorrow about it. He slipped inside, closing the door and sliding the lock in place to keep the wind from flinging the door open while he was there.

It was freezing in the barn, and as he walked down the central aisle, horses poked their heads out of their stalls and whinnied for attention. He grabbed a handful of carrots from a bucket, stroked soft noses, and patted necks before handing out the treats.

A crack of lightning struck down nearby, and a loud boom sounded a moment later. In the dim light, he saw a blanketed figure standing in front of Xanthus's stall. Perhaps Luigi had ventured out after all, which was why he'd left the door open.

Then he saw the person leaning in to kiss the horse's nose. Xanthus was a no-nonsense horse who didn't like strangers, and he wasn't a touchy-feely kind of animal that sought human interaction. Yet his soft whinny told a different story, and the way the horse blew soft puffs of air from his nostrils and nuzzled the person's hand was a sign of complete trust.

Jack stood frozen in place, completely taken aback by the interaction and realizing it wasn't Luigi. In fact, the slight figure was trembling under the wet blanket. He strode forward, his footsteps echoing his advance. In his wildest imaginings, he'd never expected to see Gaby turn to him, her eyes wide with fear.

"Gaby?" Jack slowed his pace so as not to alarm her. "Please, let me help you," he said, his voice sounding raspy to his ears. In one swift motion, he removed the soaking-wet blanket and threw it aside then wrapped his arms around her shivering form.

Her teeth chattered, "I'm s-sorry—I just came out for a quick w-walk, and then the s-storm hit so hard and f-fast. I t-took refuge in the s-stable. I hope I d-didn't do anything wrong."

"It's okay. You did nothing wrong, but you're soaked to the skin and will catch your death of cold if we don't warm you up." He removed his coat and slipped it around her shoulders. She was such a little thing, and his jacket completely dwarfed her. He wrapped his arms around her, hugged her close, and rubbed her back. Like a child, she nestled closer into his embrace, resting her cheek on his chest.

Jack could no more still his heartbeat than stop the rush of emotion that flooded his senses. When he touched her, a fire blazed through his veins, and he half expected her to pull away from the intensity of the heat. Instead, she sighed with such contentment that tears brimmed in his eyes. Nothing in his past or present could help him navigate the uncharted waters of what was happening to him.

"Gaby." Her name on his lips sounded like a prayer.

She looked up at him, and he found himself lost in her luminous hazel eyes. "Yes?"

The cords of his throat constricted from his racing thoughts, and speech deserted him. His gaze dropped to her lips, and he was lost. *Oh, Lord.* The memory of their kiss was seared in his brain and imprinted on his lips.

He did something that he'd never done before—he asked, his voice husky and deep in a sound that was more than words and more than a plea, "Gaby, I want very much to kiss you—may I?" *Am I really asking permission?*

He suddenly realized what a selfish fool he'd been. To take

from this woman of all women—the last thing he wanted was to hurt her or cause her pain. It was she who held the power and held his next breath in the balance. He feared being rejected by her again.

"Yes," she whispered.

Her sweet smile made his heart do a triple flip.

Their lips met, and their bodies came together, closing the space between them. All the visions Jack had of a mad, passionate union took wing. But pleasing Gaby took precedence over his own pleasure. She was a walk in a garden where one breathed deep and slow, imbibing the fragrances.

"Gaby, my darling, I cannot stop how I feel about you. It's not within my power, and I don't know what to do about it."

She placed her fingers on his lips. "It doesn't matter anymore. I can't fight what I'm feeling, either. I felt the same from the first moment our eyes met. I don't care about what comes later. I only know that if I don't do what my heart insists I must, I will never know what it feels like to love or be loved."

He placed his forehead on hers and closed his eyes. He knew that loving Gabriella D'Angelo was the only thing that mattered. Whatever came later, he would face it with Gaby, the devil be damned.

CHAPTER ELEVEN

Maremma, Italy
October 18, 1902

THE HOUSE WAS quiet as Jack carried Gabriella up the staircase. The carpeted stairs gave no echo of his footsteps. The creek of a floorboard made him hesitate and look around, but everyone had gone to bed, and he continued.

He glanced down as Gaby's dark lashes fluttered against her cheeks, and if not for her shivering, he might have thought her asleep. He relished looking at her without anyone questioning why, or what he was thinking. The sweep of her cheek and the exotic tilt of her eyes mesmerized him, and her mouth and the lush fullness of her lips made him yearn to kiss her. He imagined her soft and pliable lips tracing a path over his body, branding him, leaving an imprint that no other woman would ever erase.

I am doomed.

He opened his bedroom door and laid her on the bed before he set about warming the room. He stoked the coals in the hearth and added fresh timber. Satisfied that the blaze would not die, he removed her wet shoes, stockings, and dress. Her feet were ice cold to the touch, and he rubbed them until he felt them grow warm.

To see Gaby in nothing more than pantaloons and chemise slip made it difficult for him to swallow. As if drawn by a magnet, his eyes took in the swell of her breasts through the thin white cotton chemise, then followed the sinuous curves of her waist and hips and the honeyed tone of her skin. He was reminded of that first night and the inexplicable, instantaneous attraction he'd felt for her. If anything, that attraction had only grown more intense. Gaby's face and body deprived him of sleep and haunted his dreams. The harder he'd fought his obsession, the stronger it had become.

Now, at this moment, his yearning and fulfillment were about to meld into one. He doubted the reality would disappoint.

Sitting on the edge of the bed, he took her cold hands and rubbed them. Unable to stop himself from acting out his desire, he pressed a kiss to the back of each hand. Gabriella's damp hair clung to her forehead, and he gently smoothed it off her face. Her hair fanned across his pillow in glossy black strands, beguiling him.

Her teeth had stopped chattering, and her trembling lessened. Jack's heart swelled with emotion as he watched her. He felt sure he could sit staring at her, never tiring, for the rest of his life. He had learned early in their exchanges that she had no idea how beautiful she was. Maybe she couldn't see it, but in his mind, she was the most goddess-like woman he'd ever seen.

Jack could barely believe his dreams were coming true, which set his body on fire. The press of his trousers had become nearly unbearable, and having her within reach had such a powerful effect on his manhood that he could scarcely restrain himself. He was a prisoner to his lustful thoughts, which, for want of her, went no further than the bed and all the wondrous things he wanted to do to her.

Get a hold of yourself, man!

The fire burning inside him was attributable to a mysterious chef from the Americas, and the only solution to present itself was to get out of his clothes. He removed his shoes, stockings, waistcoat, shirt, and tie. Though he would love to remove his trousers, he didn't want to do anything to upset her.

Besides, her gaze alone on him might bring him to climax.

And he didn't want that. He needed to take things slow. He wanted tonight to be perfect for Gabriella.

He pulled the down comforter over Gaby, then, not knowing what else to do, he lay beside her. When she snuggled up against his chest and rested her hand on his heart, he couldn't control his sudden intake of breath. Her beautiful fingers toyed with his chest hair, and his pulse raced through his veins. He didn't dare move, not wanting to sever the connection with her. The utter perfection of this initial intimacy was bliss, and he kissed her forehead, which wasn't nearly satisfying enough when all he could think about was kissing every inch of her.

The sigh that escaped her made his blood thunder in his ears. It reminded him of what he felt when he plucked the low C on the cello—it made him yearn for the other sounds that might escape her perfect lips in the heat of passion. If only she knew how much he wanted to please her. If only she knew that every argument they'd had, every negative comment that had fallen from his lips, was an attempt to put distance between them. Everything he'd said and done was his stupid attempt to hide his feelings and throw obstacles in their way.

But Gabriella had found a way into his heart, and he feared he could no longer pretend otherwise.

Her lashes fluttered open, and their eyes met. He waited with bated breath for her to make the next move. She lifted her hand from his chest and cupped his cheek. Could she hear the thundering of his heart or the rush of blood that swelled his manhood?

What is she thinking? I must know.

His voice was so deep and gravelly that he hardly recognized it, but he had to say something. "Are you warm enough?" *An inane statement, you fool. The room is hotter than a Roman steam bath.*

"I don't think 'warm' describes what I'm feeling at the moment." Her giggle was husky and the sexiest sound he'd ever heard. It wrapped around his heart like the music of Beethoven and held him enthralled.

Whatever does she mean? He couldn't decide if it was good or bad. Did she want him to open a window?

His mouth dried up when it hit him that her proverbial "warm" might mean hot in her lower extremities.

Her mouth curved into a smile, and he could not tear his eyes away. Her tongue swept over those lusciously full lips, moistening them, and her eyes reflected the fire's glow. He was mesmerized, wondering what she might say or do next. Meanwhile, his cock was throbbing with need.

"Do you remember the last thing I said to you in the stable?" she whispered, tracing the curve of his bottom lip. *Dear Lord, who is seducing whom?*

"Frankly, I'm incapable of clear thought," he admitted.

Another delightful chuckle escaped her. "I said that if I don't do what my heart tells me to do, I will never know what it feels like to love or be loved, and I have every intention of being loved by you."

"I also remember you saying before that we would both be doing each other a disservice if we pursued this attraction." *You fool—why remind her of something that might change her mind?*

"I was wrong. The mistake would be *not* pursuing what we both want."

"Both?"

"Yes, Jack, both of us. Can you deny it?"

Was he hearing things? He nearly put his hands together in prayer mode. *Thank you, Lord!*

"I'd be a lying fool if I did, and I'm not. At least not anymore." He dipped his head, and before she could protest—or worse, change her mind—he kissed her within an inch of her life. He would not be denied, not this time, not ever if he could help it.

JACK'S KISS WAS as soft as a gentle breeze over her lips, and then he wasted no time coaxing open her lips and finding her tongue with his. What was this hold he had over her? How could one look from his eyes cause her heart to break through the confines of her chest and take flight?

She moved her hand to the back of his neck, twining her fingers in the golden waves. He pulled her closer, and she felt the bulge that filled his trousers.

There was nothing small about Jack, nothing.

His hardness pulsed against her, and her body deciphered the code, its message igniting her. She wanted to feel his hands and lips all over her. She wanted to feel him inside her. It made her wet, imagining what was to come.

Strong hands cupped her nape, and the same long fingers that caressed the strings of his cello with strength and delicacy now played upon her skin, possessing her in a way she'd never felt before. She knew there was no turning back. What she felt for Jack was unlike anything she'd felt for a man. She knew that no matter what happened after tonight, she would never feel this way about any man again.

Jack. There was only Jack. And this moment. She wanted it to last forever.

His mouth sought hers with a hunger that took her breath way, and everything she'd ever wished for was sealed in a kiss that made her moan with pleasure. She pressed herself against his shaft, hungering for him. Whatever followed, she would give freely from her heart without a promise of anything beyond this moment. Leaving or losing him would break her heart, but never loving him would rip her heart in two.

A warm plea filled her ear. "Gaby, every part of me yearns to love you, but I will not do anything against your wishes."

"Look at me, Jack." She cupped his face in her hands. She needed to dispel his doubts. In his eyes, she glimpsed vulnerability, a vestige from his past, perhaps, and she saw it for what it was—a fear of rejection. "What happens here is what I want. Is it what you want?

He nodded. "Yes."

"Then nothing can take this moment away from us."

"Oh, my darling." With a fierce passion, he claimed her lips again, and then she was drowning in a desire that could only be compared to fireworks bursting in the sky. His mouth was on her neck, kissing, sucking, and nibbling. He pulled her chemise off her shoulder as he kissed her skin and the hollows of her collarbone. "You are sweet as honey. Do you bathe in it?"

His tongue in her ear sent shivers up and down her spine, and she answered him with a breathless giggle. "Ahh, yes, you've discovered my secret. Eau de Pantry, from Paris," she teased. "It's a secret concoction of spices and seasonings meant to bring a man to his knees."

Jack chuckled. "Ah, you've discovered the secret of seducing me with your lush beauty and delectable food."

His searing kisses left a mark on every inch of her. When his lips closed around her nipple, she gasped, unable to contain her reaction to the jolt of energy or the quivers of pleasure that followed. She'd never met a man like Jack in her own time. But the sensations ricocheting through her body allowed for no analysis. The here and now of his loving her burst through her doubts. The only thing to do was embrace the sensations that took possession of her.

Jack's large hands cupped her breasts as he teased her with his wicked tongue. "Your breasts are perfection, Gaby. In truth, there is no part of you I do not covet. I want to do things to you that go beyond your wildest imaginings."

Gaby knew sensual pleasure was as much about the images evoked by words as the physicality of touch, and Jack's words flooded her senses. Between her thighs, she could feel the lush wetness of her arousal, and it made her back arch upward with need. "I want all of you. To feel you, with no space between us."

"Not yet, my beauty. Even though I want more than any-thing to drive my cock into you, I will not rush this fulfillment of my dreams. I will not make a mockery of this insane passion that possesses my very soul."

"Oh, Jack, do with me as you want, but please don't stop."

"I HAVE NO intention of stopping."

His tongue and lips danced over her. He was on a mission to explore and find all the secret places that elicited her treasured sighs. Discovering her pleasure points was a challenge that captured his imagination. Her sweet moans had him contemplating how great her capacity to drive him mad might be. He was like a bull let loose in a pasture of cows, and he was sure that once would not be enough.

His lips traveled down her soft skin to her thighs. "Will you open for me, my beauty?" he whispered. She gasped as he licked her belly button. He nudged her onto her back, and she spread her legs for him. He almost gasped at the smooth, hairless skin of her mons and labia. He'd never encountered that before.

Whether Gaby had hair or not didn't matter, but the feel of her soft bare skin against his tongue made his cock harder—if that were even possible. Her moist, tender flesh surrendered to his eagerness to taste her. He was consumed with the carnality of knowing all of her, but her effect on him reminded him he must exert restraint. His resolve weakened.

Dash it. My cock aches to find release. He grabbed a breath to steady his racing heart.

"Oh, Jack." Her moan of pleasure, accompanied by her fingers dragging through his hair, extinguished his ability to reason. These feminine signs of her delight spurred him on to only one purpose.

He'd been right about Gaby. She was the most sensual woman he'd ever encountered, but in the back of his mind, he was aware that what was happening between them was far more profound than the sexual act itself.

Dear Lord, I am lost.

Before he plunged his staff into her, he wanted her to experience a flood of bliss. The mere thought of Gaby orgasming made his organ twitch with anticipation. He focused on her flower bud; his tongue produced a series of whimpers and tremors that urged him to delve deeper. He loved a woman's natural scent and taste, but Gaby's unique scent and taste worked like a drug on him. It was addictive, and if he lived to be a hundred years old, it would never be enough.

She gripped the linens, and when rapture overtook her from his fervent ministrations, it nearly undid him. "Oh, Jack! Oh yes! Yes, Jack! Oh! I—" she cried, fingers digging into his shoulders. She quivered uncontrollably beneath his lips and tongue as he continued to suck her pearl with a firm gentleness that, he knew from experience, drove a woman mad. And he was as close to bursting as he'd ever been.

Damn! Hold on, man! He growled, regaining control. Lightly he ran his tongue around and over her sweet clove. Her satiation was complete. She lay spent, the rise and fall of her breasts as she caught her breath the last sign of her orgasm. His cock vibrated with his racing thoughts, anticipating the pleasure yet to come.

Nothing had prepared Jack for what he felt when he penetrated Gaby. He sank deep. Her softness closed tightly around him, drenching him in her dew, and he could barely restrain from hollering.

Her nails dug into his back, and her lips parted as he plunged in and out.

He opened his eyes and was surprised to find her looking at him. But instead of closing her eyes, she continued to gaze at him. At first, he didn't know what to make of the oddity. Most women closed their eyes during sexual intercourse, but Gaby held his gaze. He found it profoundly erotic, this intimacy of the gaze. He'd once heard that the eyes were considered the windows of the soul in the Far East religions. If true, this remarkable woman and he were not only physically joined, but they were connected in a way that he'd never known was possible.

This was so much more than the culmination of pent-up desire. If his mind were capable of clear thought, he would not be able to deny that their connection felt spiritual.

All rational thought took flight when Gaby wrapped her legs around his waist. Her magnificent breasts and budded nipples rubbed against his chest hair with each plunge of his organ, and the feeling was so intense that he knew he would not be able to last much longer. Their bodies were slick with sweat, and he slid over her clitoris with each penetration.

Gaby bit her lip and moaned. "Oh, Jack, I-I... Don't stop. Don't stop. You feel so good inside me."

"Come, my darling. I need to feel your bliss all over my cock." He was fighting to hold on to his composure, but his body, locked in a steady rhythm, was impelled to thrust more, deeper, and faster until Gaby fell apart again with a rapturous moan.

"Jack," she cried out, and he could feel her vagina spasming, clenching him inside of her. Her sweet sounds of pleasure undid him, shattering the last of his control, and he came with such a force that he roared with his release.

He sank into her open arms as they both caught their breaths. Her lips on his neck produced shudders as his shaft continued to empty. In addition to the harmonious rhythm of their breaths and heartbeats, the crackle of wood being turned to ash and rain pattering against the windows and eaves were music to his ears. Such a glorious finale, like Beethoven's Ninth Symphony, known as the "Ode to Joy," had taken its toll. Without a word, he rolled over and scooped Gaby into his arms, claiming her lips in a soft, lingering kiss. He nuzzled her neck, threading his hands through her glorious mane. Happiness flooded his entire being. As sleep overtook him, his last thought was how much he looked forward to what the morning would bring.

CHAPTER TWELVE

Maremma, Italy
October 18, 1902

GABY WRIGGLED AROUND to face Jack. His even breaths conveyed that he'd fallen into a deep sleep. An unruly lock of golden hair fell across his forehead, and she reached to smooth it off his face. The desire to kiss him and begin everything again was so tempting, but she restrained herself.

In repose with his eyes closed, he was even more attractive than when he was awake, if that were even possible. But the wariness and testiness that frequently crossed his features were smoothed away by his peaceful slumber. She drank him in, wanting to memorize every nuance of his face and what it felt like to lie in his arms.

Their lovemaking had transformed her. She'd seen Jack's heart, had seen into his very soul.

I love him.

She knew this down deep in her own soul.

She knew he cared about her and desired her, but she realized the truth—loving him meant letting him go.

She had no idea what her future held, and no control over her fate. This was not her world, and Jack deserved better. He needed to reclaim his inheritance, and he would never be able to do it by being with her. She had no right to keep him with her.

No matter how painful—and oh God, it would be so pain-ful—she would have to do it. She had no choice but to accept whatever fate had in store for her, but she would not drag Jack down this unknown journey.

She would forever cherish the memories of being in his arms, but that would have to be enough. Their brief time together would have to be enough. At least she now knew that true love was possible. And even if she never found it again, she knew in her soul that she had loved Jack.

She brushed her lips lightly along the curve of his neck and shoulder, inhaling his one-of-a-kind scent. He snuggled closer, and a contented sigh escaped his oh-so-kissable lips. Reality hit her like a bucket of iced water. She would never experience Jack's kiss or the blissfulness of lying in his arms again. Her eyes stung with tears, and the pain tore her heart apart.

Before she lost control, she slipped from his arms and dressed. She went to the desk and found paper and a fountain pen.

She wrote Jack a letter explaining that what they'd shared would be a beautiful memory for her, but that was all it could ever be. She told him he owed her nothing and should pursue his courtship with Cynthia. She reiterated, in case he thought she had changed her mind, that she would never be his mistress, and he should banish that idea from his mind. She also wrote that as soon as she could find another position, she would leave Nido dell' Aquila and begin a new life.

What she didn't do was tell him the truth about how she came to be there and what she needed to do.

A tear rolled down her cheek and fell on the paper, and she smeared the ink when she wiped it away. *Darn!* But the letter was still readable, and she wasn't about to start over. She folded the sheet of paper and, tiptoeing to the bedside table, left it where he was sure to find it when he woke.

With a last look at the man she loved, she whispered, "For-give me." She slipped from his room and ran up the stairs leading to the servants' quarters, her fist muffling her sobs. When she got to her room, she finally broke down. She cried and cried until she had no more tears to shed. Exhausted, she fell into a restless sleep.

The sunlight from the small window streaming in woke her, and she checked the little clock in the room. She'd overslept, but it was still early, just past six. She washed and dressed, still feeling sore from Jack's loving. She almost burst into tears again.

Get a grip, Gaby! The last of the guests would arrive today, and tonight was the dinner party. Keeping busy would take her mind off Jack, even if only for a few hours.

The kitchen was already bustling with activity when she got there. Maria and Katia were preparing breakfast, and the aroma of pancetta frying reminded Gaby that she hadn't eaten anything since yesterday afternoon. *"Buongiorno, a tutti!"*

"Buongiorno, Gabriella," Maria and Katia answered in chorus. Their greetings were echoed by Angelina, who waved her wooden rolling pin, called a *matterelli*, and Luigi, who flew through the door with a full basket of vegetables and herbs from the garden.

Gaby grabbed a fresh-baked cornetto and slathered butter and jam on it. She ate while walking around the kitchen, inspecting the workstations.

Antonio came through the swinging butler door. "Everyone is accounted for. The marquess, his wife, and the couple from Paris arrived minutes ago. They will join the others in the dining room as soon as they have freshened up." He reached for a piece of the crisp pancetta.

"Fermati, Antonio!" Maria slapped his wrist. "If you keep pilfering the bacon, there will not be enough for the paying guests. *Basta!"*

Antonio held his hands wide in the classic Italian expression of "what do you want from me?"

"I want you to act like a butler, you *idiota!"*

Antonio pinched Maria's cheek and laughed. "Ever the disciplinarian, Maria," he teased. "There is plenty of pancetta to go around. Besides, if we need more, the larder is full." He stuffed a piece in his mouth, grinning like a reprobate who'd been handed the keys to heaven's gate.

Maria waved Antonio away, dismissing him. *"Vai via!* There's work to be done."

Gaby stood with her hands on her hips, smiling. In only a brief time, she'd bonded with the hardworking members of her team, and they had begun to feel like a family, much like the employees at the restaurant, whom she missed.

Gaby sighed. *I can do nothing but live each day as best I can.*

"I'm going to the root cellar," she called over her shoulder. "I'll bring up the potatoes, onions, and garlic for the *patate e pomodori arrostiti.*" The main side dish for the boar stew would be delicious roasted potatoes and tomatoes with oregano.

"Take the torch," said Antonio. "It's dark down there. Be careful on the stairs."

Gaby climbed down the narrow stairs to what Americans called a root cellar, but the British called an earth cellar. Gaby marveled at the flashlight. It had only recently been invented by David Misell, a British scientist. The invention worked off a patented paper tube with a turn-of-the-century version of D batteries. The batteries filled the paper tube, connecting with a light bulb on one end and a brass reflector on the other. Gaby found these early versions of standard modern technology primitive, but useful under the circumstances.

She wished she could share her knowledge of the future with Jack.

She sighed. *Just get on with it.* She had tons of work to do, and daydreaming about what could never be would only make things worse.

The dark underground room had a dirt floor and thick, plastered walls. Shelves with wood-slatted backs lined the walls, filled with baskets of jarred vegetable and fruit preserves. On the ground, large baskets held several types of potatoes, turnips, yams, onions, and garlic. Gaby got on her knees and shined the flashlight on the many baskets as she looked for the small red-and-white new potatoes. She couldn't find them, so she began pulling the baskets away from the wall. They could have toppled behind the large baskets. Where the ground met the shelving, there was a gap. She shined the flashlight on it and squinted, trying to figure out what was back there. It looked like a burlap-wrapped object. *How odd.*

Standing, she began removing everything from the shelves. She moved the jars and added them to the storage shelves on either side. When everything was removed, she knocked on the wall. *Very odd.* The wall had a hollow sound. Was it some sort of hidden cantina? Or something else?

Her instincts kicked into high alert. Why had Allegretto sent her here, to this place? It wasn't a coincidence. She'd only been here a few days and felt so overwhelmed by everything, especially her feelings for Jack, that she hadn't really had time to think, concentrate, or focus on the fact that Allegretto had flung her back in time to this place. Why?

She tried to pull the shelves away from the wall but couldn't budge them. She needed help. Running up the steps, she called, "Where's Luigi? I need him in the root cellar."

Maria nodded to the back door. "He's probably in the stables."

Gaby rushed to the back door.

Maria called after her, "Is everything okay, Gabriella?"

"Yes. Just keep working," Gaby called over her shoulder.

Her heart pounded in her chest as she ran for the stable. Horse neighs and whinnies greeted her as she entered. "Luigi, where are you? I need you to come with me to the root cellar."

Luigi's head poked out of one of the stalls. "Did you see insects or rodents? I can bring the pitchfork or grab a broom."

"No, no, it's not any kind of pest. Come, I'll show you, and you can help me. I need to move something."

Luigi raised his brows quizzically and leaned the pitchfork he'd been holding against the stall.

"Come. Hurry!"

He trotted after her, following her into the kitchen. Gabriella ignored the questioning looks from Maria and Katia and ran down the stairs.

When Luigi joined her, she was already on one side of the shelf, poised to move it away from the wall. "Get on the other side and help me move these shelves."

"But why, signorina?"

"There's something hidden behind here, and I need to find out what it is."

"*Sì,* signorina." Luigi held the other side, grunting and groaning.

They managed to move the shelves an inch away from the wall before stopping to catch their breath. It was good that it was so cool in the root cellar, but the exertion brought a sheen to Luigi's brow, and he wiped his forehead on his sleeve. "They are cumbersome. Should I get Antonio? This is maybe too difficult for you."

"No, no, we can do this."

Luigi sighed with resignation. "Okay, let us try again."

Gabriella gritted her teeth, and together, they managed another few inches. Luigi bent over his hands on his knees and gasped, dragging in air. Gaby fought to regain her breath, but she was too excited to rest, and she grabbed the flashlight and shined it behind the shelving.

Excitement surged through her. She could just make out a rectangular wall panel. The bottom appeared to either have been eroded by moisture or eaten by rodents. The gap revealed the burlap she'd seen when she looked under the shelving. But the shelving needed to be moved entirely away from the wall.

She looked at Luigi and realized he was right—the two of them would only be able to move the shelves with some help. "Luigi, please go find Antonio. We do need his help. We must move the shelves farther from the wall to get to the panel and open it."

He looked relieved. "I will go get him, signorina." He ran up the stairs.

Gaby took a deep breath, trying to calm her pounding heart.

Something about the panel sparked her gut instincts. It could be nothing, simply an additional storage area that had been sealed up years ago. Old houses like this often held hidden closets and rooms meant to hide a family, treasures, or people seeking to evade arrest. She recalled the priest holes of sixteenth-century England that had hidden Catholics from Protestant persecution.

Then again, it could be something else. It could be something connected to Allegretto, the reason why he brought her to this time and place.

Hurry, Luigi.

Gaby turned upon hearing footsteps on the wooden stairs. She looked expectantly for Luigi and Antonio to appear. Instead, she was shocked to see Jack.

Oh, darn!

Anger radiated from his eyes. There was no question Jack had read her letter, and judging from the look on his face, he hated her.

"What the devil is this about *Signorina* D'Angelo?" he said in a clipped tone.

Gaby could only imagine how he felt. But she was between a rock and a hard place and couldn't tell him her true feelings—that she had fallen in love with him, and that it killed her to sacrifice her love for him. She doubted he'd believe her.

Nor could she tell him, Lady Darling, or anyone else the truth about her presence here. They'd probably think she was a thief or an escapee from an asylum and call the *carabinieri*. If only she could make him understand that pushing him away was the hardest thing she'd ever done. Clearly, her letter hadn't done the job.

But she didn't have the strength or time to deal with it now. She was desperate, and she needed his help.

Gathering her dignity and not wanting to antagonize him further, Gaby faced him with calm determination. "My lord, while looking for a variety of potatoes for tonight's dinner party, I discovered something that might interest you and Lady Darling. I don't know if there is anything remarkable here, but I encourage you to explore the possibility. Here, let me show you."

Jack's arms were crossed over his chest, and his legs were planted firmly apart. He looked cold and aloof in a way only an upper-crust aristocrat could pull off. He had every intention of intimidating her, punishing her. "What nonsense is this?"

Gaby ignored his scowl. She shined the flashlight behind the shelves and turned to see if he would budge from his stubborn stance. "I think there is something behind this wall." She knocked on the wall so Jack could hear what she'd heard, the hollow sound that indicated this was not a solid wall. "Luigi and I moved the shelf a few centimeters, but we need to move it away from the wall completely, and the shelves are too heavy. I didn't want to trouble you. I sent Luigi to get Antonio. I am sorry he engaged you before I knew better what I'd discovered." She cast a reproving glance at Luigi, but he shrugged in a typically Italian fashion. Antonio had also joined them, and was standing beside Luigi.

"My lord, will you not at least look at the panel?" she asked Jack. "With your estimable good judgment, I'm certain you will determine the best way to proceed." She bit her lip, and Jack's gaze, as if magnetized, was drawn to the action. Without saying it, she'd thrown down a gauntlet. The ball was in his court.

Jack's arms relaxed to his sides. "Very well—we will see what folly lies behind this supposed secret door. Please stand back, signorina."

Without protesting, Gaby did as he asked. Jack removed his jacket and handed it to her. The straight line of his mouth continued to display his displeasure. He took one side of the shelving, and Luigi and Antonio took the other. Jack's muscles bulged through his white shirt as they began to drag the shelving away from the wall.

Gaby couldn't help her gaze from traveling down his tall, strong body as she remembered how it felt to be held by him. And how it felt to touch him, to run her hands over his muscled chest, arms, back, and buttocks.

Heat flooded her cheeks, and she had to look away, but not before he glanced at her and arched one of his brows inquisitively.

With the shelves moved away, Jack's demeanor changed. He brushed away the cobwebs and ran his hands over the wall, knocking in places and feeling along the top and bottom. "Well, what have we here?"

The strangeness of the hidden door and the mystery of what might lie within had aroused his curiosity. He continued to knock and run his hands over the paneled wall until it made a clicking sound. His eyes narrowed, and he pressed a particular spot almost at the very top of the wall. Nothing happened, and he tried again, using his fist to pound against it.

As the wall suddenly popped open, Gaby gasped, as did Luigi and Antonio.

"*Madon!*" Luigi said.

"Give me the flashlight, please," Jack said—the "please" being an afterthought, yet indicated a softening of his anger toward her.

Gaby handed him the flashlight, hoping he couldn't hear the thumping of her heart. He opened the hidden door and stepped into the enclosure, moving the flashlight around. "There's something here," he called out. "Signorina D'Angelo, can you hold the flashlight for me?"

"Yes, of course, my lord." She stepped in beside him, and he handed her the flashlight.

"Hold it steady, straight ahead." His eyes met hers, and she could see the glimmer of excitement in his gaze. After all, Jack was an archeologist, and this was precisely the kind of mystery that he loved. It made her ridiculously happy that he'd come down here with Antonio and Luigi, that he'd been the one to discover how to open the secret door, and, most of all, that he'd asked her to hold the flashlight.

Jack turned back toward the far wall; squatting down on his haunches, he leaned forward and grasped the burlap-covered object. Gaby angled the flashlight to give him more light as he lifted the object and turned back to her.

"Let's see what we've found," he said.

Gaby turned and stepped back out of the dark room. Jack was close behind, carrying the mystery item.

He leaned it against the shelving and squatted back down.

Gaby's excitement ratcheted up to the point where it was all she could do not to try to tear the burlap off herself. She pressed her hands tightly together and squatted beside him.

"Get me a knife, Antonio, and be quick about it." Jack's eyes sought hers. "It looks like a painting, doesn't it?"

"Yes, it does. It must be precious to have been hidden like this. I hope it isn't damaged, your lordship."

Jack examined the burlap. "It doesn't look like any pests have gotten to it. And that hidden room, though dark and cool, was completely dry."

Antonio rushed back down and handed Jack a knife. He wasted no time slicing the rope that bound the protective burlap cover. Carefully he peeled the burlap away, and Gaby gasped at what she saw.

Oh my God! That's it! It was one of the same paintings she'd seen at the Met—the third and final painting in Allegretto's series, *The Three Stages of Love*. Her eyes blurred with tears as she realized what this meant.

Jack didn't miss her extreme reaction and regarded her intently. "Do you know of this painting?"

"N-no!" She shook her head adamantly. "H-how could I? I only just discovered this odd wall. I-it's just the shock of it. It's such a beautiful painting, and it's such a mystery that it was here."

"Hmm, yes. You're right; it is. Let us bring it upstairs, and we'll have Stefano examine it. Perhaps he'll be able to tell us who the artist is."

Gabriella tried to control the trembling that overtook her. She already knew who the artist was, but she couldn't say anything to Jack. And what was remarkable about the painting was how vibrant it looked. The colors were not fading, as they had been at the Met, and the portrait was as rich in tones as it must have been on the day Allegretto finished it. The green-eyed, red-headed muse stared out from the canvas, her gaze sensual and evocative. Gaby felt a shiver climb her spine.

"It's very sensual, isn't it?"

Much to Gaby's dismay, when she glanced sideways, she saw that Jack studied her and not the painting.

"I wouldn't know, your lordship." She dropped her gaze modestly.

"Of course you wouldn't." His tone returned to one of contempt. "Help me, Antonio—let's get it upstairs to my bedroom. I believe you have a dinner party to prepare, Signorina D'Angelo."

Her heart wrenched at his frosty gaze. They'd made love just last night, but it felt ages ago. How she missed the worshipful erotic heat in those gorgeous blue-green eyes. How she missed him calling her Gaby.

She swallowed the lump in her throat and gave a jerky nod. Jack was right—she needed to get back to work. And now that the painting had been discovered, it was out of her hands.

He turned back to the painting, clearly dismissing her. Though she didn't want to let the painting out of her sight, there was nothing to be done about it. Now she would have to bide her time.

CHAPTER THIRTEEN

Maremma, Italy
October 19, 1902

J ACK HAD WANTED to drag Gaby to his room and shake her. Then he wanted to kiss her senseless. He was livid at the letter she'd left on the table by his bed. How dare she suggest that after what they'd shared, he'd be so callous as to continue his courtship of Cynthia?

He ran his hands through his hair in agitation as he paced his room, waiting for Stefano to arrive.

Yes, he may have given Gaby that notion the other day, but that was before everything changed. Before *he'd* changed. How could she not know that from their night together?

Did she think he lacked a moral compass? He wanted to wring the little vixen's neck. He wanted to throw her over his shoulders and carry her back to his bed. He wanted to make mad, passionate love to her again. *Damn! Damn! Damn!* He wanted to— Well, that would have to wait.

When he tramped down the stairs to the earth cellar, he'd had every intention of dismissing Antonio and Luigi and having it out with her, but the look of shock and dismay on her face made his heart wrench. He couldn't stop the feeling of guilt washing over him at the exhaustion in her face and her sleep-deprived, red-rimmed eyes. But his guilt was quickly replaced by anger.

After all, it wasn't he who'd written that letter. It wasn't he who'd arbitrarily decided that one night was all they could ever have.

He'd managed to regain some semblance of control. And when Gaby told him about her discovery, his interest had been piqued. Finding the hidden room and the burlap-wrapped painting was a mystery that called to his inquisitive mind, it had scratched an itch, and he was compelled to find out more.

He continued to pace back and forth, leaving a path of shoe prints on the rug in front of the bed. He eyed the painting, which he and Antonio had hung opposite his bed, every few seconds. He was utterly enchanted with the sensual work of art, and it wasn't because he thought it was of great value. The painting spoke to him in a way no other piece of art ever had. It reflected his conundrum and the emotions brewing inside of him. Even more, it reflected something he'd never felt before he met Gaby.

Love.

I love her.

Shit!

Having had this remarkable revelation and knowing he would be deprived of it for the rest of his life twisted like a knife in his gut.

The more he stared at the painting, the more his jealousy grew. The beautiful redhead gazed at her lover the way he wished Gaby would look at him. Hell, she *had* looked at him that way last night. Did she feel the same way about him as he felt about her?

Then why did she write that damn letter?

He walked up to the painting. For some reason, it drew him like some sort of talisman. The woman in the portrait was clearly in love with the man, and Jack sensed that nothing could ever keep the two lovers apart. But that was certainly not true of his relationship with Gaby. The mysterious painting seemed to shout at him—*You are inadequate, shallow, and unworthy of love.*

How could he have been found wanting even after giving himself entirely to her? A part of Jack wanted to yell at Gaby, and a part of him wanted to get down on his knees and beg her to reconsider.

A rap on the door interrupted his self-flagellation. He strode to it, wishing it was Gaby coming to make atonement, but that was a useless wish. She'd made clear in her abominable missive that what they shared had been a fleeting moment of passion, not something to build a life on.

"What do you want?" he growled, opening the door. His brusqueness surprised even himself. The damn woman had turned him into a blathering lunatic, blundering through every encounter. He was irritated at his lack of control over his emotions.

Stefano eyed him critically, good manners likely holding his tongue from responding in kind. "Is there a problem, Jack? Antonio came to me with an urgent message to come see you."

Jack felt his face flood with embarrassment; he'd forgotten that he asked Antonio to do that. "Yes, ah, well, it seems one of the servants has made a discovery." He was so angry with Gaby that he refused to acknowledge that she'd discovered the secret room and its booty. "I need your expert opinion."

Jack crossed his arms over his chest and waited while Stefano acclimated to his surroundings. It took a second for his gaze to alight on the painting, and an instant change came over his composure.

"What have we here?" Stefano whistled.

Jack chuckled as his own words of surprise when he first saw the burlap-wrapped painting were repeated to him. Stefano's eyes sparkled with keen interest. He studied the painting from where he stood, and, as if drawn by a magnet, he inched closer and closer. Jack had already ascertained that there was no signature on the painting, but of course, Stefano, with his eagle eyes and vast knowledge of art history, would be able to ascertain its provenance.

Stefano stood transfixed, his eyes sweeping back and forth, taking in every inch of the canvas. He pulled a magnifying glass from the inside pocket of his coat and moved in closer to the painting.

"Jack, this is truly remarkable," he said a few minutes later. "If this painting is authentic, it is a most significant find." He looked at Jack, his eyes dancing with excitement. "We would need to have it thoroughly examined, of course."

Jack felt the quickening bump-b-bump-b-bump of his heart. "Surely you jest?"

"I never jest when it comes to art or money."

"You think this is an original, don't you?"

"Yes. If authentic, it is Marco Allegretto's third painting in *The Three Stages of Love* series of paintings, *Il Leto*. You recall I mentioned the mystery surrounding this painting and that it was last seen at the Uffizi and stolen? A rumor circulated about fifty years ago that it was somewhere in Tuscany. It would make sense." Stefano could not contain the zing in his voice. "This, *amico mio*, is the painting that Constance and I are searching for. It's worth a fortune, and Constance will certainly pay a fortune to possess it."

Jack stared at the painting with fresh eyes. He would be hard-pressed to explain why he felt protective of the picture or why the thought of parting with it disturbed him. The sensual way the two people looked at each other reminded him of what he felt for Gaby. This intense, unbreakable connection defied all reason.

There was also something else that sparked in his mind. The painting, like Gabriella, had appeared, as if by magic, at the same time and in the same place. *What are the odds?* And it was Gaby who'd discovered it.

Jack did not believe in coincidences, at least not like this. In his experience, coincidences required thorough investigation. Not to mention, how likely was it that Constance Shipley and her companion Blossom Rosalind had arrived on a search for this very same painting. And then the very next day, it was discovered in his aunt's cellar?

There's more to this than just happenstance. He was determined to uncover what it was and how everything was connected.

"If my hunch is correct, this painting might be the answer to your financial dilemma," Stefano said.

Jack's eyes flew to Stefano's face. "What do you mean?"

"Please do not take offense," Stefano said, holding up his hands. "Kitty explained to me the dire circumstances of your position, but it seems Lady Luck may have smiled upon you, Jack. I would advise you not to turn your back on this opportunity."

Kitty was highly fond of Stefano and trusted him, but Jack was torn by conflicting inclinations. He wanted to regain his estate and title. But most of all, he wanted the woman who'd blown into his life like a tornado. Before Stefano put the wheels in motion with Constance, he needed time to think about everything that had happened in the past few days and what it all meant. He needed to talk to Gaby.

"Stefano, I'd like—"

His words were cut short by the soft sound of footsteps and the tinkling of china. He opened the door and found Gabriella had stopped down the hall outside one of the guest suites. She was holding a tray with a tea service, undoubtedly delivering refreshments to one of the late-arriving guests he hadn't yet met.

Had Gabriella been spying on him? Had she overheard his conversation with Stefano? She was not a serving girl or the butler, and her duties would typically not include delivering tea to a guest. But he knew all the other staff might be otherwise engaged, and she'd likely offered to bring the tea herself.

He might have given her the benefit of the doubt, but when the door of the guest suite opened, she gasped, and the tray began to rattle in her shaking hands.

He couldn't see the guest's reaction, but a slender hand grabbed Gaby's wrist and yanked her into the room. A moment later, a beautiful woman with blonde hair poked her head into the hallway as if checking to see if the hall was empty. When she saw Jack, her eyes widened, but she quickly composed herself. She smiled serenely, nodded, and closed the door.

What in the blazes is going on? It made no sense to him. If Jack didn't know better, Gaby's shocked expression was one of recognition. The blonde woman had an elegant and aristocratic air about her. She must be Lady Danbury, the wife of the Marquess of Danbury. But how did she know Gaby? *Yet another coincidence?*

He would get to the bottom of it. There were too many mysteries surrounding his temptress, and his sanity demanded he find out the truth.

"Jack," Stefano said, rousing him from his musings. "What is the matter?"

"Oh, nothing. I just thought I heard something."

"Well, I would like Constance and Blossom to see this painting, with your permission. May I bring them to your room and show them?

"No, Stefano, not yet. If you don't mind, I want to keep the painting a secret for the time being. Besides, there's no rush, since Mrs. Shipley will be here for several more days. In the meantime, I'd like to conduct my own research."

"Of course—your investigative skills as an archaeologist can only help in the authentication. But I warn you, do not let this opportunity escape. I also noticed that the baroness was quite keen on the missing Allegretto and could be another prospective buyer. Donatella's husband, the baron, was a collector of European paintings, and she is known to have shared his passion."

Jack barely heard Stefano's comment about the baroness; his mind was still on the exchange between Gaby and the Marchioness of Danbury. It was most curious indeed. Gaby had looked like she'd seen a ghost or someone returning from the dead. How could she possibly know the woman? Another mystery to add to the growing list surrounding the woman who'd taken over his thoughts. But he would unravel the truth, no matter where it led him.

Chapter Fourteen

Maremma, Italy
October 19, 1902

G ABY WAS SHAKING so badly she could barely stand, let alone hold on to the tea tray. She had to be hallucinating. How could this be happening?

Emily gently took the tray from her hands and set it on the table in front of the settee. "Breathe, Gaby. We don't have much time, and I have so much to tell you. But first…" She wrapped her arms around Gaby and hugged her tight. "I'm so happy to see you. Jenee and I have missed you so much."

"Is it really you, Em? For a second, I thought I was dreaming."

"Yes, it's me, you silly twit," she said, leaning back. "Same Emily who left a vibrator in your nightstand in case you got randy during the night."

Gaby burst into laughter. "Oh my God, it is you, Emily." She crushed Emily in a bear hug. "I was so mad at you and Jenee because I thought you'd abandoned me at the museum."

"Never, girlfriend." Emily squeezed her back.

"And then I was—I'm not quite sure what happened to me at the museum, but somehow, I was flung back in time to this place."

Emily nodded. "Oh, sweetie. The same thing happened to

Jenee and me." She tugged Gaby down onto the settee. "Come and sit." Emily poured tea. "This calls for a strong cup of tea and a lovely scone." She added sugar and cream and handed the cup to Gaby. "I take it you were pulled into the painting just as Jenee and I were."

Gaby took a sip and sighed. "God, I've missed you. Yes, it was surreal. I still can't believe Marco Allegretto dragged me into a painting, and poof, I found myself on the edge of a cliff facing the Tyrrhenian Sea."

Emily giggled. "I found myself in the middle of Piccadilly Road, covered in mud with a carriage and team of horses barreling down on me. I ended up in London in 1892. I met the most delicious man, and though I will not admit it to him, it was love at first sight. Colin Remington, the Marquess of Danbury. I was fortunate to marry him, and we have two children. It ended well for me, but I will explain everything later.

"You are not alone, Gaby; Jenee is here too. She ended up in Paris in 1900 and fell in love with and married Chief Inspector Xavier Doumaz. He's bloody marvelous and sexier than hell. Our pimple-popping dermatologist to the stars is profoundly happy. I wouldn't doubt they will be expecting an addition to their family in a few months." Emily pulled a handkerchief out of her sleeve and dabbed at her eyes. "Colin and I attended the wedding of Jenee and Xavier. I wish you could have been there. She looked like she was in *The Princess Bride*. Jenee's in a room down the hall. As soon as Colin returns, I'll send him to fetch her. She'll kill me if I don't tell her you're here."

Gaby felt so many emotions at once that she had no idea how to identify them. "This is too much to take in. You're telling me that you and Jenee couldn't find a way back to the future, so without any options, you married? Is that what happened?"

"No." Emily smiled and reached for Gaby's hand. "Jenee and I made a choice to stay. We stayed for love." She rolled her eyes. "I know, what are the odds are that we found true love after being flung back in time. We all swore off men because the buggers we'd dated were all wankers, but we were wrong. We may have had to travel a hundred years backward in time to find them, but Jenee and I found our forever loves, and you will too. Don't give up hope; there are some good ones out there. But that's neither here nor there—I know you may want to go back, and I want you to know it's possible as soon as we find the painting."

Gaby's mind was spinning in a thousand directions. Emily's revelation of her and Jenee finding true love in another era was mind-boggling, to say the least. Especially considering she'd fallen head over heels for Jack—but for her, it was hopeless.

She pushed her thoughts of Jack away and studied her best friend. Emily looked as beautiful as ever, elegantly attired in a worsted wool navy traveling suit, her hair coiffured fashionably in a Gibson updo. She looked different, though, and it wasn't because of her clothing. Perhaps it was finding her true love and becoming a mother. Gaby could scarcely believe that Em had two children, but there was no question about it; her friend had a look of maturity she hadn't possessed before.

Realizing that she'd been lost in her own world and hadn't responded to Emily, Gaby blurted out. "The painting!"

"Okay, this is the difficult part to explain. Iris Bellerose is real. And she's also here with us in Tuscany."

Gaby gasped. This bombardment of impossibilities was getting to be too much to absorb.

"Breathe, Gaby, and listen to me. Iris Bellerose and Marco Allegretto are the reason we time-traveled. Iris wrote *The Time Traveler's Lover*. Everything in the book is true except the ending. We, the three of us, were sent back in time to change the ending. To set things right.

"Jenee and I helped Iris find the first two paintings in *The Three Stages of Love* series, *La Sedia* and *Il Divano*. Now we must find *Il Letto,* the third. Without the painting, Marco and Iris can't be together for the rest of their lives, and you can't go home. We need to find the third painting. We need to close the last portal."

"I think I'm getting a headache. Portal?"

"Drink more tea. As I said, we haven't much time. A man saw

you come into my room, and we cannot explain your presence if you stay here too long."

"A man?"

"Some gorgeous, big bloke with long golden hair."

Jack! "Did he say anything to you?"

"No, we merely exchanged a nod of greeting."

Jack would surely notice if she stayed too long in Emily's room. "I must go. You're right, my delay will be noticed." Gaby rose to leave and then paused. "You mentioned a portal. What is this portal, and where do we find it?"

"Iris explained that the portal resided within the painting and was a passage for traveling through time. The portals were opened by an oracle under pressure from an evil sorceress. The sorceress seduced Marco Allegretto, and he promised to paint a portrait of her, but when he met Iris, he canceled the commission and shunned the witch. Now she is consumed with destroying him, Iris, and his art. That is why the paintings in the Met were fading. She wants to turn Iris into a permanent time traveler and erase her from Marco's life. Then she will erase Marco's art from history. We are their only hope of defeating this horrible witch and closing the portals forever."

"But how?"

"The portal painting *Il Leto* must be returned to Marco, and then he will destroy them all."

"But the world will be deprived of them forever."

"No, the portal paintings are mirrors of the originals, which the sorceress stole from Marco. Jenee and I found the first two mirror paintings in the series, and Iris traveled through the portals and took the mirror-image paintings with her. Marco destroyed those paintings, and now there is only one left. Which means there is one portal left open. But the Contessa Caterina di Farnese is determined to find the painting before we do. We must prevent that from happening. Only when the last of the portals is closed will Marco be able to deal with the contessa and reclaim his original paintings. The curse will be over, and Iris will cease to be a time traveler. Then she and Marco can live their happily ever after."

"My God, it sounds like a Brothers Grimm fairytale. So how would I go back if the portals are destroyed?"

"If you decide to return to the future, you must leave through the portal with Iris. Once the portal closes, you will have no other way back."

"Is the contessa here? Who is she?"

The door to the bedroom opened, and both Emily and Gabriella turned their attention to the man who entered—and Gaby's question went unanswered and, in the excitement, forgotten.

"Em, my sweet, I've seen to everything—" The man stopped and regarded Gaby with a curious expression.

Emily jumped up and ran to him, delivering a kiss, which he returned with an embrace and a smile. "Darling, you will not believe what has happened."

"There is nothing, my love, in this universe that would surprise me, especially since God has blessed me with you."

Emily planted another kiss on the handsome man's cheek. "Gabriella D'Angelo, I present to you Colin Remington, the Marquess of Danbury, father of my children, and the husband I adore beyond measure."

"Your Grace, I'm pleased to meet you." Gaby popped up from the sofa and attempted a curtsy.

"Oh, fodder, you must address me as Colin, at least when we are alone. Em has told me so much about you. And without seeming presumptive—and for your information, my formal address would be my lord and not Your Grace—you are exactly as Emily described, and I am so pleased to meet you." Colin strode to her and, taking her hands, pulled her in for a warm hug.

Gaby was stunned but awkwardly returned his embrace.

"This is jolly good," said Emily, "to see my dearest friend and my darling husband embracing." She clapped her hands with approval. "Colin, my love, would you be so kind as to bring Jenee to our room? If I don't let her share this moment, I will never hear the end of it. But don't say a thing; I want to see her face when she sees Gabriella."

"Ah, yes, it would be my pleasure." Colin strode from the room and closed the door gently behind him.

"He's bloody marvelous, isn't he?" Emily's face reflected her love and adoration for her husband.

Gaby laughed. "What he is, girlfriend, is hot. You really struck the mother lode. If I wasn't so happy for you, I'd be jealous."

A compassionate smile lit Emily's face. "You'll find your forever love, Gab. I feel it in my heart—be patient."

Gaby had thought her tears over Jack had all dried up, but it seemed her eyes hadn't gotten the memo, because her vision blurred with tears.

"What is it, Gaby? Tell me, what is troubling you? Best friends don't keep secrets from each other."

The door flew open, and Jenee burst into the room. "What is going on? I told Colin to keep Xavier company and to give us a few minutes alone." She was so caught up in her objective that she didn't register Gaby's presence. Her mouth suddenly froze as cognizance came to her. Her eyes widened, and she squealed like a child seeing a puppy under the Christmas tree. "*Oh, mon Dieu,* am I dreaming?"

Gaby wiped her tears on her apron and pointed to the blemish on her chin. "Do you see this zit on my face? You're the pimple expert. What have you got in your bag of tricks? I need it gone now."

"Oh my God, oh my God." Jenee ran and threw her arms around Gaby. Emily joined the hugging reunion, and the three jumped up and down like cheerleaders at a Friday night football game.

When they finally broke apart, "All for one and one for all, united we stand, divided we fall," Emily declared—Alexander Dumas's famous quote from *The Three Musketeers*, which the three women had often toasted with during their Zoom chats.

"Oh, I wish we could sit here and gab the day away. But we must be careful not to alert the household. Jen, I'll explain everything to you after Gaby's gone back downstairs, but something must be discussed before she goes." Emily turned to Gaby. "Fess up, girlfriend. You had an emotional breakdown a minute ago, and it wasn't because of time travel." Her eyes narrowed as if she were divining a mysterious phenomenon. "It's a man, isn't it? You've met someone, and he's done something to hurt you. Who is it? I'll lop off the bloody arse's 'ead."

Jenee looked from Emily's piercing gaze to Gaby's damp cheeks. "Would someone care to fill me in on what is going on?"

Gaby's words poured from her like a rush of water freed from the spillway of a dam. "I've fallen in love with someone I can't have. I acted out my fantasy with him, and now I'm paying the price." She covered her face with her hands, and her shoulders shook with her sobs.

Jenee wrapped her arms around Gaby and hugged her. "If he's not a pirate or a thief, what could be so bad about loving him?"

"It's Jack, and he's all but engaged to another woman," Gaby blurted between sobs. She looked up, embarrassment warming her cheeks.

Emily frowned. "Who is this Jack bugger? Please tell me it's not Jack the Ripper."

"Lord John Henry Langsford, the Earl of Whitton, and Marquess of Bainbridge."

"Lady Darling's nephew? That doesn't sound so terrible," Emily said. "Wait a sec. Is Jack that blond hunk I saw down the hall?"

Gaby nodded.

"Good one, girlfriend!"

Gaby couldn't help but laugh through her tears.

Jenee patted her on the back. "Surely he can break his engagement or whatever he shares with this other woman?"

Gaby shook her head. "She's an heiress, and he needs her wealth to reclaim his title and lands, which his cousin stole from him." She sucked in a deep breath and explained as quickly as possible Jack's circumstances, ending with his offer to keep her as his mistress.

Emily looked as if she was ready to blow a fuse. "Why, he's nothing but a bastard. This is entirely out of the question. The lout needs to be put in his place, and I have a good mind to—" She turned to the door as if contemplating doing just that.

"You mustn't say a word. I would die if he knew I told you. But there's one more thing I failed to mention."

Emily and Jenee replied as one, "What?"

"I found the painting."

CHAPTER FIFTEEN

Maremma, Italy
October 19, 1902

J ACK HURRIED STEFANO out of his rooms and told him he'd speak to him soon about the Allegretto. The painting, however, played second fiddle as he poured a scotch and paced his room, unable to get his mind off Gabriella. What in blazes was she doing in the marchioness's rooms? He itched to give her what-for and squeeze the secrets from her sweet lips.

In truth, he longed to again sink deep within her, drive her to the brink of bliss, and then withhold satisfaction from her until she confessed all. Such was the madness of his thoughts as he ran his fingers through his hair, *damn her*. How had his life come to this madness?

Another depressing thought came to his mind: his required attendance at the evening's dinner party and having to endure the baroness's innuendos regarding the lack of a forthcoming proposal for Cynthia's hand in marriage. His duty to the family's legacy demanded he make an advantageous match to secure his patrimony.

I am lost on a storm-tossed sea, and whatever course I navigate will take me in the wrong direction. Have I no other option then to go down with my ship?

The tinkle of china arrested his ruminations and self-pity. He threw open the door and caught the subject of his roiling feelings by surprise, and the tray she held clattered to the carpet. The cups, saucers, sterling, sugar, and cream took flight in every direction.

"Leave it!" The force of his angry tone froze his quarry in her tracks. Jack immediately realized he needed to reel in the simmering pot of his frustrations. No good would come of his recalcitrant, unyielding position or his ballistic assault on Gaby.

Jack watched a flush of red rise from Gabriella's neck to her ears. Her expression transformed from one of anticipating the whip of his anger to her wielding the whip and finally to where he felt the stripes of the whip on his back. Her spine strengthened, and her chin rose skyward. She went from submission to battle-ready in the blink of an eye. He couldn't help but admire her stalwartness. This was a woman worth winning, and mercy on his peace of mind if he lost her.

"I beg your pardon, my lord." Her censorious gaze and formal address diminished his ability to exert power over her, and he nearly found himself tongue-tied.

"If you would please allow me to have a few words with you in privacy, I would be appreciative." It was all he could do not to stammer.

Her eyes swept the hallway. "Would that not be injurious to my reputation, my lord?"

"Oh, bollocks, you have no past to contend with, and I doubt very much that your future will be much affected." He was close to losing it again, and he modulated his voice to a more welcoming tone. "Please, Gaby, allow me to speak my mind, as I must find clarity."

"But what of all of this?" She waved her hand at the mess.

Not wanting to argue about meaningless things, he bent and began picking up the shards of broken crockery and utensils scattered across the carpet. Gaby chuckled, bending to assist him. "It isn't seemly for a man of your station doing the work of a lowly servant."

"I implore you not to tease me, Gaby. I am trying my best to diminish the differences between our stations to better understand you."

Gaby huffed, her hazel eyes glowing bright with renewed anger. "Do me no favors, my lord. It is probably best we keep the disparity of who we are in the forefront of our thoughts."

"Instead of flinging arrows, it would be better if we spoke civilly to each other." Jack left the tray by the door and, grabbing Gaby's wrist, pulled her into his room.

As he closed the door, Gaby wrenched her hand from his. It was impossible for him to believe she could feel such an aversion to someone she'd loved with such passion only the night before. It made him question the truth of the letter she'd written to him. He sensed she was struggling as much as he with the dissolution of whatever it was they'd shared.

Gaby turned and stared at the painting. It was as if their interaction pained her, and to hide her feelings, she focused on the Allegretto. "I see you wasted no time in hanging the painting; you must find it very appealing."

Jack's anger dissipated as he gazed at the work of art. "It is strange how much I'm drawn to it. The love between them is so profound and moving. It gives one hope that real love is possible." He settled his gaze on her.

He must have touched something in her, because the way Gaby looked at him made him want to profess his feelings for her, the devil be damned.

"Gabriella, what is your relationship with the Marchioness of Danbury?"

"Whatever do you mean?"

"Come now, do not play coy. I saw you deliver tea to her room, and I saw your face when she opened the door. You displayed recognition, and then you disappeared into her room and spent an inordinate amount of time there."

"Were you spying on me, my lord? Have you not more important ways to account for your time?" Gaby refused to meet his gaze, keeping her eyes on Allegretto's painting.

"Your desire to change the subject does not dissuade me from asking again how you and the marchioness know each other."

"I'm sorry, but I have nothing to tell you. At first, I thought she was someone I knew, but the ridiculous notion became apparent when we spoke. As for my time in her room, she asked me to wait for the tray and tea service. Now, I really must get back to the kitchen, or the dinner party will be a disaster."

Gaby spun on her heel and stomped out of the room in a huff. He heard the tray clatter and her muttered curses through the door, and a smile came unbidden to his face.

She really was magnificent. He pictured her curvaceous hips swaying as she marched back to the kitchen. *Madon! Che bel culo.* He'd lived in Italy long enough to know that the Italians were spot-on when it came to their vernacular expressions, and *what a beautiful ass* was a classic one.

Jack's eyes were drawn once more by the Allegretto painting. His gut instinct told him it was all connected somehow. Not for a second did he believe one word Gaby had said. To be certain, she was hiding something, which only added to the growing mountain of lies he suspected her of, including that damn letter. This had everything to do with Gabriella and all these supposed coincidences. The mysterious marchioness was just one more twist in this tale.

I'll uncover the truth no matter what happens.

Chapter Sixteen

Maremma, Italy
October 19, 1902

"Signorina D'Angelo, may I speak to you, *por favore?*"

"Of course, Antonio." Gabriella removed her apron and joined the deferential butler. Everything had gone perfectly with the dinner, and she expected he had come back to the kitchen to convey compliments from the dining room.

"I have a message from Lady Darling."

Gaby was expecting the kind of praise she'd been used to getting at the restaurant. Customers were always requesting she stop by their table so they could sing her praises. Just as it did in her family's restaurant in Chicago, it boosted her confidence when Kitty sent compliments to the kitchen. At least there was one place where she knew she belonged, one thing she knew she excelled at. In the kitchen, Gaby reigned supreme, and that singular bright spot would have to see her through the heartache and the challenges ahead.

"Wonderful. And what did her ladyship have to say?"

"She prefaces this with an admonishment that she will not accept any excuse on your part for not following her wishes."

"What?" Gaby asked. This did not sound like a congratulatory compliment, and her heart sank.

She went over the menu in her head. In what way had she

disappointed? What dish had fallen short? She couldn't imagine it being the boar stew. She'd tasted it, and it was rich and flavorful, and she'd served plenty of extra gravy on the side for the polenta. She hoped it wasn't the dessert that the guests didn't like, because it would break poor Maria's heart. The girl had put such effort into the beautiful almond cakes.

"Antonio, I'm completely bewildered about what Lady Darling's dissatisfaction could be. Was the meal not to her liking?"

"No, she is not disappointed. In fact, from what I could see and hear, everyone very much enjoyed the meal. But she wishes you to join her in the dining room after you go to her room, and Mrs. Livingstone helps you dress for the recital that Lady Darling and Lord Langsford will perform."

"But that's impossible." This was the last thing Gaby had in mind. To be in the same room with Jack and see him fawning over his future bride, Cynthia, would make her physically ill. "I-I…"

"Her ladyship said I was to tell you that she and his lordship would not perform until you take your seat in the dining room. She said if you do not want to incur her wrath, you'd best get yourself upstairs without further ado. And she also said she looks forward to seeing you and is saving you a seat next to Signore Stefano Bardino, who is most anxious to meet you."

"Oh, damned if I don't and damned if I do."

Antonio's brows rose. "Signorina, I do not understand."

"Sorry, Antonio, I spoke my thoughts aloud. Tell her ladyship I will do as she asks." There was no way for her to weasel out of Kitty's invitation, or rather her demand that she make an appearance at the recital. Kitty meant well, and Gaby had grown very fond of her, but the dear lady had no idea what had occurred between her and Jack. Nor would she, if Gaby had anything to do with it, and she was sure Jack would never reveal a thing about their liaison, especially with so much on the line for him.

Gaby resigned herself to the inevitable. She would have to sit through the recital and then feign exhaustion and make her escape. "Thank you, Antonio. I'm sorry if I made this difficult for you. Please tell her ladyship that I will join them in the dining room as soon as possible."

JACK CONSIDERED HIMSELF an erudite polemicist, which meant he was always ready for and valued a lively discussion. He had often considered standing for the House of Lords. Of course, until he regained his good name and title, his status as a peer was questionable at best. However, introducing controversial subject matter at the dinner table was not. He found it amusing to plant the seeds for a fiery debate. *Scandal is the entertainment of the rich and spoiled.*

In the newspapers he received from London, he'd read about the performance of a scandalous new play by the thought-provoking critic and playwright George Bernard Shaw. Shaw, a socialist, believed Victorian society's mores regarding women were repugnant. Aunt Kitty, an unrepentant fan of Shaw, never missed an opportunity to criticize society's mores that she believed subordinated women. She supported the suffragette movement, and she was in favor of all women being offered a chance to better themselves. Aunt Kitty found it entirely intolerable that a woman could not inherit her father's title, and she was incensed that women had little or no chance of being masters of their own ship even when they were often the more capable heir.

Jack sipped his whiskey, his gaze raking the guests. "Any of you seen Shaw's play *Mrs. Warren's Profession*? I hear Lord Chamberlain has since censored it, and it could only be performed privately at the Lyric Club."

He looked around the table, anticipating some dissension from perhaps the Marquess of Danbury. What he didn't expect was Danbury's wife to launch into a debate with such vocal conviction. His curiosity over her relationship with Gabriella increased exponentially as he realized the similarities between the two women. They were both outspoken and appeared not to be cowed by any man. His interest sharpened as he learned the marquess took pride in his wife's opinions and, if anything, seemed to encourage her in every way. *A most synergistic union.* The only other relationship he recalled that was anything like it was Kitty and Stewart's.

"Lord Danbury and I attended the private performance at the Lyric Club, Lord Langsford," said Emily. "I am a devoted fan of Shaw's work and was interested in seeing his play, which reflects my beliefs."

"Really?" said Aunt Kitty. "How delectably scandalous you are, my dear Emily. You must tell us what the play is about."

"I've heard it's a most unseemly subject," Cynthia said stiffly.

"And what subject is too sensitive for the public to see or hear?" Kitty asked with astonishment. "Censorship is the sword of tyrants, used to keep the masses in line, and it should not be tolerated," she emphatically declared.

Donatella laid a hand on Cynthia's diamond-cuffed wrist. "*Mia cara*, there is no reason to defend your statement. It is crass to shove the plight of the less fortunate under the noses of an unsuspecting audience that is out for an evening of entertainment. Life has never been fair, nor will it ever be fair. There will always be haves and have-nots. There will always be distinctions between... I need not say more." The baroness didn't have to clarify what was understood by all.

"Ahh," said Stefano. "That insufferable notion of class distinction perpetuated by the ruling class."

"Baroness, I disagree entirely with what you say. Those so-called distinctions fade even as we speak." Jack swirled the whiskey in his glass, casting an aside to Stefano. "I say, old chap, this is a fine scotch, is it not?" He winked at Colin. "Our good-old-boy's days are numbered, I fear. Do you not agree, Remington?" Jack rather liked what he'd seen so far of the marquess, but conversations such as these tended to bring forth truths about a person that in daily discourse would not be seen. Remington appeared to be a gentleman's gentleman and a straight shooter, but one never knew.

"The scotch is smooth as silk. The conversation is bloody good, too, even though I sense a barb or two here and there." Colin's eyes gleamed as he exchanged a look with his wife. He finished his scotch, setting the glass on the table. "I do believe you are right; vast changes are coming. And the march of time will stop for no one. I do not believe we will ever return to the old rules anytime soon, and I, for one, will not be sorry."

"Well, despite how good the scotch is, our little recital will begin soon." Aunt Kitty gave Jack a look. "Slow down, Jack, or that cello of yours will make a complete fool of you." She gestured to Antonio, who'd just entered the room. The butler bent and whispered in her ear. She nodded and whispered something back, and a sparkle lit her eyes. She was up to something; Jack was sure of it.

Emily picked up the thread of the conversation. "In answer to your question, Lady Darling, the play is about the relationship between a mother and daughter, but not your average mother and daughter. Mrs. Warren, Shaw's heroine, is the owner of a chain of brothels across Europe. At one time, she supported herself as a prostitute, but eventually, she managed to save up and buy into the brothels and raise herself from the streets to the upper class. Her daughter Vivie has just graduated from Cambridge with honors. I remind you although female students are allowed to attend lectures and sit for exams, they are still, to this day, prohibited from obtaining a degree. A deplorable situation, which, no doubt, must change.

"In the play, the mother and daughter are only beginning to know each other, which turns into a rather complex situation when Vivie learns her mother put her through Cambridge by earning her living as a prostitute. But what mortifies Vivie even more is her mother not only doesn't regret her vocation but chooses to continue to run her business. Despite her accumulated wealth, she has no compunction or remorse for her part in bettering herself by enslaving women in the same position as she herself was held captive.

"I found Shaw's play utterly spot-on. Shaw shines a light on the untruths perpetuated by society—that women who turn to prostitution as a profession are not only lacking in character but born depraved, so they get exactly what they deserve. Shaw reveals it for the lie it is. He lays the blame on a societal system that deprives them of other ways to feed, house, and clothe themselves. In other words, they are forced into prostitution by a society that turns a blind eye and is complicit in their disgrace."

"Bravo, darling. Mr. Shaw would be proud to know his message was heard loud and clear," Colin proclaimed.

The obvious affection between the two felt like a punch to Jack's ribs, reminding him of Gaby's rejection. Because of the interaction he'd observed between Emily and Gaby, he paid more attention to Emily's words. How did they know each other? He suspected the Remingtons' visit was no coincidence, either.

Chief Inspector Xavier Doumaz, who thus far had said little during the dinner conversation, added, "In France, attitudes are not dissimilar, and many women are driven to sell their bodies. Fortune has smiled on some of these women, blessing them with beauty, brains, and a witty tongue, giving them entree as consorts of illustrious men who keep and care for them in a princely manner."

"*Mais, oui, mon amour*, it is a deplorable situation, but it is changing thanks to enlightened men like you who understand a woman's worth is equal to a man's." Jenee leaned in and planted a kiss on her husband's cheek.

Jack observed that Doumaz, like Remington, was thoroughly besotted with his wife. And their wives were thoroughly besotted with them. The Frenchman held the hand of his beautiful, exotic wife, Jenee, who looked at him with such adoration and devotion that Jack felt another prick of jealousy. These happy couples were negating his theory about the impossibility of a happy marriage. The obvious affection these couples felt for each other disrupted his entire belief system. He'd never considered love a possibility in his life and was beginning to feel the deprivation.

"In a different world, these flowers would pursue other vocations and climb the ladder of success with their achievements and not their bodies," the inspector went on. "Their merit would be determined by their talents and their efforts. I had such a friend. Unfortunately, she fell prey to a monster and met her demise."

Jack could not help but observe Cynthia's reaction to the discussion. She looked positively scandalized, while the baroness seemed to scrutinize the chief inspector, her lips in a severe grimace.

"How tragic," sympathized Aunt Kitty.

Constance and her companion Blossom both nodded in agreement. Jack's curiosity turned into a profound respect for how the American carried herself. Her neck was roped in lustrous white pearls, and she was glamorously attired in a forest-green velvet gown. Jack found her lyrical Bostonian accent entertaining. He knew in the United States, women could inherit their husband, father, or mother's estates, even though they might be passed over when it came to running the family business.

Constance glanced at each of the women in the room. "We women who have been gifted a privileged life can change society and the world. Emily, you do it daily with the articles and essays you write urging for improving women's rights and, hopefully, the right to vote one day. Jenee, you persevered against all odds to become a physician and even now face tremendous prejudice and opposition to practicing your skill. Yet you fight to provide care for indigent women. As for you, my dearest Blossom, no one has surmounted more evil intentions than you. Yet your kindness and empathy never cease to amaze me." Constance raised her glass in a toast. "Thank you, Lady Darling, for welcoming us into your home and providing a magnificent landscape for us to unite. I am delighted to add you to my circle of friends and admired women."

Kitty looked pleased as punch. "Thank you so much, Constance. I am honored to meet accomplished women who will lead the way into this new century."

The door opened, and Gaby walked in, drawing everyone's attention. Jack sat up straight and had to consciously stop his jaw from dropping. Whenever he looked at Gaby, his world shifted, and he lost control over his senses. He recognized the gown Gaby wore—a sheer forest-green bodice with a plunging neckline that sported one of the newer, more formfitting silhouettes in crimped silk. But it looked completely different on Gaby. The way the silk clung to her curves made the blood rush to his ears.

He couldn't help noticing the hum of excitement from Emily and Jenee, who exchanged glances with each other and their husbands. Aunt Kitty, for her part, looked like the cat who'd swallowed the canary. Of course, his dear aunt had orchestrated Gaby's appearance. Aunt Kitty, his most loyal advocate, was taunting and prodding him. But why? She, better than anyone, understood his predicament.

The hair on the back of his neck stood on end, and he turned and caught the baroness's narrow-eyed glare. *Bloody great!* She, unlike Kitty, bore a readable expression that made his skin crawl. The baroness was not his advocate, although she'd been instrumental in bringing her niece and him together. Had she guessed his attraction to Gabriella?

But what was the baroness's purpose? He understood she wanted her niece to add an impressive title to her name, but with the wealth she was purported to have, surely there were many titled gentlemen with empty pockets who would be thrilled to step into the role of future husband to the young heiress. Cynthia was beautiful and rich, making her a highly desirable commodity.

So, what did the baroness think to gain from their union? There had to be another reason. Yet another question to add to the pile in his brain.

But the greatest mystery of all was Gabriella D'Angelo. Whenever he saw her, it was all he could do to restrain himself from throwing her over his shoulder and carrying her to his bed. His gut instinct told him that both Emily and Jenee knew exactly who Gabriella was and why she was there.

Gaby's gaze met his from across the room, and he couldn't help the thundering of his heart. *Who are you, and why can't I get you out of my mind?*

Chapter Seventeen

Maremma, Italy
October 19, 1902

J ACK FROWNED INTO his glass of scotch. After being introduced formally to everyone, Gaby was seated next to Stefano, who immediately engaged her in conversation. They spoke Italian, and Jack did his best to eavesdrop without seeming obvious. He had trouble hiding his consternation when Stefano openly flirted with Gaby. *Damn that wily Italian Don Juan.* When Stefano's shoulder brushed against hers, Jack was tempted to grab him by the neck, wrestle him to the floor, and give him what for.

The green gown made Gaby's hazel eyes sparkle like emeralds. He was sure Aunt Kitty had chosen the dress knowing it changed the kitchen goddess into a full-blown seductress equal to Venus. She must have asked Mrs. Livingstone to alter it, because the low neckline resembled Emily and Jenee's gowns.

Jack cursed the cool breeze coming in through the open French doors that made Gaby's nipples visible through the translucent fabric of the empire gown. *Damn!* He'd tasted her magnificent buds. Now, he could only think about his tongue flicking her nipples, his teeth nipping and tugging, making her moan and writhe beneath him. His pants grew suddenly so tight and his staff so stiff that it was a wonder it didn't poke through the napkin on his lap and join in the after-dinner conversation.

The only thing to do was drink more scotch, which he wasted no time doing. He hoped the liquor would quash the percolation of blood that raced from his heart to below his belt and hardened his staff. It wasn't often a man prayed his intromittent apparatus would grow limp, but under the circumstances, a limp dick would be a blessing.

Aunt Kitty had the uncanny ability to read him like a book. She must have sensed his dilemma, because she gave him the stink-eye. "I believe it's almost time for our recital, isn't it, Jack?"

"Quite right, dear Aunt Kitty." His voice sounded strained to his ears, making his aunt give him another warning look.

"I don't believe you've heard Jack play, Cynthia, my dear," she said.

Cynthia twittered, "Father insisted on me having vocal and piano lessons. He believed a true lady must always be practiced in the refined arts."

"And do you enjoy music?" Aunt Kitty asked.

"I must confess, I found the daily practice rather tedious and abandoned my lessons after a few weeks."

"That is a shame," Aunt Kitty said. "I find music truly uplifting, don't you agree, Jack?"

"Yes, completely." Jack downed his scotch.

"Shall we make our way to the drawing room?"

Jack needed to pull himself together. He picked up his water glass and gulped it down before setting the empty glass on the table with a thud.

"Stefano, will you escort Miss Maxwell and the baroness into the music room?" Aunt Kitty asked.

Jack noted the disapproving look the baroness shot at Aunt Kitty and the downward droop of Cynthia's lips.

He strode toward Gaby, intending to escort her, giving him a chance to speak with her. But Lady Remington beat him to the punch and linked her arm through Gabriella's. Before he could even think of protesting, Madame Doumaz took her other arm and smiled at Jack as if nothing was awry with three women breaking acceptable protocol. Emily and Jenee thought nothing of abandoning their husbands. Instead, assuming the role of a young virgin's protectors, they escorted Gabriella to the music room.

"Do not worry, Lord Langsford—we will see Miss D'Angelo to the concert," the marchioness said. "I'm sure you need to tune your instrument before the performance."

Jack's mouth gaped open at the innuendo. Was he imagining it, or had the proper English aristocrat just told him to get his cock under control and back off?

Remington and Doumaz gallantly escorted Constance and Blossom, leaving Jack to accompany his aunt.

"I hope you're not foxed!" Aunt Kitty whispered as they followed behind the others.

"I'm not foxed, but I wish I was," Jack muttered as he watched Gaby's hips' tantalizing sway as she walked just a few feet ahead.

⟫⟫⟫⟪⟪⟪

GABY WAS GRATEFUL her friends had thwarted Jack's attempt to get her alone. The last thing she wanted was to battle with him again, even if it was a whispered exchange. How could they have gone from passion to hostility?

She'd had no choice but to write that letter. She would be no man's mistress. Even if he did have feelings for her, how in the world could she live with only part of him? How could she build a life on that? How could she have children with him, knowing they would be born outside of the sanctity of marriage? She wouldn't think twice about doing that in her time, but not in this era. They would be labeled bastards, and that would scar them for life.

She may as well hop on the next portal out of here. Well, the *last* portal, according to Em and Jen. She was happy for her friends. Happy that they'd found true love with good and honorable men who adored them. Happy that they were building their own families.

But Gaby had to face the cold, hard truth. Jack could never be hers. Not in the way she wanted. In the way that mattered most to her. Besides, she hadn't even considered what it would mean to stay here. It would mean never seeing her family again. It would mean saying goodbye to her life, her career, not to mention all the modern conveniences and advances that she'd taken for granted.

And yet whenever she was near Jack, all she wanted to do was throw her arms around his neck and press her body against that prodigious bulge inside his trousers that reminded her of their night of passion. It stole her breath. If not for Emily and Jenee holding tight to her as they made their way to the drawing room, she might have swooned and slid to the floor, engulfed in a torrent of sensual recollection and dismayed denial.

Gaby might wish and dream of a repeat of last night, but she would never have the strength to walk away. Being in his presence was torture, and she wondered how she would get through tonight. *I will disappear after the concert like Cinderella at midnight.* But there would be no Prince Charming for her.

She took her seat between Stefano and Emily. Without appearing to eavesdrop, she couldn't help but listen to what the baroness seated on the other side of Stefano was saying.

"Stefano, have you heard anything from your contacts about the Allegretto painting?"

"No…not yet, but I am hopeful that, given the substantial amount of money Constance Shipley has offered, we will be successful in locating it."

Gaby could hear the hesitation in his voice, and she was sure the baroness had heard it too. Why was the baroness so keen on the painting? Was it just curiosity, or was there more to it?

From the corner of her eye, Gaby saw the baroness lay a claw-like hand on Stefano's sleeve, and her long, tapered nails dug into his arm as though to emphasize her words. "I want you to seriously consider what I have to say. Whatever Madam Shipley has offered you for the Allegretto is nothing compared to what I would offer you."

"But Donatella, that would be dishonorable of me. Constance has placed her trust in me as a client and a dear friend of many years. That is not how I do business."

"Then you had better change the way you do business," she hissed. "Heed my words, dear Stefano. You have no idea of the power I wield, nor what I can do for you…or against you."

Stefano let out a soft chuckle that was threaded with anger. "Are you threatening me, baroness?"

"Of course not, signore." She shrugged. "I am merely a woman who is passionate about getting what I want." She leaned toward him, pressing her breasts against his arm. "Come to my room tonight," she purred in his ear, "so we can discuss this further. I am sure we can come to a satisfying arrangement that will benefit both of us."

Gaby could not believe what she was hearing from the baroness. The woman had presented herself as rather cool and aloof, and here she was turning into a femme fatale. Gaby liked Madam Shipley and assumed that her feelings went deeper than friendship for Stefano. She'd noticed the smiles exchanged across the table by the American heiress and the art dealer. Would Stefano give in to the baroness's wily, seductive ways, or would he remain true to his dear friend and client?

She wished she could talk to Jack about this. She was certain he'd shown Stefano the painting. It worried her that the painting was hanging in his room, and anyone could steal it. She didn't trust the baroness, not one bit, and suspected the unlikeable Donatella might be the evil contessa Emily had told her about, a sorceress capable of taking on the identity of another.

She needed to speak with Em, Jen, and Iris, who was here under the guise of Constance's companion, Blossom. They needed to figure out what they were going to do. The fact that the baroness was keen on acquiring the Allegretto was a new wrinkle in their plans.

Gaby watched Em and Jen with their husbands, their teasing

banter, and their loving looks. Both thoroughly modern women, Emily and Jen had not only adapted to living in the past but were thriving. Neither seemed to miss the modern world or its conveniences.

Gaby herself had embraced cooking in this era. Yes, she missed her stand mixer, her food processor, and all the other fun and helpful kitchen gadgets that she loved. Then again, her grandmother and mother had also taught her to do pretty much everything by hand. She didn't think she'd have a problem adjusting as a chef.

No, the only problem with staying would be Jack. Unlike her friends, there would be no happy ending for her with the man she loved. Jack would propose to Cynthia, and that would be that. If she and the gals could get the painting to Iris soon, she could head home and wouldn't have to be around to witness Jack and Cynthia's betrothal announcement. Her heart wrenched at the thought of leaving Jack forever, but she couldn't bear the idea of staying, knowing he would be marrying Cynthia in a matter of months.

Gaby's musings were interrupted when Blossom stood and made an announcement. "You will excuse and forgive me, but a migraine has come upon me, and it would be best if I retire early. Thank you, Lady Darling and Lord Langsford, for a delightful evening. I bid you good evening." Without waiting for a reply, Blossom whisked past Antonio, who was stationed at the doorway.

"Oh my," said Aunt Kitty to Constance. "I do hope she will be all right."

"She will be fine," Constance replied. "She has a migraine powder, which is quite effective against the demonic pain that attacks her. Blossom is very sensitive."

"Very well, let us begin," Aunt Kitty said. She sat at the piano and turned to Jack. "Ready?

"Ready," Jack replied, holding his bow poised on the cello strings.

His eyes met Gaby's as he began to play. The music was so

achingly beautiful that she had to blink back tears. Oh, how she wished things could be different between them. How she wished they could have their own happy ending…

IRIS TIPTOED DOWN the hall toward Lord Langsford's bedroom. Since learning from Emily that the painting had been found and was hanging in Jack's room, she'd waited for a moment when everyone would be occupied, and she might sneak upstairs and see the painting for herself. The evening's entertainment was her best chance, and she made her escape without arousing any suspicions—at least, she hoped no one was the wiser.

The hallway was empty, and she slowed as she approached Lord Langsford's door. Glancing up and down the hall, she held her breath and listened for footsteps.

Iris tried the knob, but it was locked. She pulled a hairpin from her hair, slipped it into the locking mechanism, and, with a few twists and turns, jimmied the lock. The knob turned, giving her entry. She'd learned many survival skills during her years as a time traveler, including a few that were against the law. *All for a good cause.*

Iris slipped into the room without a sound and closed the door.

When she turned around, her breath caught in her throat. It had been some time since she'd seen *Il Leto*, and her knees almost buckled. Her senses were flooded with memories of the first time she'd seen the finished painting.

She'd been writing at her desk when she felt Marco's hands on her shoulders. His strong, elegant fingers kneaded her muscles, and she'd sighed with pleasure, her head falling back against him. Never one to miss the opportunity of expressing his love for her, he'd bent to kiss her neck and then worked his way up to nibble her earlobe. His warm breath had aroused her, and she knew the kiss was but a prelude, and they would find themselves making love beneath cool linen sheets. It did not matter that she was intensely occupied with her writing. There had never been a moment when she ever thought to refuse him. The fear that she'd be sucked away by time and disappear to another era had always been with her. She never took the miracle of their love for granted.

His warm breath in her ear brought shivers and goosebumps. But to her surprise, his intention was not an afternoon tryst. "Vieni, tesoro mio, *I want to show you something.*"

He kissed the back of her hand and helped her up before leading her through the villa to his studio. She could feel his excitement pass like an electric current from his hand to hers.

Marco's studio held at least a dozen easels with paintings in various stages of completion. On his worktable was a pestle and mortar for grinding minerals such as azurite and malachite, as well as various plants such as saffron and Brazil wood, which he mixed with walnut or linseed oil. The afternoon light poured in from the windows, filling the room with a golden glow. Iris guessed Marco had waited for this magical moment to reveal to her the painting he'd been laboring over.

When he pulled back the cloth, she was so overwhelmed by what she saw that she couldn't speak. Struggling to compose herself, she'd stared in awed silence, taking in the dramatic play of light and shadow across the canvas. Then, with more serious intent, she'd focused on the technical skills and mastery of his art. Finally, she'd simply let the beauty of the painting soak into her mind and soul.

You do not overthink a masterpiece, she'd told herself. *You simply let it speak its truth.*

Now, standing before the painting once more, she realized she'd nearly forgotten how powerful it was. She closed her eyes, and a tide of emotion washed over her as she remembered the tremor of his voice when he asked, *"What do you think,* tesoro mio?" His tone had been hesitant, as if he were worried that she might disapprove or find the painting wanting.

She'd turned to him, taking his face between her hands. *"It's* your finest work, Marco. The world will sing your praise long after we are both long dead. The third and final painting chronicles our love, and the series is complete. You have given us immortality, my darling."

Iris's soul sang with yearning as she remembered their passionate lovemaking afterward. She inched closer to the painting until she stood directly before it. She whispered, "Come to me, my love. Please take me home."

The French doors flew open, and the drapery billowed from a blustery breeze that carried the fragrance of roses, but Iris did not move. She brought all her powers of concentration and every nerve in her body to bear on the painting. She willed the man who'd created it to appear. The canvas rippled as if waves washed over its surface.

The figure of Marco in the painting came to life, and slowly he turned. He was naked from the waist up, and the desire in his gaze sent a surge of heat and tremors throughout her body.

"*Amore mio*, I love you with my very soul. But there is something we must do before we can be together. The contessa must be destroyed, and her evil must be stopped once and for all."

Tears slipped down her cheeks. "I don't know if I can do this. I'm afraid, Marco."

"Do not be afraid. We are so close to being free of her. I will be here waiting for you, and we will never be parted again."

"But what if she gets hold of this painting? She will control the portals, and I will be lost in time forever."

"You must not let that happen, Iris. You and your friends are the only ones who can stop her absolute evil from spreading. Together, you will defeat the contessa. I will do everything I can to keep the portal open for you and Gabriella if she wants to return to the future. I sense the sorceress's presence; she is here in this villa."

"I sense her, too. I suspect she's stolen an identity and changed her appearance. I think it is the Baroness of Blythe Hollow, but I must be sure. I could never live with myself if I destroyed the life of an innocent woman."

"Of course not, *tesoro mio. You* must find a way to confirm her identity. Search her room. I am certain you will find the proof you need."

"I know she is here, and I will find the proof. But how will we destroy her? The power she wields is formidable, and I fear I am not strong enough."

"The way will open to you, but you need the help of your friends, and this…" He held up his hand, and the ruby ring shot rays of light into the room. There had been no diminishment of its magical power, and Iris drew strength from it. She closed her eyes and absorbed its warming energy.

And then, as suddenly as he'd come to her, he was gone. She opened her eyes and was alone again, gazing at a beautiful painting.

CHAPTER EIGHTEEN

Populonia, Italy
October 20, 1902

T HE CARRIAGES MADE slow progress, but Jack enjoyed the sensation of Gabriella's shoulders and thighs pressing against his when the carriage hit a rut in the road. The effect on him was arousing, and he was grateful for the blanket over their legs for warmth.

They'd set out just after dawn, and Gaby sat rigidly, staring straight ahead, careful to avoid looking at him. Still, he could see the pale blue vein in her temple throbbing, and he contemplated what she might be thinking. Did his nearness affect her the way it did him? He could not imagine her feeling indifference, as he now and again detected an inhalation of breath that might indicate uncontained excitement.

Her response to him the other night was undeniably passionate, and he refused to think otherwise. Visions of their lovemaking had haunted him last night, and he'd tossed and turned in his bed, unable to sleep, reliving in his dreams her responses to his touch, her feverish kisses, and the arousal in her eyes. These were not reactions she could have faked. Hell, he'd felt the spasms in her body when she climaxed.

Yes, her letter had stung and wounded his ego, but deep in his heart, he didn't think she meant a word of it. This war of conflicting emotions held him enthralled, and nothing in his life could compare with the feelings she evoked in him. It was why he wanted to strangle her one minute, and the next he wanted to grab her and kiss her senseless.

For once, he was glad of Aunt Kitty's meddling and insistence that Gabriella join them on this outing. Gaby had used every excuse possible, but Kitty would not hear of it. In the end, she had persuaded Gaby to accompany them to the ancient coastal town of Populonia to visit the Necropolis of San Cerbone, where they would see the Etruscan tombs and then enjoy a picnic.

At the last second, Iris had bowed out of the excursion, her reason being another headache. For Jack, it had been fortuitous, for it meant there was room in Kitty's carriage. It foiled Kitty's plan that would have had him riding in the same carriage as Cynthia, the baroness, Stefano, Constance, and Lord and Lady Remington.

Using the excuse that he wished to converse with Inspector Doumaz about a discovery in the catacombs of Paris, he'd jumped into Kitty's carriage and taken what would have been Iris's seat next to Gabriella.

He'd startled her, and the delightful flush that tinged her cheeks was his reward after having to endure a long, tedious evening the night before that culminated with his and Kitty's performance of Brahms's Cello Sonata—which, despite his drinking, went off without a hitch. Music came easily to him, but not so love. At Gabriella's appearance in the dining room, he'd sobered instantly—and could not help looking in her direction as he played.

She had slipped away before he'd had a chance to speak to her after the recital. And he'd returned to his room, feeling angry and frustrated.

Allegretto's painting was another reason for his anxiety. He hadn't decided whether to sell the painting, and Stefano was exerting pressure on him to decide on a course of action.

At breakfast, Stefano had whispered in his ear that he thought there might be a bidding war for the painting. From the baroness's comments, Stefano had ascertained that she and Constance Shipley would be inclined to pay whatever amount he asked to obtain the storied Allegretto.

Stefano's revelation was stuck in Jack's head.

"Just think, Jack, you'll have enough money to regain your patrimony, and you'll be free from the need to marry. Don't think I haven't noticed your avoidance of making a commitment to Miss Maxwell, and I am not the only one who has noticed. Be careful."

Stefano hadn't mentioned who else had noticed, but Jack knew it could only be the baroness and likely Cynthia herself, although he saw no threat from her quarter.

"Dear me." Kitty fanned herself. "Had I known this was such a trek, I might have reconsidered our outing to Populonia. I'm worried about Cynthia and the baroness, as I do not believe they were looking forward to today."

"Jack has kindled everyone's curiosity," Xavier said. "Jenee and I are eager to see these ancient burial grounds of the Etruscans; we know so little about them. Besides, it's a lovely day for an outing, and the beauty of the Tuscan countryside is without parallel. For all the joys of living in Paris, to be in the countryside and at leisure is a welcome change."

"I agree," added Jenee. "We can learn so much from history. It is admirable that you, Jack, a man of title and wealth, would choose to devote yourself to a passion with a purpose that benefits humanity. I have so often witnessed quite the opposite. So many in the upper echelons live only for self-indulgence."

If they only knew that my immediate passion is sitting beside me and that my purpose today is to indulge myself in her. "You are too kind, Jenee." Jack inclined his head to the beautiful Frenchwoman while covertly watching for any reaction from Gabriella, any sign that her feelings for him were more profound than she claimed. To his dismay, she sat rigid as a statue and avoided his gaze.

"Unfortunately, this great passion for archeology is why he finds himself in such a pickle," said Aunt Kitty.

"A pickle?" Xavier turned to his wife. "What is this pickle, *ma chérie?*"

Jenee laughed, and even Gabriella could not help but smile when Jenee kissed Xavier on his cheek. "It means a dilemma, *mon amour*. Our new friend's passion has resulted in him stepping into hot water. *D'accord?*"

Jack was fit to be tied. "Really, Kitty, must you air my dirty laundry for all the world to see? You always accuse me of speaking without a filter; perhaps you should heed your own advice."

"Lady Darling meddles, as you say, because she cares about you."

It was the first thing Gabriella had said to him since he'd dragged her into his room yesterday when she was carrying that blasted tea tray. She stared at him, hands folded in her lap. He knew her discomfort had everything to do with him. It exasperated him, but she had to be aware that her confounded note had torn his world apart. He needed answers and wanted an explanation, not what she'd written in that damn letter.

"Ah, she speaks; therefore, she is." Jack couldn't resist teasing her. "Miss D'Angelo, are you of the same opinion as Aunt Kitty?" He modulated his voice, careful not to prompt an angry retort.

"I was simply making an observation in support of Lady Darling. I cannot see why my opinion should matter."

Her gaze met his.

Yes! He wouldn't let her escape that easily now that he'd finally managed to get her to look at him. "Oh, but it matters very much to me."

"What do you think, Gabriella, of Miss Cynthia Maxwell?" Aunt Kitty asked.

Jack wanted to shake his aunt for interrupting and hug her for asking such a bold question.

"Yes, what does our chef extraordinaire think of my future countess?" After what Gaby had put him through, he could not resist the barb, but he regretted it instantly. The flash of hurt in her eyes made him want to take her in his arms and beg her forgiveness for being so callous. *Damn it, hold your tongue, or she'll clam up, and you'll never get to the truth.*

"Sh-she is beautiful and cultured and—was clearly raised to be the wife of a t-titled gentleman," Gaby stammered. She took a deep breath, and a bright smile suddenly appeared on her face. "I'm certain your families will benefit from such an *advantageous match*. I wish you both the very best, Lord Langsford. I hope you will be happy." She rushed out the last few words and then turned to look out the window, dismissing him again.

Her emphasis on the words *advantageous match* stung like a swarm of hornets whose nest had been threatened. Jack hated that Gaby thought him a fortune hunter. He'd never previously considered marrying for money. But that had been before his father disowned him, thanks to Jack's nefarious cousin. It would have been easier if he'd just throttled the bastard. Instead, he'd maneuvered himself into a possible betrothal with the wrong woman and fallen head over heels in love with the right one.

The cool breeze carried the scent of salty air, and the blue water of the Tyrrhenian Sea provided a majestic view. But the scenery did not stir him. What disrupted his composure was the minx beside him, who sat close enough to touch. Close enough to have his way with, had there not been three other people in the carriage.

"To find love is difficult enough, and one must never take it for granted. I, for one, never will," Xavier said, gazing at his wife with adoration.

The observation struck home. Jack didn't miss the point, and he doubted Gaby did either.

"I couldn't agree more, *mon amour*," Jenee said, taking her husband's hand. "Love is not something to be trifled with or cast aside."

Gaby made no comment, and Jack could only wonder at her thoughts.

"Then again, one cannot merely rely on love alone," Jenee continued. "There must also be a willingness to make whatever sacrifice is necessary for true love. And the strength and honor to fight for it." Her gaze was steely as she spoke.

Jack couldn't help but feel that she was directing her comments directly at him. *Damn.* Did she know about him and Gaby?

He could feel Gaby stiffen beside him, and she turned to Jenee. The two women exchanged a look that seemed to hold a world of meaning. Jenee was as protective of Gaby as the marchioness. In fact, they seemed like three peas in a pod. Which made Jack even more determined to find out everything he could about Gaby and her past. He had to get her alone, and soon.

"I agree that true love is worth any sacrifice," Aunt Kitty added in a wistful voice. "Losing the love of my life, my beloved husband Stewart, was and is an unfillable void. It has been a struggle to find my way forward." She sniffled, pulling a handkerchief from her reticule, and dabbed her eyes.

Jack was surprised by Kitty's blunt confession. He'd always considered his aunt to be as tough as nails. His uncle had passed away five years ago while Jack was in Egypt. He'd had no idea his aunt still grieved.

Gabriella reached out and took Kitty's hand in hers. "The love you shared with your husband was the love of a lifetime, but I hope you will find happiness again, my lady."

"Alas, I dare not dream of finding another husband that will ever supplant Stewart in my affections. But if it is God's will, and a good man by some miracle comes into my life, I will not be foolish enough to turn him away."

Jack felt like an idiot for not realizing how lonely his aunt was. She was always bustling about, ensuring her guests at the villa were comfortable and content. And she had always had time for him. He made a mental note to speak privately with her. No matter what happened in his life, he would always be there for her.

"I do hope everyone finds the luncheon to their satisfaction," Gabriella said. Jack had the feeling that she was trying to distract his aunt from her sad musings. He knew that Gaby cared about Kitty, and that warmed him from the inside out.

"Oh, Gabriella, I am certain we shall," Kitty said, giving Gaby's hand a squeeze. "Everything you make is so delicious. I have never tasted the like. And your ability to make each dish so unique and different... You are truly a culinary artist." Her smile returned. "Jack might be your biggest fan, cooking-wise, as I've never seen him refill his plate so often."

Xavier laughed and patted his stomach. "I could not concur more; your cuisine is *formidable*. As a Frenchman, I have a most discerning palate and pride myself on my cooking. Jenee is quite the aficionado of my bourride. Dare I say it was instrumental in winning her heart." He winked at his wife.

Jenee slapped his wrist. "Xavier, your fish soup is excellent. However, I was far more taken by your other talents," she said, returning his teasing, the innuendo not lost on Jack.

Everyone in the carriage could not help but laugh, and no one laughed harder than Xavier.

"Your witty tongue, *mon amour*, is second only to your great beauty, which holds me spellbound as always."

Jack could feel the tightening in his chest. The inspector and his wife made no secret of their adoration of each other—neither did the Remingtons, for that matter—and he couldn't avoid the prick of jealousy. He studied Gabriella, wondering if she, too, wished to know such bliss. She was smiling at Jenee and Xavier but was, once again, avoiding his gaze.

"Goodness, all this rocking in the carriage is jarring these old bones of mine," Aunt Kitty said. "How much longer, Jack?"

"You are the furthest thing from old, Aunt Kitty, but you're in luck because we've arrived." Jack jumped out of the carriage before it had come to a stop and helped his aunt down. Then he turned to assist Gaby, feeling heat shoot through him at the touch of her hand in his.

"Thank you, my lord," Gaby said, barely meeting his gaze. "Please excuse me. I must see to my staff." She hurried off in the direction of the wagon pulling up behind the second carriage.

Jack almost whooped with glee when Aunt Kitty made a

beeline for the wagon and, quite loudly, told Gabriella that Luigi, Maria, Sofia, and Antonio were more than capable of unloading and setting up the picnic. She insisted that Gaby join them in exploring the necropolis.

Unfortunately, the baroness practically dragged Cynthia up to Jack, exclaiming how excited her niece was about the ruins. He couldn't help but notice that Cynthia looked anything but excited about the tour, but he had no choice but to offer her his arm.

Damn! Thwarted again! But he was not daunted. Jack was determined to come up with a plan to get Gaby alone. And even more determined to get some answers.

Cynthia held a parasol and grabbed Jack's arm for support as he led the party through the ruins. "What you see scattered about are burial mounds and family tombs, which we can explore at leisure after the picnic. I thought hiking up the hill to the necropolis caves would be amusing and invigorating."

"I say, Jack," said Colin, "I've heard the Etruscans had some interesting proclivities."

Jack's lips twitched with humor at Colin's meaning. "You are correct—the Etruscans were quite open about certain activities. Tomb paintings have been found that depict naked young women serving meals, which is quite a risqué proposition to contemplate."

Stefano guffawed. "That would certainly add flavor to any meal."

"Or ruin it," the baroness said with disdain.

"How very shocking and distasteful!" Cynthia added.

"My dear, one must learn tolerance when judging cultures different from your own," Jack said. "Remember, we are talking about a thousand years ago, and by all indications, they were quite advanced for their time."

"How very decadent," said Stefano. "I imagine the Romans must have incorporated much of the Etruscan culture into their own."

"They did. So much of what we consider Roman culture, accomplishments, and customs stem from the Etruscans. The

Etruscans influenced them in many ways, including art and design. It is a shame I can't take you to Tarquinia and show you the tomb paintings. They are extraordinary and give an excellent picture of Etruscan culture and everyday life. Unfortunately, Tarquinia is a two-day journey from Nido dell' Aquila."

"Jack, I'm certain our guests will be quite satisfied with this small introduction to the Etruscan world," Kitty said with a chuckle.

"Righto, I forget myself. Not everyone shares my fascination with history and archaeological discoveries."

"My friend," said Stefano, "your passion for antiquity is not very different from my passion for painting and sculpture. Art also reveals much about the past, though not such a distant past."

"Ah, yes, and that includes the work of Marco Allegretto? I am curious, Stefano, have you received any leads as to where the painting might be?" asked Donatella.

Stefano exchanged a quick glance with Jack. "Not yet, but I have my feelers out, and I am hopeful my inquiries will lead to someone coming forward with information."

"Forgive my bluntness, Donatella, but you have shown an inordinate interest in Allegretto's work," Constance said as she walked beside Aunt Kitty. "Are you also interested in acquiring one of his paintings?" The American heiress studied the baroness with a sharp-eyed look.

"My late husband and I amassed a sizeable collection of Renaissance art," the baroness replied in a smooth tone. "As a collector, I am intrigued by this missing painting that Stefano has spoken about. Although Allegretto was a lesser master than Leonardo or Michelangelo, his work would be a fitting addition to any Renaissance collection."

"I see," Constance replied with a slight smile. "I am certain Stefano will keep us both apprised as to any revelations of the whereabouts of, as you say, this lesser master."

Jack noticed Constance was not surprised by the baroness's interest in the painting, nor did she seem concerned that the woman might offer a challenge to her acquisition of it. It also confirmed what Stefano had said—the baroness might be maneuvering to secure the painting for herself. Her belittlement of the artist seemed to be a strategy to achieve her end. Donatella was a sly fox, and Cynthia might also be part of a larger plan. Stefano may have, against his wishes, revealed that the painting had been found.

Jack hadn't decided to reveal or sell the work, but his gut told him he'd better secure the artwork in a safer location. He'd kept his bedroom locked, but he didn't trust anyone except Aunt Kitty and Gaby…

That surprised him, given she had yet to reveal the truth about her past. But in his heart, he knew it just as he knew every inch of her body.

CHAPTER NINETEEN

Populonia, Italy
October 20, 1902

G ABRIELLA'S HEART TWISTED into knots as she watched
Cynthia holding tight to Jack's arm for support. The last
thing she'd wanted was to be on this outing, but she'd had no
choice. She couldn't say no to Kitty.

The carriage ride had been hard enough sitting next to Jack,
feeling the heat from his tall, gorgeous body. But the conversation had only added to her anxiety.

Not to mention the added strain of seeing how Jen and Xavier
loved each other, how they were so in tune with each other's
thoughts and feelings—and then feeling the press of Jack's
shoulder or thigh as the carriage rolled over each rut in the road
was frustrating, to say the least.

She was also worried about the painting, but Jen and Em had
whispered to her that Iris would keep an eye on things until they
returned. Gaby wished she could have had a chance to speak
privately with Allegretto's muse and the author of her favorite
book, but she'd had no idea that Blossom was Iris Bellerose until
Emily and Jenee explained everything to her. Iris must have
known who Gaby was; she and Allegretto had been responsible
for her going back in time.

But why didn't she reach out to me? Perhaps she had been biding her time, knowing that Em and Jen would arrive the next day? Still, Gaby felt so discombobulated, so out of the loop. She still had no idea how they would help Iris and destroy the contessa.

Gaby sighed as she walked alongside her friends and their husbands. At least she'd get to spend a little more time with her besties before this was all over. And then what? There was no future for her and Jack. What reason did she have to stay? Yes, she'd miss her friends like crazy, but knowing they had both found true love and were both so happy filled Gaby's heart with warmth. *If only I could have the same with Jack…*

Em reached for Gaby's hand and gave it a slight squeeze. Jen took Gaby's other hand, and they fell back, walking a little slower, their husbands forming a protective wall in front of them.

"Iris stayed behind for a reason," Em whispered in Gaby's ear. "She'll be searching the baroness's room."

"Does Iris thinks it's her?" Gaby whispered back.

"Yes," Jenee replied. "And she went to your room the night she and Constance arrived to tell you who she was and tell you of her suspicions about the baroness, but you weren't there."

"Something tells me you were with a certain hunky archeologist," Em said.

Gaby's face heated.

"We need to have a good, long chat before the shit hits the fan," Jen added. "We don't have much time as it is. And we want to make sure you're okay, Gaby."

"I—I don't know if I am, to be honest."

"Honey, Jen is right," Em said. "Once we've worked out a plan with Iris, things will move quickly. You have to really think hard about whether you want to stay or go home."

Gaby swallowed the lump in her throat as she realized her friends were right.

"Gaby, I was sitting across from you during the carriage ride," Jen said. "The sparks between you and Jack could light up the night sky."

"But he's going to marry Cynthia," Gaby said, her voice breaking.

"Do you know that for sure?" Em asked.

"How can he not marry her? He needs her money to win back his title and estate."

"I'm sure with Colin's influence, we can help."

"But I wrote him a letter, and now he's pissed off at me. Besides, he never told me he was in love with me."

"Well, did you tell him how you feel?" Jen asked.

"No. Everything's happened so fast. I just can't think straight anymore."

"Colin and Xavier are good judges of character, and they both think Jack is a good guy," Em said.

"I know that too."

"Then you need to tell Jack how you feel," Jen said.

"And soon," Em added.

Gaby nodded, but her insides were churning with anxiety. She had practically memorized Iris's book, she'd read it so many times. Knowing that the story was all true made her tremble with fear at what the contessa was capable of. She feared for her friends, Aunt Kitty, and especially Jack.

Em and Jen were right, though. When the time came, Gaby needed to figure out if she would stay or leave with Iris. She needed to talk to Jack, to tell him everything about herself. She needed to take the biggest risk of her life and tell Jack she loved him.

⟫⟫⟫⟫⟫⟫⟩⟨⟨⟨⟨⟨

THEY SETTLED INTO silence as the path steepened, weaving through a forest of towering cypress, umbrella pine, and gnarled olive trees. When they reached the summit, a cliff face was carved with doorways and windows. A ladder rested against the bluff face, and a man climbed out of one of the upper openings.

A big smile filled his suntanned face when he spied them. "Jack, is that you? Where the devil have you been? It feels like years since we've seen each other." Suddenly realizing Jack was in mixed company, he said, "Forgive my spicy language, ladies. It's one of the side effects of being an archaeologist, as I am rarely in the company of the fairer sex."

"Sir Edward Marlborough, may I introduce you to my aunt, Lady Katherine Darling," Jack said.

Kitty smiled warmly. "No need to apologize; I hate censorship in any form." She took Sir Edward's hand and shook it firmly. After introducing everyone to Sir Edward, Jack asked how the dig was progressing and what might interest his guests.

"That depends on how daring everyone is," the older man said with a chuckle. "We've just opened a hidden section, but it requires climbing down a ladder into a newly discovered secret chamber. I think it might have been the tomb of a priestess, based on the cave paintings and artifacts we've found thus far."

"Well, I'm certainly in," Jack enthused. Cynthia was the last to agree, and Jack was sure she only did so when she realized that everyone else was going and she'd be left alone.

The group fell in line behind Sir Edward. Jack was surprised to see Kitty take Sir Edward's arm, inviting him to escort her. Jack couldn't help but notice the man's broad smile as he chatted with his aunt. Stewart Darling had been an adventurous man, and Kitty loved him fiercely. Sir Edward was cut from the same cloth as Jack's late uncle. Tall and fit, with penetrating dark eyes and a trim silver beard, he had carved out a career doing what he loved. Like Kitty, he refused to conform to what was expected of him.

Jack wished he'd thought of inviting Sir Edward to the villa long ago. But he'd been so wrapped up in his own problems that it hadn't occurred to him. And, remembering what Aunt Kitty had said in the carriage, Jack wanted to help her find contentment in her life. Knowing that Sir Edward was around would ease Jack's worries about returning to England to deal with the estate.

Now, if only I could get my own life sorted. Gaby was never far from his thoughts, even though physically, she'd stayed close to Emily and Jenee throughout the tour.

"I imagine being a coastal city, this must have been a hub for trade," Constance observed. "I noticed the harbor was small but more than adequate."

"You might compare Populonia to your American city of Pittsburgh in that it was as famous for its iron ore smelting as Pittsburgh is for its steel production," Sir Edward said with a smile. "Now, I must warn everyone to please stay as close to the group as possible. Please do not wander off; some chambers have not been fully secured or investigated."

They entered the brownstone cliff face through one of the chiseled openings, following Sir Edward through a narrow passageway. "In case you're wondering, I gave my crew the day off," he added, stepping over a set of chisels and a stack of paintbrushes in various sizes. "I will light a lantern before we begin our descent, and I will go down first to light the way. And Jack and the other gentlemen can assist from here. Ladies, mind your gowns. You may want to hold your skirts slightly higher as you climb down the ladder. For safety, of course."

"Now don't you peek, Sir Edward," Kitty teased, setting off a litany of giggles from the women.

The archaeologist roared with laughter and added with a Scottish brogue, "Ah, lassie, nothing I haven't seen before. You can trust my eyes will not wander...much."

Barely able to control her amusement, Kitty managed to respond, "Touché!"

Jack's heart did a somersault as Gaby reached for his hand. He looked at her and saw her beautiful eyes were luminous in the darkened cavern. "Careful on the ladder," he said, and his voice sounded strained to his ears.

"I will, thank you," Gaby said softly.

Once the women were on solid ground and had rearranged their skirts, the men followed them down. Sir Edward led them down a dimly lit passage and into a chamber.

The lantern's light filled the room with a golden glow. Inside the room were benches and carved stone pillows where the dead must have lain. The ceiling was low, and painted on the back wall was a faded fresco depicting a sun with golden rays shining down on a collage of figures in armor and on horseback.

"It feels so eerie, and the air is so stale," Cynthia said with a shudder.

"I suppose you are right, my dear," Sir Edward said. "It is an ancient tomb, but I can assure you I have not come across any ghosts here, simply the remains of a woman and the necessities needed to accompany her into the afterlife. Extraordinary well-preserved finds, such as a bronze mirror, an amphora and cups with wine residue, candelabra to light her way, cans of crystallized honey, and a pair of beautiful gold earrings that would indicate she was a young priestess from a wealthy family."

"Sir Edward, you must join us for our picnic," Aunt Kitty said. "I have so many questions I want to ask you about the Etruscans and your work."

"I would be honored to join you and delighted to answer any questions you might have."

"Shall we—" Jack's words were cut off by a woman's scream.

"Gaby? What's wrong?" Emily cried out. "Please, wake up!"

Jack's heart leaped to his throat, and he pushed through the group to get to Gaby. "What happened?"

"She fainted," Emily said in alarm.

Jenee had reached Gaby's side a moment after Jack did, and, kneeling, she reached for Gaby's hand and pressed her finger to her wrist to check her pulse.

"Please move back," Jack barked over his shoulder. "You're crowding her, and she needs air."

"I'll fetch water." Sir Edward was already halfway up the ladder.

Jenee called to him, "Have you any smelling salts, Sir Edward?"

"Yes, I'll grab the medical kit I keep on hand for emergencies."

Jenee's attention returned to Gabriella. "Her pulse is elevated, perhaps a reaction to something down here; it is quite musty."

Jack scanned the cavern, and his eyes landed on the baroness.

It suddenly occurred to him that he'd noticed the older woman had been standing close to Gabriella and whispering something at one point. Had the baroness said something to upset Gaby?

He didn't have long to dwell on the mystery because Gaby suddenly began to speak in an odd voice. "It will never be allowed."

Emily exchanged a look with Jenee. "What won't be allowed, Gaby?"

"A priestess cannot marry. The gods will never allow it." Gaby's eyes remained closed, and whatever she said appeared to be filtering through her unconscious.

"Whatever is she talking about?" the baroness said impatiently. "The girl must be touched in the head. You did say, Kitty, that she has no recollection of where she came from. Perhaps she escaped from a lunatic asylum."

"No, she seems to be in a trance of some kind," said Stefano. "I've heard of this kind of occurrence before, where a person channels another life. You cannot deny the existence of spirits, especially in a place such as this."

"Don't be ridiculous," Jack barked. "There is nothing wrong with her mind."

Gaby finally opened her eyes and looked directly at Jack. "It doesn't matter whether you love me, or I love you," she said in that strange voice. "They will never let me break my vows, and they will do whatever it takes to separate us."

CHAPTER TWENTY

Populonia, Italy
October 200 CE

WHAT'S HAPPENING?

One minute Gabriella was in the cave with the others, and the next, their voices had faded away, and she was surrounded by darkness. Had the lantern gone out?

She blinked several times, and her vision cleared, but she was no longer in the cavern. Hearing the roar of the surf, she realized she was standing on a bluff overlooking the sea. Just *like last time*. The sun had set, and a fog was rolling in.

Gaby's heart pumped like she were a runner heading for the finish line. She stumbled back from the edge, hoping to hear hooves pounding turf and a horse and rider barreling toward her. She regained her balance and looked around, but no one was there. No Jack to rescue her this time.

A sob escaped her at the thought of never seeing Jack again. She'd never be able to confess to him that she'd made a mistake. Never tell him the truth about who she was and where she came from. Never be able to tell him how much she loved him.

Xavier's words repeated in her mind: *To find love is difficult enough, and one must never take it for granted.*

She hadn't fought for Jack, hadn't even tried to hold on to what they'd shared, and her chance at true love had sifted through her fingers like grains of sand in an hourglass. She could see it now so clearly. Somehow, some force in the universe had connected Em and Jen and herself with Iris and Marco. Emily and Jenee had traveled back to the past and found their true loves. And she'd been given the same chance. Fate had brought her to Jack, but she'd been too scared to see it. She'd thrown her chance away! And now she would be forever separated from the man she loved and the friends she cherished.

Oh God, what a fool I've been!

The sound of footsteps came from behind her. She whirled around, fearing the worst. Instead, walking toward her, out of the mist, came Jack.

Am I dreaming?

But there was something different. This was Jack, but not the one she knew. Although he looked like just like Jack, his clothing was different. He was dressed in an ancient style of costume, a short white linen tunic and a red woolen mantle with gold embroidery and trim, clasped at the shoulder by a jeweled brooch. His golden hair fell well below his shoulders, and he carried a spear with a bronze arrowhead tip, using it as a walking stick.

Dear Lord, where am I?

"Velia, you left the temple with such haste before the sacrifice and without taking the auspices," he said.

He even sounded like Jack.

"You set tongues wagging, and the elders are not pleased," he went on. "Whatever can be the matter? It is dangerous to invoke their displeasure."

Gaby looked about her, expecting to see someone else standing near her. *Who is Velia, and what is he talking about?* The man spoke in a language unlike any she'd ever heard. Yet she understood his every word.

Before she could contemplate this strange turn of events, Jack, or whoever he was, wrapped his arms around her and pulled her against his broad chest. He dipped his head and swept his lips over hers, hungrily kissing her with such passion that without his strong arms supporting her, she would have fallen to the ground. This Jack kissed her just like her Jack. Her body responded the same way as whenever he kissed her—she utterly melted into him. As with Jack's kisses, she wanted it to never end, and when he finally pulled away, she was tempted to wrap her arms around him and pull him back for more.

His deep baritone descended into a husky thickness as he stared into her eyes. "There is not a woman in our city-state that I cannot have, but I desire only you. The one woman I cannot have. A priestess who is forbidden to me. You and only you are my one true love, now and forever more.

"Tell me, Velia, why have the deities denied me? You have bewitched me, and I would not have it any other way." He closed his eyes, resting his forehead against hers. "You, who reads the future from the entrails of sacrificed beasts—can you not see a future for us?"

This man was pleading for her love. She almost laughed at the irony. And then it came to her, and she realized she was in the throes of a vision. Whether it was time travel or a dream, her past life was being revealed to her. How crazy was it to believe in time travel, yet it had happened, and now she was in the middle of another unexplainable event.

Perhaps this was fate righting a past wrong.

She cupped his face, lost in his loving gaze, and the words of her past life came to her. "They will never allow it, and I cannot live without you. It would be better for me to die than to live without your love. We have wasted too much time already. I am yours already in spirit; make me yours in body."

It suddenly didn't matter what the future held or what obstacles impeded their love. She was determined not to let this moment pass without being one with the man she loved.

"You cannot mean this," he said. "The punishment will be severe."

"I do mean it. Will you deny me my one and only wish?"

"I can deny you nothing. Since we were children, I have

always loved you. They did their best to separate us, but I won't let them. I, Aranthur, pledge myself to you, Velia, now and for eternity. Let the gods decide our fate. I will be one with you even if it costs me my life, for life is meaningless without you."

She caressed his cheek, his lips curved into a smile, and then they were kissing again. That spark surged through her, the same spark she'd felt from the first moment she saw Jack galloping through the fog. Only she didn't realize it then. But she realized it now—Jack was her destiny. Past, present, and future.

A foreboding crawled up her spine and interrupted her bliss. It seemed a whisper at first but grew louder with each passing second. Men were shouting, their voices filled with anger. "What is happening?" she asked.

Aranthur lifted his head and listened. "You must leave. Now!"

"Why?"

"They are coming for us, my love. They seek to destroy us."

"But—"

"You must get away from here. I will distract them and hold them off."

"But you are one man. And they are many."

"Do you doubt my skill as a warrior?"

She gazed into his eyes and saw Jack, the man she loved. The man she would always love. "Never."

He cupped her face and claimed her lips in a fierce kiss. "Run, Velia—go to our secret place and hide. I will find you. No matter what. I will find you, and we will leave Populonia for good."

"Never forget I love you," she said, her eyes blurred with tears.

"I'll never forget. I promise. Now, go!"

Gabriella ran as fast as she could. The light from the full moon guided her toward a grove of pine and cypress trees. She ran deep into the forest. When she could run no more, she bent over, gasping, trying to catch her breath. Her heart pounded so hard it throbbed in her ears. She leaned against a tree and slid down the trunk to the moss-covered ground. Tears rained down her cheeks as she contemplated this past life that felt as cursed as the one she'd been transported to. Would she ever find happiness with Jack?

She heard the sound of the surf in the distance, and then it came to her in a flash—*What if I can change our fate?* Whether it was a vision or not, she was meant to know that she and Jack were destined to be together. And she would rather die with him than alone in the wilderness.

Gaby took a deep breath and ran back. When she got to the edge of the forest, she saw that Aranthur/Jack was holding his own. And then she saw a soldier. He was lean and short, no match for Aranthur physically, which was why he was sneaking up behind him.

Not on my watch, you son of a bitch.

She glanced down and found a branch, picked it up, and crept out from behind the tree. Hefting the branch, she swung with all her might and hit the bastard in the back of the head. He toppled to the ground with a thud.

Aranthur had dispatched the two soldiers he'd been battling. He swung around, and his eyes widened. "What in Hades are you doing back here? I told you to run."

Her hands went to her hips. "Well, that's the thanks I get for saving your life?"

He looked down and saw the dead soldier.

Gaby heard more shouts in the distance. "There are more coming. Hurry. There's not much time!" She grabbed his hand and laid it on her heart. "Do you trust me?"

"With my very soul."

"Good. Then come with me." She held tight to his hand and led them back through the trees.

"Where are we going?"

"To the place where it all began." She led him to the bluff. They stopped at the cliff's edge, and she looked up at him. "This is where I met you. And where I will meet you again. I love you with all my heart."

"Oh, my beautiful Velia. There is no escape, and this is the end."

"No. This is the beginning. Trust me. I will find you again. I promise."

He drew her into his arms and kissed her fiercely. The shouts from the soldiers were getting closer.

"Come, my darling," she said. "Let us go to meet our destiny."

He lifted her in his arms and whispered, "I will love you for eternity."

Gaby wrapped her arms tightly around his shoulders and whispered, "I will love you for eternity."

Holding her tight against his chest, he ran as fast as he could and leaped off the cliff.

"Don't let me go, Jack. Don't let me go…"

"IT'S ALL RIGHT, I've got you. You're safe."

Gaby opened her eyes and stared into Jack's beloved face. "Are we dead?" she whispered.

"Gaby, you fainted. I've been half-mad with worry."

"What year is it?"

Jack rolled his eyes. "It's 1902, the twentieth of October."

"Oh, thank God!" She wrapped her arms around him and held on tight.

"I take it you're feeling better?"

"Yes, now that I know where I am." She leaned back in his arms.

"Good, because I've got a few questions for you," he said as he kept walking with her in his arms.

"What questions?"

"Who is this Aranthur chap, for one thing?"

Butterflies flapped their wings against her rib cage. "I—I'm not sure," she lied. She felt the heat of a blush in her cheeks as she remembered the searing kisses she'd shared with Aranthur.

But it was really Jack, so it doesn't count.

She would tell him everything, but not now, not here among the ruins, where others could overhear.

Then she saw his smirk and realized how well Jack knew her. He'd become an expert at reading her expressions. She was a lousy liar, and he was an expert observer.

He lowered his voice. "I've never heard you mention him, and I must admit, I'm jealous."

Jack is jealous? She couldn't help but be surprised at his admission.

"Don't look so surprised. You must have realized that you've completely turned my world upside down, Miss Gabriella D'Angelo."

I can't wait to tell him how much I love him.

"So, who is this man?" Jack growled. "Is he someone from your past? Is he the reason you're here?"

In more ways than one. "Must you always suspect the worst of me?"

"It wasn't me that left that cruel and indifferent note." His self-deprecating laugh revealed his pain.

"I'm so sorry. I thought I was doing the right thing at the time," she whispered. "To allow you a way forward. I was such a fool. Can you ever forgive me?"

"Forgive you?" He gave her a fierce kiss, too short for her liking.

"Does that answer your question?"

"Jack! Someone will see."

"They're all back in the cave. I carried you out as fast as I could out of that tomb."

She placed her hand on his cheek. "Jack, I need to tell you the truth, about me, about everything. No more lies. There is too much at stake."

"No lies—now that would be a welcome change." He grinned.

"I'm sorry about that too. I was afraid."

"Gaby, please trust me. I won't judge you or think less of you, regardless of the truth."

Gaby nodded. "I trust you, Jack. Now take us home."

CHAPTER TWENTY-ONE

Maremma, Italy
October 20, 1902

T HE HOUSE WAS quiet, the servants likely busy downstairs cleaning and readying for the guests to return from their outing. Iris crept down the hallway, pausing once or twice to listen for footfalls.

When she got to the baroness's room, she pulled a hairpin from her bun, and with a few twists and turns in the lock and a last glance down the hallway, she opened the door.

Her suspicions had been growing that the baroness was not who she claimed to be. It shouldn't have been hard to determine, but Iris had only met the Contessa Catarina di Farnese once at the palazzo of the Medici. The contessa was a chameleon, just like her former minion, the Nazi time traveler.

Iris had first crossed paths with the Nazi when she witnessed him shooting and killing her parents in cold blood after dragging them off a train in Bordeaux. He then aimed his pistol at Iris and pulled the trigger. But just as the bullet passed through her heart, she'd vanished into thin air. Fate had plucked her from certain death and hurtled her from era to era, forcing her to survive by her wits and an inner strength that grew with each new journey. Her life was not her own, and she feared she would be destined to live as a time-traveling vagabond for the rest of her days.

Until the day she arrived in the Mercado Vecchio in Florence. Her heart soared and her soul rejoiced when her eyes met Marco's across a crowded market square.

Little did she know that the Nazi had been hunting her all along and would eventually join forces with Catarina.

At least the bastard is dead. She and Marco had dispatched him in Paris with the help of Emily, Colin, Jenee, and Xavier. Now, she and her friends were reunited again to battle the contessa herself and destroy her once and for all.

Iris scanned the lovely bedchamber decorated with burgundy velvet drapery and carved mahogany furniture. A beautiful jewelry box drew Iris's attention. She ran her finger along the smooth, lacquered surface of inlaid marquetry. Iris lifted the lid, and a haunting melody filled the room. She recognized the tune, for she'd heard Marco hum it many times, a lullaby from his childhood. Iris was still unsure, because the lullaby was common to the period and could have been known to anyone.

A glint of green caught her eye, and her pulse quickened. She hooked a finger through a gold chain and lifted it, gasping at the magnificent emerald dangling at the end. Her knees went weak, and she dropped into a chair, overwhelmed by a vision from the past…

The fortress-like palazzo shone brightly with hundreds of torches as Marco introduced her to his friends Leonardo da Vinci and Sandro Botticelli. When a woman approached, they were laughing at one of Leonardo's entertaining witticisms. She was beautiful, dark-haired, with eyes that glittered like a cat's. She took Marco's arm, her nails biting into his skin; she pinned him with her gaze and leaned in to whisper, *"Amore mio*, there is always a price to be paid for betrayal. Yours will cost you everything."

Marco pulled away from her grasp. "Do not dare threaten me or anyone I love," he replied through gritted teeth. "For I will fight you to the end of time." He took Iris's hand in his and turned his back on Catarina.

"You have made a choice that will only lead to your destruction," the contessa hissed.

Marco bade his friends goodnight and tucked Iris's arm through his. "Come, *amore mio*." He bent and kissed Iris on the cheek. "It is time to go home."

As they made their way to the doors, Iris could not help but look back over her shoulder. Her heart leaped in her throat as she saw Caterina watching them with a venomous gaze. And Iris knew in that instant that she and Marco would never be safe from Catarina's wrath.

Iris shook off the chill from the vivid memory and regarded the emerald pendant. It was the same one that had glittered between Catarina's breasts the night she confronted Marco at the Medici palazzo. It was proof that Donatella Falaguera, the Baroness of Blythe Hollow, was really Contessa Catarina di Farnese, a Florentine noblewoman of great wealth and a sorceress of great power. But would Colin and Xavier accept her as such? Em and Jenee would, and no doubt Gabriella. But Iris had gotten to know the marquess/investigator and the inspector quite well. They'd want more proof.

She turned in a slow circle as her eyes swept the room. An eerie feeling made the hairs on the back of her neck stand on end. *There is something else. Something that will prove that the baroness is the contessa.*

Her gaze settled on the desk opposite the bed. One by one, she searched the drawers. She didn't know what she was looking for, but she needed to keep looking. There was something here. Something that she needed to find.

The desk yielded nothing, and nor did the bedside night table. She ran her hands around the mattress's edges as frustration built in the pit of her stomach, then approached the elegant armoire and opened it. Everything inside was meticulously organized by color, with day and evening outfits separated on either side. A dozen pairs of shoes were arranged on the lower shelf. On the upper shelf were hatboxes, some bearing labels from the famous department store in Paris, Bon Marché. The contessa did not travel lightly nor deny herself the finest of luxuries. Iris inhaled the scent of lavender from the potpourri sachets that hung from silk ribbons between each garment.

Dragging a chair over, she climbed up and examined the hatboxes. She shuddered. Stuffed birds decorated several of Caterina's hats, reminding Iris of Emily's aversion to this gaudy style. Unfortunately, the hatboxes contained nothing but hats, but Iris refused to give up. The contessa was hiding something.

Iris ran her hands down each gown, and her heartbeat accelerated with excitement as an object in a dressing gown pocket took shape in her hands. She pulled it out and gasped at what she beheld. *The Time Traveler's Lover*, the novel Iris had written that would be published more than a century into the future.

Knowing that the contessa had gotten her hands on a copy of her book and read it filled Iris with fury and fear. Donatella Falaguera, Baroness of Blythe Hollow, was, beyond a doubt, the Contessa Catarina di Farnese, her mortal enemy.

Iris needed to strengthen her resolve. She flipped through the pages, curious to see if Catarina had written any observations. There were none, but when Iris reached the book's last chapter, she blinked back tears. Emily and Jenee had told Iris that her book had become a bestseller. They also shared that it had brought the three friends together. Holding the book in her hands brought all the emotions rushing back, and Iris feared the ending she wished for would not be realized. Unable to refrain, she read what she'd written.

Marco's heart-wrenching plea to keep her with him overrode the howling winds that roared in her ears. The winds of time had come as she knew they would, taking her away from the man she loved. But even though she knew that she and Marco were already parted by centuries, she could still hear his words echoing in her mind. "Dio, ti imploro, non portarmela via." God, I implore you, do not take her from me.

Tears stung her eyes. As much as she hated the cycle of traveling through time to strange places where she was forced to survive by her wits, she realized it was time travel that had delivered her to her soul mate. *She and Marco were born hundreds of years apart. Yet fate had miraculously brought them together, and she would be eternally thankful for that. Even though her fate with Marco remained unknown, she would not rest until the contessa and her evil were destroyed…*

Iris closed the book and held it to her heart. *The ending to my love story has yet to be written, and I pray it will be a happy one.* She slipped the book back into the pocket of the dressing gown and returned to her room to formulate her plan.

CHAPTER TWENTY-TWO

Populonia, Italy
October 20, 1902

A GUNSHOT BLAST broke the silence. "OMG, what was that? Gabriella asked.

"I don't know," Jack replied, "but that was the report of a firearm." He squinted, searching in the direction from where it was likely the shot emanated. "Stay here while I investigate. I don't want you in any danger."

"Don't worry about me; I'm fine." She smiled to reassure him.

He set her down, but his hands remained on her waist. "I'm afraid it's too late for that." His lips curved in a wry smile, but his eyes were laced with worry. "Worrying about you has become integral to my existence, and I cannot stop."

She longed to throw her arms around his neck and feel the press of his body against hers. She longed to tell him what was in her heart, but now was not the time. Something might be terribly wrong.

"For your safety, stay behind me."

She didn't argue with that. Her mind was still trying to catch up with her heartbeat as she recovered from her fainting spell and that strange vision of her past life with Jack.

Turning, he began to run toward where the shot had come

from, and Gabriella picked up her skirt and ran after him, trying to keep up. When they reached the picnic area, they saw Sir Edward walking toward them, cradling a bloody, unconscious Cynthia. The baroness trotted beside them, looking pale and distraught.

"What happened, Edward? Who shot her?" Jack called.

"It's not she who was shot but a wild boar, and he's very much dead. I heard a scream and ran to find out what had happened. It's unusual for a boar to attack in this area. The baroness and Miss Maxwell had gone for a stroll and must have somehow raised the beast's ire, because he viciously attacked. I shot the beast, but not before he impaled Miss Maxwell, and she needs medical attention. I know a surgeon in Populonia, but we'd better hurry; she's had significant blood loss."

Jenee rushed forward, holding a medical bag, and took Cynthia's wrist to take her pulse. "Before we see this surgeon, I want to examine her. I'm a physician, and time is of the essence with blood loss. At the very least, I can bathe the wound and stem the blood flow. I have the medical bag you brought when Gabriella fainted. I grabbed this blanket from the carriage. Please lay her down, and I will examine her."

Sir Edward laid the unconscious Cynthia on the blanket Jenee rolled out on the ground.

"Sir Edward, there are no clean bandages in this bag. So, I'll need as many as you can find, and a bottle of whiskey or brandy would be helpful."

"Of course—I will see to it at once," said Sir Edward. He rushed off in the direction of the tents.

The baroness wiped her eyes. "This would not have happened, Jack, if you hadn't gone off with the cook. Cynthia was upset and embarrassed over your callous treatment. The poor girl needed to talk, and I suggested a walk so she could air her distress. The beast came out of nowhere and attacked Cynthia without provocation. I, too, would have no doubt borne the brunt of his rage if Sir Edward had not arrived on the scene and destroyed the animal."

"I resent your inference, madam," Jack retorted. "Gabriella required attention at the time, and your accusations are only distracting us from attending to Cynthia."

Aunt Kitty, who'd just rushed over with everyone else, came to Jack's defense. "Blaming my nephew is not helping Cynthia. Let Jenee do what she can for her. In the meantime, everyone not essential to Cynthia's well-being should return to the villa. The poor girl doesn't need all of us hovering over her."

"You're right, Aunty. Cynthia is our guest, and her recovery is the only thing that matters. I will attend to her and accompany Sir Edward to Populonia if she requires further attention after Jenee cares for her." Jack glared at the baroness and added, "I know your first concern, baroness, is Cynthia's well-being; however, I can see how distraught you are. You should return with the others to the villa. Jenee, Sir Edward and I will do what is needed, and then get word to the villa as soon as we have news."

Jack's innuendo was not lost on Gabriella. She could see the last person whose presence he wanted to be in was the woman who dared insinuate he was to blame.

"I will not leave my patient," Jenee declared.

"Do you wish me to remain here?" Xavier asked Jenee. Taking her hand, he pressed a kiss to her palm.

"Of course, *mon amour*, an extra pair of hands will be helpful—but Lady Darling is right. The less commotion, the better for Cynthia. She is in good hands." Jenee smiled reassuringly and turned her attention to her patient.

THE DAMPER ON the day's activities made for a quiet ride back to Nido dell' Aquila. The picnic had been quickly packed up, as everyone had lost their appetite. Kitty went into drill sergeant mode and had Constance, Stefano, and Donatella accompany her in one carriage. Gabriella, Colin, and Emily rode in the other. It had been decided that Sir Edward would see Jack, Jenee, Xavier, and Cynthia to the doctor in his wagon.

Gabriella fidgeted. She was worried about Cynthia. There had been so much blood on her dress that Gaby could not even discern where she'd been wounded. Jenee was an excellent doctor and would do everything she could to help Cynthia.

But Gabriella couldn't get the baroness's words out of her head. Her blaming Jack for neglecting Cynthia only underscored the situation. Gabriella was no expert on the psychology of men or what caused them to behave in one way or another. But Jack was a gentleman through and through, despite his roguish ways. What if he was overcome with guilt over Cynthia's injuries and Donatella's accusations? Would he decide to go through with his proposal to Cynthia? The pain would be unbearable for Gabriella, especially given her vision that Jack and she had loved each other in a past life, and the love deprived them.

In her vision she'd forced them both over that cliff, believing it was the only way forward. Dying together in that spot meant they would meet again and be given a second chance. Surely, Gaby being flung back to this era had been fate asserting itself. Yes, Marco and Iris had picked her to go back, but it must all be connected. It had to be. It was fate righting a past wrong.

But what if I'm wrong? What if history was just repeating itself?

Gaby realized she was thinking incoherently. Why would Jack suddenly propose to Cynthia when he had all but said he loved her, and why did she doubt his sincerity? She hated when her insecurities surfaced, but Jack was from the aristocratic class, wealthy, and unpredictable. At least, he *would* be wealthy when he recovered his father's estate. He was also brilliant, confident, and too good looking, and she couldn't help feeling insecure. She was dangerously in love with him, and it scared her.

Talk about "opposites attract." Gabriella was an Italian American chef from Chicago, the daughter of a hardworking couple who ran a successful restaurant. Her grandparents were immigrants and had carved out a life for themselves through sheer hard work and determination. She was born almost a century apart from Jack, and her lack of experience with men made her vulnerable. Jack was an earl, Oxford-educated, and a man who assuredly had plenty of experience with women. The very idea of their finding lasting happiness was as ludicrous as her traveling back in time.

And yet here she was. Here they were.

Emily interrupted her reverie. "Since our time is limited, why don't we get to the juicy part? What the hell happened to you in that burial chamber?"

Gaby shook her head, driving the image of her death from her mind. "I know it sounds crazy, but being in the chamber triggered what could have been a past-life memory." She fidgeted, her hands unable to remain still in her lap. If Emily thought she was insane, then, without a doubt, Jack would think so too.

"OMG," Emily said, forgetting she was an elegant marchioness and lapsing into twenty-first-century speak. "I knew something was up, but I never dreamed it could be a blast from the past. So, what did you see? What happened? This is too brilliant!"

Gaby released a sigh of relief. Emily believed her. That was something, but the reality of what she'd experienced, though exciting, was tragic beyond what any words could convey. "I experienced my death in another life."

"Oh." The excitement on Emily's face transposed into an expression of sadness and empathy. "That must have been awful." She grabbed Gaby's hand and squeezed. "What happened?"

Discussing reincarnation was surreal, but Gabriella supposed it wasn't any more bizarre than the realization that time travel existed. "It felt so real, as if I was there, thousands of years ago, in the Etruscan world. The clothing, the architecture, the jewelry, everything. I even spoke the language, which was unlike any other I've ever heard."

"Wait, you were the priestess Sir Edward found in the burial chamber, weren't you?"

"I think so."

"But then, from what you are saying, you didn't die of natural causes."

"No. I was in love with a man, which was forbidden. The elders and leaders believed physical love compromised my spiritual ties to the gods and goddesses."

"Who was he? Who were you in love with?"

"Jack. He didn't know he was Jack. But it was him all right. His name was Aranthur, and he tried to save me. To save us. He tried to hold off the soldiers they'd sent to kill me. He told me to run. But I couldn't leave him, and I ran back and took him to a bluff much like where Jack found me when I first arrived here. And there was nothing we could do, so we...jumped." Tears streamed down her cheeks.

"Oh, Gaby, I'm so sorry. But don't you see? You are here, and it must mean something. Something good for you and Jack."

"I don't know, Em. What if it's just history repeating? What if we are powerless to change anything and we're stuck on a terrible fate loop?"

"Oh, bullcrap! Have some faith! You and Jack have already had sex. Believe me, love will find a way. If Colin and I could figure it out, you can." Emily grabbed Gaby's hand, giving it a warm squeeze. "I think you're being encouraged to follow your desire, and you must exert yourself and win him completely. You want to, don't you?"

"Yes. I love Jack." Saying the words aloud to someone other than herself made Gaby realize the truth—she did want to stay, and she wanted to make a life with Jack.

"I knew it! And I'm certain he loves you too. Jenee and I can see the hot looks he gives you when he thinks no one is looking. That guy has it bad for you."

"But what about Cynthia? And what about his inheritance and estate? I bring nothing to the table."

"You bring *everything* to the table. With your love, he can surmount any challenge. We need to talk with Jenee and Iris.

Someplace where we can't be overheard or observed." Em squeezed Gabriella's hand again. "I'm terribly worried about you."

"I'll bring tea to your rooms."

"Brilliant. And bring some of those delicious scones. Being away from the children has brought out the stallion in my dear, beloved husband. I could be pregnant because I'm so bloody hungry all the time."

Colin, who'd been reading a newspaper, peeked over the page and arched his brow. His eyes sparkled devilishly. "Really, darling, have we no secrets?"

Gabriella covered her mouth, stifling a giggle. You could take the twenty-first-century woman out of the modern world and plop her down in Victorian England, but you couldn't take Em's sense of humor away. Emily was Emily, and although she looked and dressed like a lady, she was as blunt, direct, and irreverent as always. Gaby had to hand it to Colin: none of his wife's eccentricities bothered him. The man simply worshipped the ground Emily walked on, as Xavier worshipped Jenee.

"Go back to your paper, Lord Remington, and stop eaves-dropping," Emily said.

Colin chuckled, giving the newspaper a good shake, and his face disappeared behind the paper. "As you wish, my dear."

It made Gabriella's heart swell, knowing her friends had found such happiness. "You certainly haven't changed in the least, Em."

"Of course I haven't. I'm still the same, Em. I've even become a bloody suffragette, although I dare not march through the streets with signs. It wouldn't look well for Colin in the House of Lords. But I sometimes imagine burning my corset and riding my horse butt-naked through the streets of London like Lady Godiva." Emily chuckled. "Wouldn't that cause a scene? Oh, if only I could."

Colin lowered his newspaper again and arched an amused eyebrow. Emily blew him a kiss and waved him back to his reading.

She turned back to Gaby. "I do try to temper my words and actions somewhat for Colin and the children's sake. I write for the *London Times* under a pseudonym to spare them the wrath of the *ton*. However, I must say even the women of the aristocracy are beginning to pay heed to women's rights. My articles sell newspapers, especially among the female demographic, and my adoptive father, Sir Arthur Weatherby, couldn't be more pleased. He is training me to succeed him as the publisher of the *London Times*, something unheard of in early twentieth-century England—or anywhere else, for that matter. It would shake up the status quo so completely I might be the cause of a revolution." Emily giggled. "My darling husband is the epitome of patience. How I bless the day I landed in his arms."

"I imagine it's exciting for you to be doing what you always dreamed of doing, serious journalism. I'm very happy for you. I wish...I wish..." Tears filled Gabriella's eyes.

"Hush, sweetie, don't cry. Stiff upper lip."

Gabriella tried to believe everything Emily said, but her thoughts returned to the baroness and her motives. The less contact she had with this annoying woman, the better.

A premonition crawled up her spine, that the baroness meant her harm. Of course she did. She wanted her stepdaughter to marry Jack and saw Gabriella as a threat.

But Gaby couldn't help but think there was more to it. She just hoped that Jack didn't do anything rash. If he did, she would have no choice but to return to the present day without telling him who she really was.

CHAPTER TWENTY-THREE

Maremma, Italy
October 20, 1902

T WO HOURS LATER, Gabriella was picking fresh herbs for dinner when a carriage drove up the long drive and stopped in front of the villa. Jack jumped out, and Jenee helped him gather Cynthia into his arms. He carried her into the house, with Jenee and Xavier following close behind.

Gabriella wistfully remembered what it felt like to be held in those strong arms. It was a feeling of security compared to none other. A twinge of jealousy coursed through her veins, and she tried not to let it get the better of her.

She wanted to believe that they would overcome the obstacles that arose at every turn in the road. How odd that from the moment she "landed," she'd tried to avoid telling Jack anything about herself, but now she was desperate to tell him the truth. Would he believe her?

The blood drained from her face as she wondered what she would do if he didn't. Then again, Em and Jen, their husbands, and Iris were there to confirm her story. But Colin and Xavier were completely and utterly in love with Em and Jen. They had believed them. But what if Jack wasn't in love with her? After all, he hadn't declared his affections. Gaby figured he had feelings for her that went beyond a physical attraction. But what if finding out the truth was too much? What if it only propelled him into Cynthia's arms? Facing a future without Jack would be unbearable.

She was so immersed in her thoughts that she didn't hear Antonio call out from the kitchen, nor did she hear his approach until he was upon her. "Gabriella, Lady Remington has requested tea in her rooms, and she asked that you bring it to her."

Gabriella wiped her hands on her apron. "Of course. Thank you, Antonio." She was anxious to talk to her friends. She wanted to tell them everything, and together they needed to figure out what to do about the painting.

Carefully balancing the tray, Gabriella walked down the hallway. As she passed Jack's room, she was tempted to knock. Still, she didn't, because explaining everything to him while holding a tray and standing in the hallway would be impossible.

Jack emerged from Cynthia's room as if he'd heard her thoughts, and when their eyes met, Gaby froze. The tray shook, and the teapot and cups rattled. Jack rushed to her, grabbing her elbows and steadying her. His eyes glowed as clear and blue as a mountain tarn, and the touch of his hands awoke the embers of love that sparked when he was near.

Finding her voice, she stumbled over her words. "H-how is Cynthia?"

His beautiful lips curved up in a smile. "She will recover. Her injuries are not life-threatening. How are you? I hated staying behind without you, but it was my duty. You understand that, don't you?"

"Yes, I understand. Cynthia's injury required immediate attention, and there was no point in the group remaining there. We would have only gotten in the way."

His hands still cupped her elbows, and he looked down with consternation. "I see you are once more the servant girl delivering tea."

The tray in her hands remained a barrier between them. Perhaps it was just as well. It kept them at a circumspect distance; otherwise, Lord knew she might have wrapped her arms around him and pressed her lips to his.

"Y-yes." Her passion-filled thoughts sent a rush of blood to her cheeks, and a wave of heat below that made her quiver. "Lady Remington requested I bring her tea."

Jack's brows rose, and Gabriella wanted to tell him everything right then and there, but she couldn't. Not in the hallway.

"Emily and I are friends. Jack," she whispered. "I promise to explain everything soon. I have so much to tell you."

"I suspected there was something between you and Lady Remington. I confess I look forward to hearing more about this friendship of yours. You continue to surprise me, Gaby, but why would I not believe you? I do not imagine you are a spy, a foreign agent from the Americas, or an art thief…" Amusement curled his lips into a smile. "Although, given you were the one who found the Allegretto painting, I am more than curious to hear what you have to tell me."

"I am not a spy, a foreign agent, or an art thief, but the painting is why I am here."

Jack's brow furrowed. "Dear Lord, Gaby, what folderol is this? You have set my head reeling."

"I cannot explain this to you now, but I swear I will enlighten you at the first opportunity."

"I shan't be able to think of anything else until you do. When might this meeting of ours take place?"

"I—uh—after dinner. Perhaps you can steal away. I'll meet you in your bedchamber."

She saw the excitement that lit his eyes and wanted to kick herself. Maybe meeting alone in his bedroom wasn't such a good idea. Being in such close proximity to him and that big bed might be too great a temptation.

"Would you prefer the stable? I could meet you there." The sensible part of her hoped he would agree to the stable, but the head-over-heels-in-love part prayed for the bedroom.

The excitement drained from his face so quickly that she wasn't sure it had ever been there. "If you're worried that I won't be able to contain my desire, fear not. I think I can control myself long enough to hear you out. Besides, you know I would never force myself on you."

"It's not you I don't trust—it's myself." Her face flushed with her declaration.

"Well then, we will both have to maintain control over our yearnings as best we can." He gave a low chuckle and let go of her elbows, and she shuddered, causing the china to rattle again. A smile caressed his lips, and he looked pleased as Punch that he had affected her so powerfully. "I will excuse myself after dinner and meet you in my room. I promise my behavior will be respectful."

Gaby nodded. "I must go before the tea gets cold," she said.

For a moment, it crossed her mind that the last thing she wanted was for Jack to control his desire for her. If she was honest with herself, respectful was not what she wanted.

⥲⥲⥲⥲⥲

"THERE YOU ARE." Emily glanced down the hallway and shut the door behind Gabriella. "I've been on pins and needles. Here, let me take this." Relieving Gaby of the tray, she set it on the tea table in front of the fireplace.

"I was delayed by Jack when I ran into him leaving Cynthia's room."

Emily scrutinized her with as much intense focus as a mom about to grill her teenage daughter after catching her sneaking back home well after curfew.

"I think he's in love with you, Gaby. If you could have seen his face when you fainted..." She fanned herself. "He snatched you up and carried you out of that cave like a superhero."

"Really?" Gaby's face heated, and she looked down as if somewhere in the richly colored magenta and gold carpet beneath her feet lay the answer to her future.

Emily tugged Gabriella onto the settee with her. She poured tea and handed Gaby a cup. "As for Cynthia, I suspect she's no more in love with Jack than he is with her."

"Why do you say that?"

"Okay, confession time." Emily pulled an envelope from her pocket. "I saw this telegram in the basket where the post is left, and it was from London. I was worried it was about my kids or parents, so I picked it up and opened it. I didn't realize I was reading a love letter until it got really racy."

"Emily Christie! You are as irreverent as ever! And snoopy beyond words!"

"Well, maybe not quite." She sipped her tea, teasingly holding back on any details.

"Okay, spill. I can't take another second of this suspense." Gabriella's spirits were buoyed by Emily, being around her girlfriend was like coming home.

Her heart constricted. She missed her family so much, but knowing that her friends were here and hoping that Jack loved her as much as she loved him would give her the strength to stay.

"You're not going to believe it," Emily replied in a singsong voice.

"Give me the telegram, dammit. I'll read it myself." Gaby grabbed the paper that dangled from Emily's fingertips. She couldn't read it fast enough. When she looked up, her mouth hung open. "I have to tell Jack."

"You can't. I took Cynthia's telegram, and should it come out that I pilfered it, Colin will be angry with me, and I can't bear to cause him any more grief than I already do."

"Okay, I understand, and I wouldn't do anything to hurt you," Gaby said. "My lips are sealed, but there has to be a way to let the cat out of the bag. Think, Emily. No one is cleverer than you. I have to forewarn Jack that his cousin Beauford Bastion Broome, the man who schemed him out of his earldom, is on his way here. But the most unbelievable aspect is that Beauford is Cynthia's lover." She jumped up, unable to contain her nervous energy, and began to pace much the way she'd seen Jack do.

Emily gazed at the embers in the hearth, ignoring her, but

Gaby knew the look on her friend's face meant she was busy searching for a solution to the situation.

"I have it!" Em said. "We must convince Cynthia to confess all to Jack."

Gabriella stopped pacing and regarded her friend with disbelief. "That's insane. She's a prim and proper woman."

"Not that prim and proper," Emily's pursed her lips mischievously.

"No, but she does whatever the baroness tells her to do. Otherwise, why would they be here in the first place? The baroness wants Cynthia to marry Jack. Although I'm not sure why, given that he no longer has the title nor the estate. It's all very odd."

"Yes, it is. I'm sure it also has to do with Donatella's obsession over Allegretto's painting."

"Yes, I noticed that too," Gaby said. "Everything about the baroness is suspicious. She's like a character from the game of Clue come to life."

"Spot-on, Gaby!" Em giggled. "Maybe she already knew the painting was somewhere in this area. Stefano told us about the history of the painting and that it was thought to have been hidden somewhere in this area centuries ago... What if the baroness already knew the backstory?"

A knock on the door made both Gaby and Emily jump. "Who could that be? I sent Colin and Xavier on a horseback ride while Jenee was tending to Cynthia. Everyone else retired to their rooms to rest up before dinner."

"Should I hide?" Gabriella's gaze flitted around the room, searching for a viable hiding place.

"Don't be ridiculous." Emily rose, smoothed her gown, pinned her shoulders back, and regally walked to the door to open it. "Oh, for goodness' sake, Iris, come in."

Gabriella had moved out of sight to a corner of the room, and Iris didn't see her. "Emily, I made a startling discovery."

Emily's lips quirked into a smile. "This day has become one revelation after another. Iris, say hello to Gabriella. I'm sure she, too, will be interested in everything you have to say."

Iris whirled around, facing Gabriella. "It is good to see you again, Gabriella. It is past time we took you into our complete confidence, *mon amie*."

Emily clapped her hands like a child about to receive a long-dreamed-of gift. *"Dites nous vos nouvelles."*

"Yes," agreed Gaby, "tell us your news."

CHAPTER TWENTY-FOUR

Maremma, Italy
October 20, 1902

J ACK PACED HIS room with his hands clasped behind his back. After his chance meeting with Gabriella, he'd been at his wits' end trying to piece together the odds and ends of her revelations. What he didn't know about her far outweighed what he knew. Instead of his solving the mystery of the woman who'd captured his imagination, the secrets continued to grow. He felt further than ever from the truth.

He was frustrated, unsure of what to do. When he saw her in the hallway earlier, with that blasted tea tray again, it was all he could do to stop himself from carrying her to his room, and damn everything else.

Every few minutes, he stopped and turned to the painting. It enthralled him nearly as much as his mysterious lady love. Like all connoisseurs, when in the presence of beauty, he fell completely under the spell of the magnificent painting and could not stop looking at it. There was something about the woman in the portrait that was familiar. Admittedly, beautiful women all shared something in common, an allure that stood them above the crowd. Gaby, Emily, and Jenee all possessed it, even if they were unaware they did.

When Aunt Kitty made her debut as a debutante at eighteen,

she'd been considered an original. Acclaimed as a beauty, she completely took London Society by storm. Artists had clamored to paint her. To this day, a portrait of her by John Singer Sargent hung in the library at Singly Park, the Langsford family's earldom seat in Staffordshire.

It angered Jack that he might never set foot in his family's estate, never see Kitty's remarkable portrait, and never be able to take his place in the House of Lords because of his seedy, sneaky cousin.

He was itching to confront the bastard, but he needed proof of his cousin's perfidy. Meeting Gaby had changed everything. Had it been only a few days since he'd rescued her from the edge of that bluff? It felt like he'd known her forever. From the moment he'd set eyes on her, he was lost. He'd never believed in love at first sight, but it had hit him like a thunderbolt.

He'd failed to acknowledge it until after they spent that incredible night together. But everything had gone sideways when Gaby disappeared from his bed and left that abhorrent rejection letter, which had undoubtedly thrown him for a loop.

Anger and frustration had dogged him until that moment in the burial cave. Gaby had collapsed and fallen unconscious, and he went berserk. He was so scared of losing her that he'd swept her up in his arms and carried her out before Sir Edward had even returned with the medical bag.

Thank goodness she'd only fainted, but that didn't explain those strange things she'd said. She had admitted she needed to speak with him and seemed anxious to do so, and she acknowledged the letter had been a mistake. So, there was that. But he was still confused, still in the dark.

If only they had had more time to talk before Cynthia's accident. He was grateful for Jenee's superb skill. Never had he seen a doctor act so quickly and efficiently. Xavier looked at Jenee like she walked on water. Hell, Colin looked at Emily that way too. Jack envied what they had, and he wanted it too. What was more, he wanted it with Gaby.

Jack's eyes sought out Allegretto's painting, and he again pondered Stefano's suggestion to seriously consider selling the artwork. The mere thought brought a tightening in his chest. Could he give it up after falling in love with it?

A work of art has stolen my heart, as has the woman who found it.

He was a man who didn't act impulsively. He considered his actions before making important decisions, except when it came to Gabriella. With her, his best intentions went awry. With her, he could not control his words or desires.

He pondered the two things he knew he must do. Both were persistent in his mind. He must confirm that the painting was indeed a work by Marco Allegretto, and he must tell Cynthia that he would not marry her. The sooner, the better. Yes, she was spoiled and prudish and not passionate about anything, and his conversations with her were stilted at best. Still, she wasn't a horrible person, and she was beautiful and rich, so she would have no trouble finding a husband.

As for Allegretto's painting, he must take it to the Uffizi Gallery in Florence and have it authenticated. Only then could he decide what was best. Selling the Allegretto would solve all of his financial problems. But no matter what happened, he would never, in no uncertain terms, marry Cynthia.

❯❯❯❯❮❮❮❮

"IRIS, MY DEAR, you look like you've seen a ghost," Emily said.

"In a way, I have. My suspicions were correct, and I found all the proof we need."

"Your suspicions?" Gaby asked.

"The Contessa Catarina di Farnese, my nemesis. The woman behind all this destruction is here under this roof. That sorceress has completely changed her appearance. But I know it's her."

Gabriella was unable to contain her curiosity. "You found proof that it's the baroness?"

Iris nodded. "I found a copy of my book hidden in her room. In addition to an emerald necklace she wore the day I met her."

Emily scrunched her brows together. "And Cynthia—do you think she is somehow part of the baroness's scheme?"

"I don't know, but I doubt it. More likely, Cynthia is being manipulated." Iris sank into a yellow brocaded bergère chair across from the settee where Em and Gaby sat.

"I think you're right." Emily poured Iris a cup of tea, milk, and sugar, and handed it to her. Gaby marveled at Em's calm demeanor. Em, who'd been the editor of a popular online fashion magazine, would never have been considered patient. Gabriella could only imagine it to have come about from Emily's new life as a marchioness, her marriage, and motherhood.

Iris took several sips and sighed. She set her teacup on the small table next to her chair. And it hit Gaby how beautiful she was. Gone were the tinted spectacles. Her striking green eyes regarded them with keen intelligence. She'd released her hair from the tight bun, and it cascaded around her shoulders like a beautiful red halo. It struck Gaby that Iris was a chameleon as well. But she'd been forced to take on many guises to free herself and Marco from the evil contessa. Anyone would recognize her as his muse if Iris stood next to Allegretto's painting. Gaby still had trouble believing the heroine of *The Time Traveler's Lover* was real. That the book was accurate. That everything was actual, including her traveling back in time.

Handing the pilfered telegram to Iris, Emily said. "Read this."

With a quivering hand, Iris scanned the note from Beauford Bastion Broome to Cynthia. When she finished, a knowing smile spread across her lips. "But of course. This all makes sense now. The baroness is blackmailing Cynthia into marrying Lord Langsford to get her hands on *Il Leto*. She is the reason and the mechanism for Jack losing his earldom. Caterina has clearly coerced Jack's cousin into doing her dirty work. Her machinations are endless. She has been planning this for quite some time."

"I need to warn Jack, to tell him what's going on," Gaby said. Her heart was in her throat at the danger they were all in with that witch under the same roof. And she was apprehensive about

Jack and Kitty because they had no idea what was happening.

"You will, sweetie. But first things first," Em said, patting her knee.

Another knock at the door, and they all turned their heads.

"If this keeps up, we'll soon have everyone in the house here." Em chuckled.

This time it was Jenee who bounded into the room. Taking everyone in, she proclaimed, *"Bien, on est tous là."*

"Yes, we are all here, and soon we'll need another pot of tea," Em said. "Iris, show Jenee the letter so we may bring her up to speed."

Jenee read the missive and handed it back to Iris. "Aha! The plot thickens. Prepare yourselves for a shock. I have news."

"What now?" asked Gaby. She didn't think she could stand any more plot twists.

"It all makes sense now," Jenee added.

The new Emily wasn't as patient as Gaby had thought, because her consternation displayed a growing annoyance. "Jenee, darling, please just spit it out. I can't take any more of this dilly-dallying."

"Cynthia is pregnant!"

They gasped and leaned forward, nearly spilling off the settee to the floor.

"Well, if that isn't the most stunning revelation, I don't know what is," Emily said.

"Is the pregnancy okay?" Gabriella asked. She held no ill wishes toward Cynthia.

"Oui—fortunately, the pregnancy appears to be fine," Jenee replied. "Cynthia is shaken but resigned, delighted to be with child. She swore me to secrecy and doesn't want the baroness to find out."

"Damn, double damn," Emily cursed. "My theory that the baroness was blackmailing her could be wrong, then."

"Not necessarily," said Jenee. "The baroness may know about the dalliance between Beauford and Cynthia, but she has no idea that Cynthia is pregnant. Cynthia only just figured it out. But a compromised reputation would eliminate her from the Marriage Mart and leave her no other option but to marry Jack. The baroness would be secure in her quest to control them and take possession of the painting."

Emily tapped her finger to her lips. "This explains Beauford moving heaven and earth and racing to get here. Maybe there is more to him than we think. Perhaps something the baroness never counted on has happened—Beauford fell in love with Cynthia and can't bear the thought of her marrying Jack."

"The baroness must be aware that the painting is here," Gaby said. "To get her hands on *Il Leto*, she'll do anything and everything. Even threaten to ruin Cynthia's reputation if she doesn't marry Jack, and with her holding all the money and power, he will be forced into a corner." Gaby wanted to burst into tears, but she had to be strong. They had to stop Caterina.

"So, why keep up this charade?" Jen asked. "She might have already gotten the inside scoop from Stefano that Gaby and Jack found the painting, and it's in Jack's bedroom. A locked door won't stop her. After all, she's a sorceress. So why not break into Jack's room and leave through the portal, taking the painting with her?"

Iris, quietly listening to the rapid-fire conjecturing, said, "Because she can't. Marco now controls the portal, thanks to the ruby ring. Without me, she cannot get through."

"What do you think she means to do?" Gaby asked.

"I do not know. Yet. Unfortunately, I cannot leave through the portal either. Not until the Contessa Catarina di Farnese is neutralized once and for all."

"What do you mean by neutralized?" Gaby asked, already feeling dread creeping up her spine.

Em slid her finger across her throat, making it clear that they had to kill the contessa.

"There is no other way," Iris said. "If you thought the Nazi was evil, you have no idea what this woman is capable of. If she gains possession of the portrait through Jack, I will be forced into a devil's bargain with her."

"We will find a way," Emily stated adamantly.

"I'm worried," said Gaby. "If Jack's cousin is on his way here, another problem arises. Jack hates Beauford after what he did to him. If he sets eyes on Beauford, he will challenge him to a duel. I would not put it past the baroness to somehow cause havoc and kill Jack. Then the painting, I assume, will belong to Beauford as the heir to everything Jack possesses."

"You may be right, Gaby." Emily turned to Iris. "How do we stop this from getting out of control?"

"We must get to Beauford before he arrives and divine his true intentions and secure his cooperation," Jen said. "I was able to gain Cynthia's trust. And from what she told me, he is deeply in love with her, and she is with him."

"When he learns of her condition, he will be desperate to marry her, and fast, to prevent a scandal," Iris added.

Emily's dimples deepened with her smile. "Think of this, Gaby—if Beauford marries Cynthia, he will become wealthy beyond measure. He won't need Jack's earldom or his inheritance. What we need to do is persuade him to reinstate Jack's inheritance and his title. And issue some sort of public apology for the egregious error."

"I get the money part, but the title is something Beauford wanted very much," said Gabriella.

"Don't worry. Between Colin and I, we can give him the push he needs. The fact that he swindled Jack's father on his deathbed will not sit well with the aristocracy. They are a close-knit group and naturally would feel threatened by what Beauford did. It is very disruptive to the continuity of Society for a title to be wrested away from a member, regardless of what he has done."

"We must enlist Cynthia's help in this plan," Jenee said.

Gabriella moaned. "Yes, but it would mean standing up to her stepmother, who controls everything, including her dowry. How can we get her our side?"

"Because we are going to make it worth her while," Emily said.

CHAPTER TWENTY-FIVE

Maremma, Italy
October 20, 1902

J ACK STARED AT the flames that flickered and danced in the fireplace hearth as if in a trance. He was so lost in his thoughts, he hardly heard the crackling of wood smoldering into red embers. He'd gone to Cynthia's room to speak to her, but she was sound asleep from the sleeping draught that Jenee had given her. Jenee wasn't in the room, but she'd enlisted one of the maids to watch over her. Mafalda was Antonio's cousin and had a heart of gold, but was also as strong as a man, and nothing and no one could get past her when she cleaned one of the rooms. She told him the doctor had ordered no one to disturb the young lady's sleep, including Signore Jack.

Distracted by his worries, he'd been poor company at dinner. Even though the conversation was lively, Jack had been gloomy and quiet. Aunt Kitty had invited Sir Edward to the villa, and Jack was pleased to see his aunt basking in the glow of Edward's attentions. She deserved to find happiness again, and Sir Edward was charming, intelligent, and, most of all, honorable.

Jack's own romantic inclinations had been thwarted at every turn. It seemed like an eternity since he'd held Gaby in his arms and even longer since he'd kissed her. Still, he held hope, if not patience, as he stared at the flames. He couldn't wait to see her, and he was impatient for her to come to his room after she finished in the kitchen. It felt like he'd been waiting forever for her. And perhaps he had.

His frustrations manifested in his drinking too much and overeating. Shamefully, he'd indulged in two helpings of the thinly pounded veal scallopini served with angel hair pasta.

Aunty Kitty had insisted that Gabriella join them. She did come out to greet everyone but said she was needed back in the kitchen. She blushed prettily at the praise heaped on her. The soul-satisfying meal dressed in a delicate lemon, white wine, butter, parsley, and caper sauce, which Stefano proclaimed *squisito*, had garnered applause from everyone.

The kitchen goddess was as tempting a morsel as her creations. But unlike her exquisite food, tasting her would not thicken his waistline.

He should have gone for a ride on Xanthus, but the only ride he craved had a long mane of luscious, dark curls, sultry hazel eyes, and lips the color of pomegranate.

Get a hold of yourself, man. Your mind has turned to pudding.

He expelled a deep breath, knowing he would have to be a little more patient. They needed to talk before he would allow his amorous intentions to take over.

Jack was worried, but he tried to think of something other than Gaby. Unfortunately, true to his obsession, his mind found its way back to her. He was not a man given to daydreams, but staring at the blue, red, and yellow flames dancing above the logs was hypnotic. His thoughts turned to Singly Park, the seat of his family's earldom—his stolen earldom. He was determined to confront Beauford and force a reckoning. Jack refused to let his cousin get away with ruining his good name. He would fight to the death to reclaim his rightful inheritance.

But how to lure Beauford into the open and force him to relinquish what was not rightfully his? History would not label him as the Langsford who did not take his place as the Earl of Whitton and Marquess of Bainbridge.

But beyond that, he wanted to provide a worthy life for Gaby. She would bring life and love to Singly Park, his ancestral home. She would change darkness into light. Deep in his heart, Jack knew he would have no happiness without Gaby. He saw his sons and daughters in her eyes, and something else he never believed possible. He saw that marriage and love were not antithetical. The estate, which had never provided the nurturing he so desired, would become a place of love and an enduring legacy for their progeny.

Gaby had yet to learn of his intentions, and nor would she until he reclaimed his earldom. But now that he saw the future with such clarity, he would not be deprived of that dream.

He'd tamed Xanthus with patience and a gentle hand, and he would do the same to his thorny rose, Gaby. Jack chuckled. At *least I will have fewer bruises to show for it. I hope.*

A gentle rap sounded at the door, and he stood and took a deep breath, flooding his senses with oxygen. He would need a clear head and all his focus to deal with his temperamental temptress. He would need to listen to everything his lady love said and control his sometimes-acidic tongue.

When he opened the door and saw her, he wanted to pull her into his arms and kiss her, but he did not, fearing she'd bolt like a frightened colt. He reined his impulses in as he'd promised he would. "Come in," he welcomed her. He could tell by her flushed cheeks that she had come straight from the kitchen.

She seemed nervous as she crossed the threshold with one hesitant step after another. Her eyes skittered around the room, landing on the bed. As he followed her gaze, his recollections flooded his senses, forcing him to look away. Dear Lord, how he wanted to sweep her up in his arms and kiss her doubts away.

"Please sit down, Gaby. Would you care for a glass of wine?"

"I probably shouldn't, but yes, please." She sat at one end of the settee and stared at the flames like he had been before she arrived.

"I do love a fire burning in the hearth," he professed. Striding to the side table, he picked up a crystal decanter from a silver tray and filled two goblets with claret. After handing a goblet to her, he sat on the opposite end of the settee, leaving a suitable distance between them. He raised his glass in a toast. *"Cent'anni!* May we both find happiness in what we seek."

"A hundred years," she whispered, and sipped.

Jack sat back and rested his arm atop the sofa frame. He extended his legs in front of him and did his best to appear relaxed and calm. Jack hoped it would encourage Gaby to do the same. He wanted her to confide whatever troubled her without feeling threatened.

"My congratulations—you outdid yourself tonight," he said. "I still can't get over that you are a chef, and a brilliant one, if you don't mind my saying. I'll have you know I had seconds. If your desire is to fatten me up, I daresay you are succeeding." *Keep it light. Give her time to unwind.*

It was the first time she'd smiled since entering his room. It cut the tension hovering between them and dissipated it into nothingness. Her smile lit the heavens, as far as Jack was concerned, and the one thing he was sure of was that he wished to bask in the sunshine of her smile for the rest of his life.

"Maybe you should consider taking up a hobby instead of indulging so heavily in the art of eating," she teased.

"Oh, I can think of one hobby I'd like to completely immerse myself in." *You dunderhead! Keep calm, for God's sake.* He took a drink of his wine, worried she would get up and run for the door.

"I beg your pardon?" She lifted her brows, but a flame of red climbed her neck and tinted her cheeks. He was relieved to see his innuendo's effect on her was not off-putting but sensually acknowledged.

There was no denying she was thinking the same thoughts as him. With great effort, he did not look at the bed where he longed to lie with her.

"Gaby, I want you to be able to say anything to me and not worry about the consequences."

She smiled again, and his heart thundered in his chest. "I'm trying, but I'm not sure where to begin."

"Perhaps a fable would work, or an allegory."

Her look showed a thoughtful contemplation of his suggestion. "We would never have met if everything in the universe had proceeded according to plan. Has the notion of time travel ever entered your mind?" she asked.

Of all the things in the universe she might have said, that was the last he'd expected. "In all honesty, I am firmly rooted in the here and now, and I can say my thoughts have never wandered to such unrealistic possibilities."

A slight frown creased her brow, and her gaze returned to the smoldering embers in the grate. She drew a deep breath and let it out slowly. "Jack, I never suffered from amnesia. I just couldn't tell you the truth about where I came from. You wouldn't have believed me. At least not when we first met."

Jack had no idea where this conversation was going, but reassuring her was of primary importance. "I will now."

"Maybe, maybe not."

"We will get nowhere if you provide only cryptic answers." He reached across the settee, taking her hand. "Try me."

Their eyes met, and he feared all control would be lost to him. A fire ignited, and he released Gaby's hand and sucked in a much-needed breath.

Her eyes darted to where the Allegretto painting had hung, and the color drained from her face. "Where is the painting?"

Confusion and a growing sense of dread made his pulse pound. "Why do you ask? What difference does it make?"

"I told you I am here because of the painting."

"You also told me you are not an art thief, a spy, or a foreign agent. I haven't decided what to do with it, and I moved the painting to a safer place."

She nodded and expelled a giggle of relief, and he hoped it was not hysteria that provoked her sudden change of mood. "You haven't asked me what happened to me in the burial chamber."

"Fair enough. Why did you faint in the burial chamber?"

"Are you familiar with the term déjà vu?"

"Yes, of course. It's a rather recent term coined by a French philosopher, and it relates to a sense of having lived through an experience or been in a place before." His curiosity piqued, Jack leaned forward. "Is that what happened? Did you experience déjà vu in that chamber?"

"Yes. It was my burial chamber. The shock awakened memories of another life, and you were there with me."

"In the burial chamber?"

"No, not in that chamber. I was a priestess, and you were an elder. I believe that is what they called the councilmen of the Etruscan cities. I think perhaps you were also a warrior. The finest I had ever known."

She smiled at him, and he felt ridiculously giddy.

"We'd known each other all our lives, since childhood, and we fell in love." She stopped and took a sip of wine. "Forbidden love, as I was chosen to be a priestess. Our families had placed us on different paths. Different destinies. But nothing could keep us apart, and we planned our escape. Unfortunately, the elders got wind of it and sent soldiers to slaughter us. You told me to run and that you would hold them off. I didn't want to leave you, but you were most insistent. Typical Jack, if you ask me."

She quirked another smile, and his heart did a backflip. How well she knew him.

"But I couldn't leave you," she continued. "So, I turned around and ran back. You were holding your own against a group of soldiers. You were magnificent. Although you missed a sneaky guard who'd crept up on you. But I dispatched him readily enough. We managed to get away. But we both knew it would not be long before more soldiers came after us. There was nowhere we could go. I looked at you, and you understood what we needed to do. The only thing that we could do—" Gaby's voice cracked as she stared at the flames in the hearth. "W-we ran to the bluff, but the s-soldiers were getting closer… Soon they would be upon us. Y-you picked me up and carried me to the edge. We gazed into each other's eyes and told each other that we would love each other for all eternity. And then we jumped."

Gaby's shoulders shook, and a sob escaped her.

Jack had sat frozen in silence as he listened to her story. But now, he leaped into motion. Taking the glass out of her hand, Jack set it on the side table with his. Then he pulled her onto his lap. Relieved she didn't resist him, he held her close against his chest, his arms wrapped tightly around her as she cried.

His heart ached; his soul ached. Her story had rendered him speechless. And yet it explained so much. It explained why he'd fallen in love with her from the moment he set eyes on her, why it felt so right to hold her in his arms, and why he never wanted to let her go.

When her sobs had ceased, and her tears had stopped flowing, he kept holding on to her.

"Jack, we loved each other in that life, and we lost each other," she whispered. "Do you believe me?"

"Yes." He nodded. It also explained why he'd felt a strange feeling come over him at the archeological site. But more importantly, it explained why he'd always been so drawn to that bluff. Why when he visited Piombino he rode Xanthus past the spot, long before he'd ever met Gaby. "Well, those Etruscans clearly scooped you up and put you in that burial cave. I must have ended up a midnight snack for the lions."

Gaby's shoulders shook again, but this time from her giggles.

She leaned back and looked up at him, and the sight of her tear-streaked face made his chest constrict. He reached into his pocket and pulled out a handkerchief. "It's clean, I promise."

She giggled again as he gently wiped the tears from her face.

"This was quite a revelation," he said. "But this can't be the grave secret you've been keeping from me."

Gaby reached out and caressed his face. "No, it is not. What I have to tell you, you'll find far more difficult to believe, and I fear the vision of our past life is a warning."

The warmth of her touch sent the blood surging through his veins. He cleared his throat and tried to rein in his desire for her.

"I am a time traveler," she whispered.

"A what?"

"I am from the future."

Surprise was the least of the emotions he was feeling.

"When you were riding Xanthus and came upon me on the bluff, I had literally just arrived in that spot. Before that, I had been sitting in an art gallery in New York City. The Metropolitan Museum of Art, to be exact. I was born at the end of the twentieth century, in 1996."

"I was certainly not expecting to hear that." Although he tried, he couldn't subdue the trembling in his hand as he continued to wipe away her tears.

He didn't know *what* he'd been expecting... She'd sobbed in his arms after telling him about her vision. He believed her. He believed her down to his soul. He also believed that something unexplainable had brought them together. Perhaps it was fate. He was an archeologist, a man of science. But archeology was also about unraveling mysteries and discovering how people lived and died centuries ago—and, yes, how they loved. But this? This was utterly unfathomable.

"I know it is unexpected, unbelievable, unfathomable," she said.

"You just echoed my own thoughts on your revelation. How is it possible for a human being to travel through time? I have spent my life studying the past, but I also read about the brilliant minds taking science to new realms. And I have never read about this."

"Jack, I understand how you're feeling. I felt the same way before it happened. But it is the truth. And I will prove it."

⇥⟫⟫⟪⟪⇤

GABRIELLA REACHED FOR Jack's hand and held it tight. Surprise flickered briefly in his eyes at her public gesture in front of Iris and the others, but she wanted him to feel comfortable and to show him that, no matter what, she cared about him. She took it as a good sign that he didn't pull away.

"Jack, we all realize how incomprehensible this must be for you," Emily began. "But I want you to know that every one of us has stood in your shoes. Not one of us believed time travel was possible. Please hear us out with an open mind, and you will understand why this has happened. And what your role is in this unbelievable story. If you would please save your questions until we've had our say, I think it will be easier for all of us."

Gaby squeezed his hand encouragingly. "I promise you, once you have heard everyone out, you will completely understand what is at stake. Trust me." She held his gaze, imbuing hers with as much warmth as she could muster.

"Trusting you is my first inclination, and it seems I have no choice but to follow your lead."

Gaby smiled at Jack and then nodded for Iris to begin.

In her lilting French accent, Iris started the story with the horrific moment when the Nazi time traveler killed her parents and fired a pistol aimed straight for her heart. She told Jack about being transported to the Mercato Vecchio in Renaissance Florence and meeting the artist Marco Allegretto. She admitted that love blossomed between them from the first moment they set eyes on each other.

"Seeing my parents murdered in front of my very eyes was the most painful thing I had to endure, but finding love with Marco and then being torn from his arms was unbearable." Iris wiped an errant tear from her eye. "Marco is my true love, my very soul, but if the contessa succeeds, we will be torn apart forever. The Contessa di Farnese is a destroyer of life and love, and she will wreak havoc on the world if she gets her hands on the painting in your custody, Lord Langsford. To stop her from her evil quest, the painting must be returned to Marco."

"As you are aware, Jack, Stefano procured the second painting in *The Three Stages of Love* series, *Il Divano,* for me," Constance added. "I had no idea that the painting I owned was a mirrored version of the painting and a time-travel portal."

Constance explained her part in this remarkable story, and

Gabriella was a little in awe of her. The American heiress was intelligent, intuitive, kind—a gracious lady who'd opened her heart and her mind to believing the unbelievable. She was truly a woman ahead of her time. If they were living in the modern day, Gaby had no doubt that Constance could have run for president of the United States. *She would have had my vote!*

"I had no qualms about letting that painting go," Constance continued. "I did it to help my dear friend Iris, whom I adore. Iris vanished with the painting through the portal." She chuckled. "I was left with an empty frame, but not for a minute do I regret my decision. An evil serial killer was brought to justice."

Gabriella noted all the nods of agreement as Constance spoke.

"But Iris's reunion with Marco was only temporary, because the third painting was still out there. And the contessa was still plotting. That is why our lovely Gabriella was brought here."

Constance smiled, and Gaby felt her face heat with a blush as everyone in the room echoed her sentiment. She was too nervous to look at Jack's face, but her heart soared when she felt his hand give hers a gentle squeeze.

"That is also why I enlisted Stefano's assistance in finding the third painting," Constance continued. "Not because I wanted to acquire it for my collection, but because I wanted it for Iris. You can see how thrilled we all are that the painting is in your possession. It is the third and final time-travel portal. Jack, it is within your power to end the contessa's treachery and help Iris reunite with Marco once and for all."

Gabriella chanced a glance at Jack and could see he was still processing what Iris and Constance had told him.

"Colin, I see you nodding in agreement," Jack finally said. "But are you satisfied with the truth of all of this? How can a sensible man like you put your faith in what seems to be a fairy tale?"

"I was every bit as skeptical as you, old chap," Colin replied. "Had I not witnessed it myself, it would have been hard to swallow. Both Xavier and I are investigators of brutal crimes in our respective cities. We are men of facts. We believe in the science of forensics." He nodded at Xavier.

"But with each murder case we investigate, we also seek to understand the darkness that lies in the criminal mind," Xavier added. "We know there are mysteries that are unexplainable. Things that both Colin and I have witnessed that are *formidable*." He reached for his wife's hand and kissed it. "And there are mysteries that I am truly thankful for."

"I second that," Colin said, grinning at Emily. "I met the love of my life thanks to time travel, as did Xavier. I think I speak for both of us when I say we are grateful to Marco Allegretto and to Iris. We are committed to helping them and will do whatever it takes to reunite them."

"But are you not both concerned that both Emily and Jenee might be transported back to the time they came from?" Jack asked. "As Iris was wrenched numerous times from Marco's arms."

"No, we are not," answered Xavier. "We believe that these four remarkable women are connected by something we cannot fathom, and once the final portal is closed, it will enable all of us to live our lives as normally as anyone else."

"I must explain," Iris interrupted. "Emily, Jenee, and Gabriella were each transported through a different painting portal. Emily and Jenee both made a choice to remain here in the past. They knew that when I returned the portal paintings to Marco, their chances of returning to the future would end. If we are successful, and I leave with the last painting, Marco will destroy them all, and the portals will close forever. I will be reunited with the man I love and live out the remainder of my days with him. If Gabriella wishes to return to her life in the future, she must leave with me. It is her choice, and one she must not take lightly."

Gaby saw the shock flash in Jack's eyes at this realization that she could go home if she chose. He turned to look at her, and oh, how she wanted to tell him right then that she didn't want to leave. That she would stay for him.

But she couldn't. Not in front of everyone. There were so many things she still had to say. So many questions she still had to ask.

"It would mean you would have to give up the painting, Jack," she said softly to him. "You wouldn't be able to sell it."

They'd thrown so much at Jack. Were they asking too much of him? There was the crux of the matter. Gaby knew that if Jack couldn't sell the painting, he would have no choice but to marry Cynthia or another wealthy heiress.

"You would have to marry well to fight for your estate."

Her heart wrenched when he pulled his hand from her grasp. His vivid blue-green eyes were shuttered. It was all Gabriella could do to hold back her tears.

The painting had been his ace in the hole, but now he'd have to go through with marrying Cynthia. If she returned home, then he could move forward with his plans. Her presence was only complicating his life. Gaby couldn't do that. She loved him too much.

"I think we have given Lord Langsford a great deal to think about." Gabriella stood on wobbly legs. "I have a lot to do tomorrow morning and must be up at the crack of dawn. I bid you all goodnight." She walked to the door and opened it without a backward glance.

"Gaby, wait," Emily said.

But Gaby couldn't wait. She had to get out of there. She closed the door behind her and ran to the only place where anything made sense to her. She would not allow Jack or the others to see the tears that blinded her.

The reality had hit her like a sucker punch from behind. If she returned to her life in the future, she would never see Jack again, and her heart broke as the truth sank in. She would be reunited with her family, and that would give her solace, but she would never see Jack again and would have to live with that for the rest of her life. A life doing what she loved and making other people happy, but a life bereft of her own happiness. She would spend it as an outsider watching happy couples holding hands and exchanging kisses, watching mothers holding their babies and taking their children to the park or shopping for school clothes.

Her long, exhausting days at the restaurant would end with her returning to an empty apartment with no one to talk to, no one that loved her—and without the only man she'd ever loved. She'd foolishly wanted Jack to declare in front of her friends that he didn't want her to leave, that he needed her. That he didn't care about the painting or fighting for his title or estate. That he loved her and couldn't imagine living his life without her.

But he'd said nothing. And she'd said nothing. And whatever hope she had was crushed.

CHAPTER TWENTY-SIX

Maremma, Italy
October 20, 1902

S *HE'S GONE.*
Gabriella had rushed out before he'd even had a chance to process everything. He needed to find her. Needed to speak to her in private.

Jack jumped up and, with a quick goodnight, ran from the room. He rushed down the hall, hoping she was in his bedchamber, but his room was empty. *Damn!* He'd known her less than a week, yet she'd changed his life forever.

Robert Burns said it well: *The best laid plans of mice and men often go awry.*

He ran up the back stairs to the servants' quarters and barged into her room, but her chamber was empty.

And then it hit him. Gaby would seek refuge in the place that gave her comfort—the kitchen. The dwelling place of the kitchen goddess.

Jack rushed back down the stairs, his heart pounding as he neared the kitchen. The aroma of last night's dinner, its pungent spices and seasonings, fragranced the air. In his mind, those scents were as erotic as a rare perfume because those were the scents that lingered on her skin, the scents that drove him mad with desire.

The woodburning cooking ranges had cooled and wouldn't be lit until early morning, when Angelina would rise at dawn and bake the day's bread. There was an eeriness to being in a dark, empty kitchen where the heat and bustle of the day were dormant. But this was Gaby's place, where her creativity took wing.

He scanned the room, worried she wouldn't be there, but then he spotted a shadow moving along the far wall. He took a few steps closer and saw her sitting on a bench beneath a shelf stacked with aprons and towels. Stilled by the silence and not wanting to approach without invitation, he waited, hoping she would acknowledge him.

"A part of me wants to go home, back to my family," she finally said. "I know they must be suffering deeply because of my disappearance. My heart hurts just thinking about it."

His body tensed at her words. So, it had come to this. She missed her family and her life and couldn't bear it.

"But my heart hurts thinking about leaving here, too."

Jack's breath caught, and he took a few more steps toward her. Her heart hurt about leaving. Then that meant that a part of her wanted to stay. She wanted to stay even though he'd offered her no reason to do so. She might consider giving up her family and her life in the future for nothing more than the chance to be his mistress.

For that was what he'd offered her. What he'd thoughtlessly offered her. And he hadn't revised that offer. In her view, he still felt that way. And in light of the very real, very tangible issue of his finances, she would have no reason to think otherwise.

He would have to give up the painting so that Iris and Marco could be together and the contessa's reign of evil would end. In Gaby's mind, he'd have to marry Cynthia or another heiress in order to fight for his birthright.

Jack swallowed the lump in his throat. No wonder she was torn. No wonder she'd had such a difficult time telling him the truth. No wonder she'd run off. No wonder she was here, hiding in the kitchen.

All he'd offered her was the great honor of being his mistress and bearing him bastard children. Even thinking of that word made it hard for him to swallow. How could he not have seen the insult to her dignity? A million questions filled his mind, and he nearly laughed, thinking of how he'd wasted so much time already. If he began asking her right now all the things he wished to know about her life, there would not be enough years remaining in their lives to answer them all.

"Why does your heart hurt to leave here?" he asked, waiting with bated breath.

"What does it matter why I am torn? It's just a projection of my own silly, stupid heart. My desire for something that will never be."

Jack couldn't see her tears, as the shadows hid her face, but he could hear the hopelessness and resignation in her voice.

"You asked me to trust you," he said, "and I did. Now I'm asking you to trust me. I believe you. I believe everything you've told me. Everything your friends have told me."

"You do?"

"Yes, as incredible as it is, I do." He took a few steps closer. "May I sit down?"

She scooted over on the bench. "Yes."

He sat next to her, not too close, but near enough that if she showed the slightest encouragement, he might pull her into his arms and kiss her. At least now he could see her face and read her emotions. Being near her gave him the courage to face his fears and uncertainties. The acknowledgment of his love for her was so recently realized that he ached to share it with her, but he couldn't rush this. Gaby deserved to be courted.

"I didn't tell you, but after I saw you in the hallway this afternoon carrying that tea tray, I went to Cynthia's room to speak to her."

Gaby looked down at her hands. "Did you go to propose your engagement?"

"Good God, no. I went to tell her the truth. That I didn't love her, and she deserved someone who did."

"You did? What did she say?"

He chuckled. "She was asleep, and Jenee had left Mafalda to stay with her. And, well, you know how formidable Mafalda is."

Gaby giggled. "I spend most of my time with my kitchen crew, but yes, I've had dealings with Mafalda. She's a force to be reckoned with. Your aunt is very lucky to have her."

"Indeed. Well, suffice it to say, I never got a chance to speak with her, but I can assure you I will at the soonest opportunity."

"But what of your inheritance?"

"My inheritance is not what I'm thinking about right now. I'll figure out another way. The point is, I've discovered a great deal about myself since we met."

"Have you?"

"Yes, I have. I thought it didn't matter whether I married for love or not, but I've realized that it matters very much to me."

Gaby nodded, and though he yearned for her to look him in the eyes, she stared down at her hands.

"What about you, Gaby? Does love matter to you?"

"Yes, it does, but I've resigned myself to living without it."

"Why would you do that?"

"I-I… Because the man I love doesn't love me."

"And you know that for certain? Because I cannot imagine any man not falling in love with you."

She looked up at him, her eyes wide and questioning. "You're just saying that because you see I am distraught, and you're feeling guilty about what we shared."

"Is that why I'm here? Speaking to you about love and what is in my heart? Do you really think my actions are motivated by guilt? Search your heart, Gaby. Would I be willing to give up everything for the woman I love for the unworthy emotion of pity, or even empathy?" He chuckled. "I do not believe I am that altruistic or saintly."

A small smile formed on the lips he longed to kiss. "You are definitely not a saint."

"Ah, something we can both agree upon."

"There might be other things we can agree upon."

His heart thundered in his chest. Had their conversation taken a turn for the better?

He could not disguise the thickness in his voice, given his excitement. "And what might those things be?" He took her hand, drawing circles with his thumb, an impulsive caress he could not suppress. "Perhaps you should give me an example, something I can wrap my dense head around."

Flirting with Gaby was like diving into a bed of rose petals. His senses were spinning with the need to hold her. He couldn't deny that he was head over heels in love with her, and it filled him with strength admitting so to himself. It made him realize that his future possibilities were embodied in this enigmatic, beautiful creature sitting next to him. If she reciprocated his love, there was no mountain he couldn't climb, no obstacle so great that they couldn't conquer it together, and no storm that could tear them apart.

He had to believe she felt the same, but he needed her to say it. In truth, he wanted her to shout it from the rooftops so the entire world would hear her say she loved him. Then and only then would he be satisfied.

"There is nothing dense about your brain. You are clear thinking, even if a stubborn know-it-all streak runs deep in your psyche," she said with a chuckle.

He laughed. "Now, who's calling the kettle black?"

"Never have I met a man who confused me more than you. Yet all I want is to know your every thought, and I don't understand why."

Did he dare put words into her mouth? If he didn't do it once and for all, he doubted she would ever say what she truly felt, and he needed to know. What he planned would change his life forever, and he had to be sure. The possibility that she didn't love him wasn't something he could bear. The thought of living the rest of his days without her brought a wrenching pain to his chest.

"Is it possible you're in love with me?"

She examined his face—now, he had her complete attention. It was as if he could see his desire manifest itself in her expression.

"If I tell you that I love you, what will you do?" she asked. "Will you offer me a castle to live in where you visit when the opportunity presents itself? Will you keep me there while you pursue another heiress to regain your estate and title? Will you regret your impulsive commitment?"

"What if I tell you that I can't bear the thought of living my life without you?" Jack said. "That my heart is yours to do with as you wish? Nothing else matters if you are not by my side today, tomorrow, and every day after that."

His face was so close to hers that he could feel her breath whisper across his features. Her lips were so close that he could already taste their sweetness. The ache that filled him was palpable and delicious. It was more powerful than any emotion he'd ever experienced. It felt addictive, and he was sure that when he kissed her, he would never kiss another woman ever again. There would be no substitutes for Gabriella. This was his only chance for love, and that realization was strangely liberating.

"I want to believe you, Jack," she said. "I really do."

"Then take a chance, Gabriella. Stay here with me and let us build a life together."

"What are you saying?"

"I'm saying I love you more than my very next breath. More than all the titles and lands in the world, it is you I want. It is you I want to bear my sons and daughters. I love you, Gabriella D'Angelo, and I beg you to consider me for your husband. Grant me this privilege, and you will never regret it."

Gaby blinked rapidly, seeming stunned into silence.

"Sometimes, when I look at you, I can't bear it," she said.

"But why?" Fear constricted his heart, and he didn't dare breathe.

"I love you so much, Jack, that it hurts." Her hand on his cheek was warm, and he covered it with his.

"Say it again."

"I love you, Jack, and I will never leave you. And before you change your mind"—she giggled—"yes, I will marry you, but—"

Before she could finish the sentence, his lips were pressed to hers. His desire would allow for no more conversation. She could finish her thought after he'd ravished her and brought them both to satisfaction.

He pulled her onto his lap and pulled up her skirt, and his fingers sought the source of her pleasure.

"Jack, what are you doing?" she said breathlessly.

"Don't speak, my love, just enjoy. I've dreamed of this moment since the night we spent together. Please don't deny me." He circled her with the pad of his thumb while his middle finger entered her.

"I... Oh, Jack!"

Her nugget had swelled, and a little more pressure from his thumb sent her head back against his shoulder, silencing her. Moans replaced words, and she spread her legs apart, giving him greater access. He swallowed her moans with his kisses, and when his middle finger slipped inside her again, her back arched, and her beautiful breasts pressed against her bodice. He shifted her on his lap and pushed his finger deeper. All the while, he kissed her passionately, fervently, allowing her not a breath of protest. One day he would make love to her in every room of Singly Park, and all of the lonely memories of growing up there would be put to rest once and for all.

Every time she worked in this kitchen, this would be her memory. It would always be where he asked her to marry him, and she accepted. But her private erotic memory would be this, his making love to her here.

His incessant fingering of her brought the desired response. She whimpered and stiffened simultaneously. It was glorious to feel her quivering and tightening around his finger, and her gasps as he felt her explode were music to his ears. But the cry of his name on her lips made his cock pulse against his trouser leg, demanding satisfaction.

He ran his tongue up her neck to her ear and whispered, "My

darling love, I adore you with every fiber of my being. Now, may I please fill you with my heart, soul, and *cock*?" He resumed caressing her clitoris, and he felt it harden again.

"Yes! Yes! Yes!"

>>><<<

GABRIELLA RESTED AGAINST Jack's chest. Their passionate lovemaking had wrung whatever doubts she may have harbored. His fingers rubbed the back of her neck, and his warm lips pressed to her temple. She could hear his thundering heartbeat that only now began to return to a normal rhythm. Her head was spinning from their passionate lovemaking and his declaration of love for her.

Jack loved her, and no dream could ever compare to that reality.

Gabriella snuggled against Jack's chest, drifting on the buoyancy of satiation as the truth of things slowly returned to her. She wanted to forget every pressing matter not resolved, but she could not. Jack may have hidden the painting, but wherever he hid it, it would never be safe from the baroness.

Iris's words returned to her, and a realization followed. Until the portal was closed and destroyed, she would not be safe. None of them would.

Gaby opened her eyes and studied the face of the man she loved. With his eyes closed, she had a moment to admire his strong, bold features in repose. He was so handsome, virile, and impossibly determined in everything he did. She marveled at the twist of fate that had brought them together. Her heart swelled with love, and she was reminded that anything worth having was worth fighting for. If Jack and she had a future together, she would have to risk everything.

"A penny for your thoughts, lovey." A quirky smile graced his lips.

"Were you watching me watching you with your eyes closed?" Was there nothing she could keep secret from him? Not that she wanted to, but still, how easily he could read her mind was perplexing.

He wrapped his arms around her, trapping her against his hard chest. "I will not have you second-guessing what just happened and bolting away from me like last time. Let us just say your recovery from our sweet liaison was more rapid than mine; however, my sixth sense remains ever conscious of you, and I will not have you doubting my feelings for you."

She cupped his face in her hands. "I would never have run from you then if I didn't think it was for your benefit. I promise I will never run from you again, and you can cast aside any thought that I would ever doubt you."

"Good. Now that that's settled, where were you a moment ago? Certainly not on this bench with me."

"I cannot ignore the possibility that unless Iris stops the baroness, or contessa, or whomever she is, and returns with the painting to Marco, you and I might suffer the same fate as them. It frightens me to think that I might suddenly be taken from the life we built together and sent to another time and place. Time travel has brought us together, and time travel could pull us apart." Voicing her fears brought tears to her eyes.

"I will never let that happen. Although I would love to keep the painting because it brought you to me, I will gladly relinquish it to Iris if it means keeping you with me for the rest of our lives." He gently wiped away her tears with the pads of his thumbs, the same pads that had brought her to bliss. He kissed her forehead more like a husband than a lover.

"Knowing Em and Jen, they've probably been hatching a plan with the others while we've been playing hooky. But what do you think? Should we hang the painting in a prominent location where everyone can see it?"

"We'd be making it easier for the contessa to steal it, wouldn't we?" He smoothed her hair back over her shoulder.

"Iris says the contessa can't pass through the portal unless she is there. But if you wish to rid yourself of a dangerous beast, would it not be better to lure it out in the open and confront it on your own terms? At least then you are prepared to do battle."

"I see the wisdom in your plan. If we ready ourselves, I am sure we can succeed in putting an end to her evil machinations. It would be heartening to know that Iris and Marco were reunited and that we, too, might know the bliss of a life shared together."

Gaby threw her arms around his neck. "Oh, Jack, you never cease to surprise me. I was sure you'd argue endlessly over my suggestion. I was so foolish thinking you would think us all mad with our tales of time travel. All of this has felt like a dream, and I fear I'll wake up tomorrow, and you'll be gone."

"You can disabuse yourself of that notion. You will not rid yourself of me that easily. I'm afraid you are stuck with me, my beauty."

"And you are stuck with me if you'll have me."

"Oh, I'll have you all right," he said, giving her a quick kiss on her lips. "In fact, I'd love to have you right now, but I'm afraid your friends will come after me with torches if I don't bring you back to them safe and sound. Come, my beauty—let us plan how we shall slay the beast."

CHAPTER TWENTY-SEVEN

Maremma, Italy
October 21, 1902

RAYS OF SUNSHINE burst through the cloud cover like gleaming swords penetrating the clouds and piercing the ground. Soon the density of clouds rolling in from the sea would overwhelm the meager fingers of light, and rain would follow in their stead.

Gabriella, holding a basket, took advantage of the lull before the storm, snipping herbs and pulling vegetables for the day's meals from the rich earth in the garden beds. The declarations of love she and Jack gave to each other played in her mind as she worked. And though her heart sang with the memory, the necessities for guests and staff had to be addressed. She chuckled to herself as she mused—as fulfilling as love might be, one could not survive on love alone, and breakfast must be served with a villa full of people.

Standing, she brushed the dirt from her skirt. A raindrop hit her cheek, and she wiped it away. Gaby glanced up at the gray, leaden clouds that filled the sky, and she was glad that the basket was filled and she'd be inside before the downpour began. The darkening sky did not dampen her spirits, and she looked forward to the cleansing rain that would wash away the dirt and the troubles that assailed her. She sensed it would rejuvenate her hopes and dreams. Everything felt possible when in love.

Turning, she heard the unmistakable clip-clop of horses' hooves and the rattle of carriage wheels. The carriage's arrival was unexpected at such an early hour. Still, she was reminded of the letter Emily had intercepted from England. The man who could destroy her future happiness was on his way to Nido dell' Aquila, and a premonition fingered its way up her spine, depriving her of some of the happiness in her heart.

Gaby watched a tall, dark-haired man jump from the carriage wearing a fashionable brown inverness cape. He brushed back a lock of dark hair from his forehead. She saw no resemblance to Jack except in his stature and strength. The man was shorter, to be sure, but realizing that this was Jack's hated cousin was enough to ignite her worry.

He looked up at the villa's façade and seemed hesitant, as if waiting for a sign or someone to bid him entry. Antonio exited the house, and Gaby could see confusion lining the butler's face when he saw the carriage driver emptying the boot of its luggage.

Gaby did not wait to observe their interaction; picking up her basket, she ran for the kitchen door. "Maria." Gabriella set the basket on the counter. "Please begin prepping the frittata." She quickly unloaded the red bell peppers, broccoli, mushrooms, red onions, parsley, and tarragon. "We'll make a vegetable frittata with gruyère, fontina, feta, and Parmesan cheese. Would you be so kind as to pull these from the cheese larder? I must take care of something. There will be no less than twelve for breakfast; another guest has arrived. Cynthia will most likely take her breakfast in her room, and I think this newly arrived guest will join her."

"Lady Darling did not mention any other guests. Should I have Mrs. Livingstone prepare a room?" Maria asked.

"I think that is a good idea. I believe he is another nephew of Lady Darling's. If he survives the morning, I assume he will be staying here."

"I beg your pardon, signorina?"

The sound of raised voices from somewhere in the house caused everyone in the kitchen to stop what they were doing and turn toward the butler's door. They could hear the mistress of the manor reprimanding someone, who replied loudly.

"Never mind—just do as I ask, please." Gabriella ran from the kitchen to the vestibule of the villa just in the nick of time. Beauford stood poised at the bottom step of the staircase, and his sizeable, muscular body cast a shadow.

Kitty stood at the second-floor landing. "Beauford, what are you doing here? Have you lost your mind, arriving unannounced?"

"Step aside, Kitty—this doesn't concern you. I'm here to see one of your guests, Miss Maxwell."

"Have you gone mad? As you well know, Jack is here and will be none too pleased to see you. What possible business do you have with Miss Maxwell that you would leave the comfort of Singly Hall for the countryside of Italy? After what you've done, you are not welcome here. My sister, were she alive, would not approve of what you've done to our good family name. Your mother had great respect for the rules as to the line of succession. That your father gambled away his estate is not Jack's fault."

"My mother is dead, and Jack is your problem, not mine. He is not worthy of your protection, Aunt Kitty. He's a cad, and though his father implored him to return, he did not. As for Miss Maxwell, we have unfinished business to attend to."

"I cannot imagine what you and Miss Maxwell have to dispute, but I can tell you she is indisposed and has taken to her bed," Kitty replied. "As far as Jack is concerned, I know your cousin better than anyone alive. It is you that manufactured accusations against him. Somehow you poisoned my brother's mind and turned him against his own son. It is you who have brought conflict into our lives with your lies and deceit. You have stolen his earldom, his wealth, and his lands. I will not be responsible for the consequences of your actions. This is my home, and you are not welcome here."

"I do not give a tinker's curse for your consequences or your accusations. I'm not here because of Jack; I'm here to see Miss Maxwell. I will not allow her to marry Jack under any circumstances. Now, please do not—"

A roar of anger erupted. Jack hung over the balustrade, his face contorted with rage. "What in bloody hell are you doing here, Beauford?" His gaze shifted when he caught sight of Gabriella. He pushed past Kitty, who grabbed his arm, trying to stop him. He shook loose with no trouble and stomped down the stairs, his eyes filled with murder. "And what are *you* doing here, Gabriella? Please return to the kitchen; this is of no concern to you."

Gaby's first impulse was to wrap her arms around him to restrain him, but she dared not and addressed him formally, unable to disguise the tremor in her voice. "Do not order me about, Lord Langsford, as I am here to stop you from doing anything rash." *Where is his so recently professed love for me?*

Jack's eyes rounded. "Do you know who this man is?"

"I do, my lord. He is your cousin, Beauford Bastion Broome."

"You know what he's done to me, how he's stolen my inheritance, and you would have me welcome him into my aunt's home? Why would you protect him?"

"Don't be foolish, my lord. I'm not protecting him, and my only wish is to prevent you from making a terrible mistake. He has good reason to be here, but I cannot say more."

"How could you possibly know what his reason is?" Jack's mouth hardened into a thin line. Gaby could see she was losing him, and she didn't know what to do. It wasn't her place to tell him why Beauford was here or about his relationship with Cynthia. As for the pregnancy, any discussion of that was entirely off-limits. That was between Beauford and Cynthia, and Jack needn't know about it.

As if she arrived in a puff of smoke, the baroness appeared. "Lord Langsford, this man"—she pointed at Beauford—"is a seducer of innocent women. He has defiled the good name of your countess-to-be! You must exact vengeance on him."

Jack looked as if he was about to explode. By this time, nearly everyone in the household had gathered. Kitty seemed mortified and looked to the others for help.

"I say, old chap," Colin said, "let us keep our heads."

"Keep my head? I assure you, Colin, that were you subjected to such treachery, you would not go gently into the night. You would exact your justice at any price." Jack delivered his grim indictment while staring at Gabriella. In a pained whisper, he told her, "For you to protect this man cuts me to the quick. I am betrayed by the one person in whose hands I placed my deepest trust and belief. What is your connection to my cousin?"

Gabriella was stunned by Jack's misreading of her, and her throat constricted, making it impossible for her to respond. How could he believe her intentions were impure after everything they had shared? She barely formed a response, choking out, "Lord Langsford, I have never laid eyes on this man before. Please do not say anything we will both regret."

He laughed, and she could see he was possessed of a madness that precluded his reason. He whispered under his breath so that only she could hear. "My only regret is that I didn't see you clearly before I gave my heart to you. You have betrayed me, and the kindness shown to you by my aunt."

"Jack, stop!" said Kitty. "You are speaking without thinking."

Gaby clamped a hand over her mouth, and tears sprang to her eyes.

Emily ran down the stairs and wrapped an arm around Gaby's shoulders. "You, sir, are the cad. How dare you speak to Gabriella like this? Can't you see the pain you are causing her?"

Iris's voice broke into their standoff. "Lord Langsford, do not believe this pretender; the baroness leads you astray to further her own agenda. You are being used, sir."

Jack spun. "I am being used, but it is not only by the baroness. How could I have been so blind to put my faith in a woman who cloaked herself in mystery and kept so many secrets?"

Beauford took advantage of the focus being directed elsewhere. "I must see Cynthia. I care not what barbs you fools hurl at one another, and I have already expended too much effort on your meaningless blather."

He ran up the stairs but was momentarily prevented from his goal by Jenee's staying hand. "Monsieur, you will find Miss Maxwell's room at the third door on the left. I pray your conversation will illuminate the answers you seek and bring you to your senses."

Iris nodded. "You made an evil alliance with an unscrupulous woman." She pointed at the baroness. "She will destroy not only you but all whom you hold dear. You will lose your soul and whatever happiness you might have known. Choose wisely, my lord."

The baroness's shrill voice broke in, and she looked from Beauford to Jack with indignation. "You cannot allow this scoundrel to sully my niece's reputation more than he already has. These people know nothing of my intentions or the young woman I protect."

Emily kissed Gabriella's temple and whispered, "You will be fine, my friend. Trust me." She released Gaby and called up the stairs, "Lord Broome, allow me to take you to Cynthia and act as chaperone." She sneered at the baroness. "I believe that should satisfy your concerns, baroness."

"Well—"

"As I surmised, you are not of pure intent, but I digress. If it is Cynthia's reputation that you are truly concerned with, you should be satisfied that I will stand watch." Emily ignored the baroness and held out her hand to Beauford to shake. "I am Lady Emily Remington, the Marchioness of Danbury." She nodded toward Colin. "My husband, Colin Remington, the marquess, will readily agree that my presence should provide ample propriety and assuage the baroness's concerns. Baroness, I assure you Cynthia will be carefully tended to by me, and Lord Broome will have no opportunity to besmirch her." She turned to Beauford. "That is if it is acceptable to you, sir."

"Yes, yes, let's get on with it," Beauford said. "I've wasted too much time already listening to this farcical cast of characters. You, my lady, are a breath of fresh air."

Emily quickly ascended the staircase and, without a look back, continued down the hall.

"Beauford," Jack yelled up the stairs, and Beauford halted and turned to face his cousin. "You will leave this house immediately after seeing Miss Maxwell or suffer the consequences."

"I will take my chances." Beauford turned and was gone, leaving everyone in a state of shock.

CHAPTER TWENTY-EIGHT

Maremma, Italy
October 21, 1902

E MILY GAVE HER husband a conspiratorial wink as she passed him, and received an imperceptible nod. Never was Emily more effective than when she took up a cause or helped a friend. Under the direst circumstances, she took the reins wholeheartedly with intense focus. She projected a winsome charm that could tame a lion, slay a monster, or even change the course of history.

Most assuredly, she would need every bit of ingenuity to convince Cynthia that she had the best intentions. It was imperative Cynthia break free of the talons of her aunt, the baroness, gain control of her inheritance, and marry Beauford.

The thin line Emily must tread without falling made the task more difficult. She could not reveal too much of the paranormal pitfalls at play. In such a short window of time, it would be impossible to convince Cynthia and Beauford they were being used by a sorceress. Forget about convincing them of the existence of time travel, painting portals, and the real identity of the baroness, a time traveler who preyed on the goodwill of others—if Iris was right, and Emily had no reason to doubt her. She had been spot-on until now, and the baroness likely followed the same practices the Nazi time traveler had used in London and Paris. The Countess Catarina di Farnese had probably murdered both her husband, the baron, and Cynthia's father to wrest control of her fortune and use her as a pawn in her game to gain possession of *Il Leto* and control the time portals.

Jack was another matter altogether. His obsession with Beauford had clouded his reason. When he vehemently turned on Gaby, he fell into the baroness's trap.

To see her friend suffering had awoken Emily's mother-tigress instinct. She would be damned if she'd let Jack get away with demeaning Gabriella. Emily had him dead to rights, and he would have to be made to see his error, or else he would lose the love Emily believed he desired.

She would deal with Jack later. This moment required her full attention.

She could hear Beauford's footsteps behind her as he shadowed her down the hallway. Having reached Cynthia's door, she rapped softly. "Cynthia, it is Emily. May I come in?" There was no sense in alerting Cynthia that she had not come alone. Far better to hold the upper hand of surprise and let the moment play out. Much would be learned in Cynthia's reaction to Beauford.

The door opened to a dark room, where the heavy brocaded drapery was pulled shut. Emily pushed the door wide, giving Beauford entry. "Cynthia, my darling." His voice was tender and filled with affection. He entered but a few feet and, like Emily, needed a second for his eyes to adjust to the dim light.

Propped on a mountain of pillows lay Cynthia. She blinked rapidly as if not believing her eyes, and then, like a sprite with no injury at all, she bounded from the bed, running into Beauford's arms.

Case closed—actions speak louder than words.

"Beauford!" she cried, her joy echoing through the bedroom. "You came!"

"Of course I came. Did you not receive my letter? I've been such a fool. Forgive me?" Beauford kissed her cheeks, her eyelids, and her forehead.

"I thought you'd forsaken me." Cynthia gazed into his eyes adoringly. "My aunt insisted I was compromised, and you didn't care. She said my only chance to keep my dignity and not sully my father's name was to marry Jack. She whisked me away from London and brought me here to Lady's Darling's villa, intending to marry me off as quickly as possible to Jack."

"It's all a damned lie. The witch used us both. She black-mailed me into helping her get some blasted painting, promising me that I would keep the earldom, and in the end, you would be mine. I'm afraid my greed and jealousy of my cousin influenced my actions. You will not marry Jack!"

"Beau, my darling, you must not blame Jack. He is a good man who cared well for me when I was attacked by a wild boar."

"I will thank him for that, but forgive me for not asking about your health? I have been beside myself with worry, but when you ran to me with such energy, in my joy, I forgot you'd been injured. Forgive me, my angel. If you are well to travel, we will leave at once for England."

"But the baroness will never agree."

Emily had stood silent witness to the lovers' reunion. They were so caught up in their emotions that they hadn't even acknowledged her presence.

She cleared her throat. "Cynthia, you must tell Beauford your news. You must not worry that I know your condition. I mean you no harm. Jenee confided in me, and I believe your news will be well received."

Bright spots of red flushed Cynthia's cheeks, and Emily hoped the girl possessed a backbone and would rise to the occasion and show strength.

Cynthia looked embarrassed, and Beauford looked concerned. "What is she talking about, Cynthia? What news have you to tell me? Is it about your injury? Are you all right?"

Cynthia cupped his cheeks. "My darling, it is wonderful news, and I hope your joy will be as great as mine." She whispered, "I am with child."

Emily could not help but be moved by the emotion that played across Beauford's face. His mouth opened, but no sound came out. He was speechless, but Emily could see his eyes fill with tears. "And you would have let another man raise our child?"

"No, I was going to run away from here back to England and beg for your protection, but the attack by the beast waylaid my plan."

"Oh, my darling, I am the worst of men to have put you through this."

"No, sir, you are the worst of men for taking what wasn't yours," said Emily.

"I beg your pardon?" Beauford asked.

"If you truly mean to do right, you must give Jack back his earldom and estate and clear his name."

"Never!"

"Would you risk your life and future in a duel? Because that is what I fear will follow if you don't."

"A duel?"

"Yes, I believe Jack will challenge you to one, and I cannot blame him if he does."

"If I were to clear his name and cede to him all he has lost, I would condemn myself to ignominy."

"Perhaps you haven't heard the rumors that have spread throughout the *ton*," Emily said. "You are already disgraced, and it is only a matter of time before you are called before a tribunal of your peers and brought to judgment. It is likely you will lose the earldom in any event. Better to do the right thing and restore order."

"But I would be penniless and unable to provide for my bride and child."

"That is ridiculous. Cynthia stands to inherit both her uncle's and father's estate, which, as you know, are quite large. In fact, you would possess wealth beyond your wildest dreams."

Beauford chuckled. "You forget, Lady Remington, that Cynthia's aunt, the baroness, holds custody of her inheritance. If we decamp, she is sure to refuse us her blessing and challenge us in court. Cynthia has not come of age and must abide by the legal stance of her trust."

"I have not forgotten," Emily replied. "We are dealing with a treacherous woman with evil intent who will do whatever it takes to hold on to power and fortune. But she does not know what we know, and I have a plan to destroy her, and Cynthia's fortune will then be yours. My husband could then assume guardianship and grant you entitlement. You will have the means to start anew and build a meaningful life. That is, if you agree to my terms."

"Beauford, we must listen to Lady Remington. I believe she is right," pleaded Cynthia.

Beauford studied Cynthia's face, and Emily read the unmistakable impression of love in his eyes.

A look of resolve filled his features. "What is your plan, and what would you have me do?"

CHAPTER TWENTY-NINE

Maremma, Italy
October 21, 1902

GABY RAN TO her tiny garret in the servants' quarters and flung herself on her bed. Tears poured from her as she relived the last few minutes. Jack's reaction, his misreading of her intentions, and his accusations devastated her. Had she fallen in love with a heartless monster? Or worse, a Doctor Jekyll and Mr. Hyde? It didn't seem possible. She knew the pressures he was suffering under, but she felt like she was on a roller coaster, and the ups and downs were getting to her.

How would she survive this latest disappointment and the truth of having fallen in love with a man so changeable and mutable that the slightest provocation could cause him to change direction midstream? He claimed to love her but didn't trust her, which was irreconcilable in her mind. For her, there could be no love without trust, and it was heartbreaking to realize that was where their relationship stood. She wanted to shake him like a rag doll until he came to his senses.

She cried until her nose felt as red as Rudolph the reindeer's, and her eyes were swollen to where she could barely see out of them. She stared at the ceiling, wondering how to make the best of a terrible situation.

He might have listened if she could only have told him everything Jenee and Iris had told her, but she could not betray their confidences. Emily had said to trust her, but what could she possibly do to make things right? Now, all Gaby wanted was to go home to her family and try to forget Jack.

But in the deepest part of her psyche, Gabriella knew she would never get over him. The only man she had ever loved seemed lost to her, and she didn't know how to get him back and make him see that the only losers of this disaster were she and he.

>>><<<

JACK PACED THE grounds of Nido dell' Aquila, puffing on a cheroot. He was bereft, like a person in mourning, waiting for something to happen that would change everything he thought to be true. His chest ached as if his heart was broken into a million pieces. He wanted to punch his fist through a wall or ride Xanthus to the bluff, spur him forward, and gallop over the edge, disappearing into the rocky waters below.

Suicide—he'd never considered it in his entire life. Not even as a boy living in a loveless, motherless manor, or when he'd returned from Egypt and been devastated by Beauford's ghastly deeds. He always rose above his troubles, swore to do better, and vowed to fight for what was rightfully his.

He'd tried to be a good son and live a worthy life, and then the false rumors began. At first, he'd paid them no mind, thinking they would disappear with time, as idle gossip usually does, but they persisted. He wasn't sure how they traveled back to England from Luxor, but they did.

But never had Jack lost heart or belief in himself—until now. Thank God Kitty had believed him, although she worried over the damage done to him and whether it could be amended. But he didn't really care whether he was accepted in civil society ever again. So long as he reclaimed his earldom and inheritance, he would be just as happy living as a recluse at Singly Hall, so long as

Gaby was there. But now he'd certainly mucked that up.

Replaying everything he'd said to Gaby, he cringed with self-loathing. He'd seen the pain in her face, yet continued, cruelly taking aim at her as if she were the cause of his misfortunes. What kind of man would do that to the woman he loved?

And love her he did, more than anything in this world. Somehow in the few days since she'd come into his life, she'd become the source of his hopes and dreams—and look what he'd done to her. He'd doubted her sincerity, questioned her loyalty, and made her feel less than worthy of his love, when it was he who was unworthy.

He could take the coward's way out and blame Beauford for his actions, but that would be a lie. Taking responsibility was the only course open to him. He needed to get on his knees and beg her forgiveness. And then, perhaps after his contrition, she might mercifully forgive him.

Then would come the hard part—penance. He had to make amends by giving her something she desired, no matter the cost to his pride or ego. Not a monetary compensation or meaningless words, neither of which would right the wrong he'd done to her. For Gaby, only an act of absolute emotional truth would reach her heart, allowing her to forgive the unforgivable—but where to start?

EMILY RAPPED SOFTLY on Gabriella's door. She was distressed to see her friend living in the servants' quarters, even though they were nicer than many in London. Still, she was mainly worried for Gaby after Jack's rebuke. Emily knew her friend was a sensitive person with a fragile ego. Gaby was accomplished and strong, but her childhood had left her with scars, and a past relationship had left her with a broken heart—the bastard wine salesman who had not only cheated on her with women throughout the country but failed to mention that he was married. The creep was a serial cheater. Emily would have liked to kick him in the arse, but ladies didn't do things like that. Still…

"Gaby, it's me. May I come in?"

"Yes, oh Em, please do!"

When she opened the door, Emily was careful not to show her distress with the dismal, dingy room that reminded her of a prison cell, with only a tiny window too high up to provide much light. She did notice and took heart from the crockery and vase filled with roses.

She sat on the bed and took Gaby's hand. "I know you're in pain, but I promise you, it will all work out. I know he behaved like an arsehole, but give him some time to figure it out. Men are daft when it comes to love. They know how to deal with situations, but their emotional vulnerability sometimes overwhelms them."

"I know you're right, but he's so unpredictable," Gaby said. "The way he turned on me surprised me. I just didn't expect it."

"He's an arse for sure, but I need you to be present for Iris. Her life truly hangs in the balance, and we must stay focused on helping her."

"You're right; I'm being selfish. All I want is to go home and leave this all behind, get back to my kitchen and family, and do what I'm good at." Gaby chuckled through her tears. "It's obvious I'm not good at love, but I can cook."

"You sure can, as my thickening waistline can testify. I've been eating like a horse, but there's nothing wrong with your ability to love or be loved. By the way, where in God's name is the painting? Stefano told me that Jack has moved it, but to where?"

Gaby looked surprised. "I don't know. I suggested that he hang it in a prominent place for all to see, and we'd find out what fish our bait attracts, but we'll have to ask him."

"Let us go look for it."

"You haven't told me what happened with Beauford and Cynthia."

"Let's start with the fact they are truly in love, and he is the father of the babe growing inside of her," Emily said. "Iris was right—the baroness is at the root of his actions. She put him up to disenfranchising Jack. It's all part of her evil plan to possess *Il Leto* and the time-travel portal. Beauford is the source of the lies against Jack."

"I don't even know what the rumors were, but they were terrible enough to cause him to be shunned from society and for his father to disinherit him."

Emily wanted Gabriella and herself out of the depressing room and into the sunlight. She threw her arms around Gaby, and they hugged one another tight. Their embrace was interrupted by a knock on the door.

"Gaby, may I come in, please?"

Gaby shook her head no and grabbed Emily's hand. "It's Jack. What should I do?" she whispered.

Emily whispered back, "Let him in, of course. You know you want to. Do you want me to leave?"

"Absolutely not!"

"Gaby, I know you're in there. I beg you not to turn me away."

Emily rose from the bed and smoothed her skirt. With her hand on the doorknob, she looked back at Gaby, who was running her fingers through her hair, neatening it as best she could. "Are you ready?"

"As ready as I'll ever be."

Emily swung the door open. Jack's gaze shifted from her to Gabriella. He looked confused and unsure of what would come next, but seemed to quickly regain his composure.

With his shoulders back and the intensity of his gaze fastened on Gaby, he began. "I've been a complete ass, and I'm sorry. I beg you to forgive me." It was apparent he'd given what he said immense thought.

Emily nodded, looking pleased. "That's a very good start, my lord." She closed the door behind Jack. "Don't you think so, Gaby?"

"I-I..." The tears that had all but dried up sprang forth replenished, and Gaby wiped at her eyes. "I'm sorry too."

"Oh, bother," said Emily. "You have nothing to apologize for, so please don't. Frankly, you two need to get your act together, as we have bigger problems to solve. Now, get on with it and kiss and make up."

Gaby jumped from the bed and ran into Jack's arms. "I love you Jack, but you must curb your suspicions and trust that I would never deceive you. If we don't have trust, we have nothing."

"I know you're right. I promise I will never doubt you again. I'm just a fool."

"That you are, my lord." Emily giggled.

CHAPTER THIRTY

Maremma, Italy
October 21, 1902

J ACK CLOSED HIS eyes and opened his mouth.
"Holy hell, that's simply scrumptious!"

"Do you want more?"

"I do!" He bent and kissed her lips.

"Jack! Your lips are all chocolatey." Gaby erupted in giggles. "I might have to swirl this all over your body and lick it off."

"Don't even think about trying that again, my lady." He helped himself to another bite and shook the spoon at her. "You don't think I'd stop you, do you?"

"Remember, what's good for the gander is good for the goose," Gaby said, licking the chocolate from the spoon.

Watching her made him hard. Never had he thought the kitchen could be a place for sensual delight, until Gaby came into his life. And now it was his favorite place to spend time with her. Next to in his bed, of course.

Gaby had made him breakfast and concocted something he'd never seen or tasted before, and he couldn't stop eating it. The eggs and fried pancetta were delicious, and the fruit-filled crepes were lighter than air; but the chocolate and hazelnut spread tasted simply decadent.

"You know we could make a fortune producing this on a

large scale."

Gaby chuckled. "Yes, we could. But I didn't come up with this idea. It's called Nutella, and it will be invented by an Italian baker named Pietro Ferrero in about forty-five years. So, it wouldn't be right to deprive him of that. Besides, the Ferrero family will go on to make wonderful and amazing treats for the entire world to enjoy. Trust me on this."

"What an incredible woman you are," he said. "You could take advantage of all the knowledge you have of the future, but instead, you've brought joy back into my life." He lifted her hand to his lips and placed a gentle kiss on her palm. "I'm sorry, my darling, for how I behaved yesterday. I lost control of my infernal temper, and I know I hurt you with my callousness. Please forgive me."

"Of course I forgive you." She placed her hand on his cheek. "I know how hard it must have been to see. I'm proud of you for restraining yourself from beating the shit out of him."

"Beating the crap out of him. What a unique way of putting it." He grinned.

"It's an expression from my time."

"Yes, I gathered. I can't wait to hear more of your unique expressions. But first things first." Jack pulled Gaby into his arms and kissed her with all the love he had inside.

"We're bloody starving, and you two are in here making out?"

Gaby and Jack pulled apart to see Emily standing there with a wide grin on her face. Colin, Jenee, and Xavier were standing next to them, with equally wide grins.

"W-we were just having breakfast," Gaby said.

Jack loved the blush coloring Gaby's cheeks. She was the most passionate woman he'd ever met, and here she was blushing like a debutante at her come-out ball. There were so many facets of her personality that he'd yet to discover, and he couldn't wait to know them all.

"I hope there's more, because if we're to be successful with our plans, we'll need sustenance," Colin quipped.

Jack chuckled. "Well, you'll have to ask the kitchen goddess to whip you something up. She's already done wonders for my mood."

"Jack!" Gaby gave him a playful smack on the arm.

Emily squealed. "OMG, is that a fruit crepe with Nutella?" Emily rushed over to them and hovered over the plate.

Gaby smiled. "It is."

"Stand back, madam." Jack held up his fork as if ready to duel. "I am sorry, but nothing and no one will come between me and this chocolatey delight."

Emily laughed. "My kingdom for a bite."

"Never you mind, Em," Gaby said. "There is plenty to go around. While I whip up some more crepes, fill us in on what happened with Cynthia and Beauford."

Everyone sat at the staff table and ate while Emily and Colin related what had transpired.

Jack could not believe his ears at first. He was still angry at Beauford for not having the twiddle-diddles to stand up to the baroness or contessa, or whoever she was. At least now he knew there were extenuating circumstances and he no longer wanted to, as Gaby so wonderfully put it, beat the shit out of Beauford.

"I can't eat another bite," Emily said. "Gaby, you must give me this recipe—the children will love it." She watched Colin clean his plate. "Of course, probably not as much as their father."

"You know more than anyone, my love, what a sweet tooth I have," Colin said with a grin.

"*Oui*," Xavier declared, "you know the French insist that no meal is complete without dessert."

"Oh, I want the recipe too," Jen said. "Xavier, *mon amour*, I've had croissants filled with this chocolate from my time. They were incredible."

"Well, then we definitely have to make it when we get back to Paris, *ma chèrie*."

Jack looked at the smiling faces seated around the table. New friends. Remarkable people that Gaby had brought into his life.

"Since we are all gathered here now, I cannot think of a better opportunity to say what I've been wanting to say for a while."

Everyone turned their attention to Jack.

"Oh, Jack. If you want another crepe, just say so." Gaby shook her head, chuckling.

"I know this may surprise you, but this is not about food." Jack knelt and took Gaby's hand.

Emily squealed and clapped her hands. "Oh, how I love a happy ending."

"Darling," said Colin, "you are such a romantic."

"Oh, Xavier." Jenee wiped her eyes and giggled. "This reminds me of when you had the concussion and kept telling me you loved me."

"*Mais oui*, it affected me like a truth serum."

Gaby put her finger to her lips, shushing them. "If you please, this is my special moment."

"What say you, my dearest Gaby?" Jack said. "Will you make me the happiest man in the world and marry me? I promise to love you until the day I die and will do everything I can to make you happy."

"Yes, yes." Gaby's hands flew to her mouth and her eyes filled with tears.

Jack jumped up and, wrapping his arms around the woman he adored, swung her around and around.

"Oh, Jack, I love you so much!" she shouted. "Now put me down. I'm getting dizzy."

Emily and Jenee looked at each other and squealed. They grabbed Gaby and pulled her into their arms as Jack accepted enthusiastic handshakes and congratulations from Colin and Xavier.

"We are very happy for you, *mon ami*," Xavier said. "And when all this is done, we will have a proper celebration—but for now, may we return to the problems at hand?"

"Quite right, old chap," Colin added. "We have a host of them to resolve."

"And most importantly, the reunion of Iris and Marco," Jenee added.

"Oh, is that all?" Jack chuckled. "Would you like to see where I've hung the painting?"

"You've read our minds, my darling," Gaby said.

"Lead the way, my good fellow," Colin added.

⤜⤜⤜⤛⤛⤛

"I STILL CAN'T get over the changes in the painting from the one we saw hanging in the Metropolitan," Gaby said, staring at Allegretto's *Il Leto*.

Jack had opened a secret door in the wall of books lining the wall on either side of the fireplace in the library, revealing a hidden room. Inside were mementos and heirlooms from his childhood and his mother. Xavier and Colin helped him remove the painting and hang it above the carved mantel. Jack had kept the painting hidden away in the locked library, and the only key had been hanging around his neck.

They all stood and admired the painting. This was not Allegretto's fading muse; instead, Iris could be seen in her full glory, with her red hair flowing over her shoulders. Her catlike green-eyed gaze was fixed on the artist, whose muscled back was turned to the viewer. The final portrait in *The Three Stages of Love* was so beautiful and sensual that it was hard for Gaby to tear her eyes away.

"Such an incredibly beautiful painting," Emily said. "And at least we know the real paintings will survive, because we saw them at the Met."

"Yes, but unfortunately, Iris's likeness will start to fade away in the paintings," Jenee said.

"Perhaps not," Gaby said. "Perhaps what we are doing here will reverse the fading of the paintings, and they will remain as beautiful as today."

"This painting will always remind me of you, my beauty," Jack said, slipping his arm around Gaby's waist. "It would have made a lovely addition to the collection at Singly Park, but I shall engage an artist to paint a portrait of you. That will satisfy my eye for artistic beauty."

"Did I hear mention of Singly Park, cousin?" Beauford strode into the room with Cynthia beside him, arms entwined.

Gaby felt Jack's tall frame stiffen beside her and saw his eyes darken with anger. She laid her hand over his hand resting on her waist. "It's all right, Jack. Remember everything we told you."

"Yes, I remember," Jack replied, meeting her gaze. When Emily and Colin had told them of Beauford's father, Jack's eyes had filled with sadness. He had told Gaby that he'd always liked his Uncle Bennett and loved his Aunt Beatrice, who'd been kind to him after his mother's death. He'd expressed regret to Gaby about having no idea the extent of the financial troubles his uncle had gotten himself into, and he doubted his father had known either.

"I know you must hate me for what I did, and I am here to apologize to you, cousin." Beauford stopped to clear his throat. "I must also tell you that with Colin's assistance, I will admit to what I have done, and your title, lands, and legacy will be returned to you and your good name reinstated."

"I must apologize to you as well, Jack, and to everyone here," Cynthia added. "I have been less than cordial and behaved like a spoiled child. I hope you can all forgive us. And in the future, I would welcome you all to our townhouse in London for a quiet celebration in about nine months." She blushed, and Gaby could see the strain that must have been lifted from her shoulders with the truth coming out.

Gaby knew more than most how the truth was a healing balm.

"We shall be returning to London as soon as possible, with a short detour to Gretna Green for a quiet and speedy ceremony," Beauford added, gazing down at Cynthia with adoring eyes.

"Over my dead body." The baroness strode in. "Cynthia, I am your guardian and the executor of your father and uncle's estates.

If you know what's good for you, I suggest you return to your room and send this four-flusher on his way. I—"

She spotted the painting, and her words died in her mouth.

"Cat got your tongue, baroness?" Jack said.

"Of course not. It is just a surprise. I did not know you'd found the Allegretto painting." She stared at the portrait, unable to drag her eyes away.

"Yes, the mysterious portrait you and everyone else seem to have an inordinate amount of interest in," Jack added.

"Did Stefano not inform you of my offer? I will pay you double whatever that American upstart has offered."

The baroness moved closer to the painting, and Gaby couldn't help but notice how her eyes were mesmerized by it.

"I thank you for your offer, but I have made other arrangements for the painting," Jack replied with a calm smile.

"What sort of arrangements?" the baroness asked in a sharp tone.

"That is none of your concern, *baroness*," Iris said, entering the library with Constance by her side. "Or should I call you Contessa Catarina di Farnese?"

Gaby's breath caught at how beautiful Iris looked. She had changed into a lilac-colored gown that appeared identical to the one she wore in the portrait. Her glorious red hair cascaded about her shoulders, and her glittery green eyes showed serenity and strength. She glowed with an inner radiance that matched the painting. It was as if she and the painting fed off each other's energy.

"You! It is you!" the baroness sputtered. "What madness is this?"

"The only madness here is you, who have been conniving to take possession of Allegretto's masterpiece. Your last attempt at cementing your power."

"How dare you!" the contessa said. "You're nothing but a cheap French whore and a Jewess. Marco was mine until you waltzed into his life and lured him away."

"Don't you dare speak his name," Iris said in a calm but deadly voice. "You are responsible for destroying numerous lives, including the deaths of Albert Maxwell and his brother Reginald."

Cynthia's hands flew to her mouth. "Oh my God, Papa and Uncle Bertie?"

"You can prove none of your wild accusations," the baroness said.

"*Oui*, I think we can," Iris replied. "With a simple exhumation of the bodies, we will find that both the baron and his brother died of poisoning. That is how your minion, the Nazi time traveler, operated. He not only murdered my parents and tried to kill me, but he defiled and murdered countless women in London and Paris. He was a serial killer, and Marco's elimination of him was a gift to mankind. You have tormented us long enough, Caterina." Iris smiled at Emily, Colin, Jenee, Xavier, Gabriella, and Constance. "These good people are my witnesses to your treachery; they know who you are and what you've done. Your evil ends here."

⇶⇸

A BLINDING BEAM of light shot from the painting, and Gaby moved closer to Jack. He tightened his arm around her waist and could feel her entire body tremble. He knew she must be afraid that the painting portal might drag her away.

"Don't worry, my beauty," he whispered in her ear. "I won't let anything happen to you."

She looked up, and her eyes met his. "I love you, Jack. No matter what happens, I will love you forever."

"I love you too, sweet Gaby. More than anything in this world, and I will fight anyone and anything to save you and keep you here. You know that, don't you?"

"I do, Jack. I do."

"But if you decide to go home—if you want to go back to your family—I will go with you."

"What?" Gaby seemed shaken by his admission.

"I mean it. I love you too much to lose you. Nothing else matters more than you." Jack had been so intent on regaining his title and lands that he hadn't stopped to think about what Gaby was giving up in staying with him. "Remember what you told me about your vision of Velia and Aranthur?"

"Yes."

"Fate has given us another chance. And I don't mean to waste it. I would go to the ends of the earth for you. So, if it means traveling to the future, I'll do it."

"Oh, Jack. I love you so much for saying that." Tears flowed from her eyes. "I will miss my family with all my heart and soul, but you are my home. And I want to make my life with you here."

"I love you, Gabriella D'Angelo."

"And I love you, John Henry Langsford."

"You have done all you can to destroy us, baroness, and you have failed," Constance declared, stepping closer to Iris in a protective gesture. "Evil like yours can never defeat true love."

"It is not over, Mrs. Shipley," the baroness said. "You know not what you are up against."

❊⟫⟫❊⟪⟪❊

A RADIANT GLOW surrounded Iris, an aura-like cloak that wavered and shimmered like a ruby. Gabriella remembered reading in a magazine that the ruby symbolized love, loyalty, creativity, and passion. Everyone was drawn to the strange light beam that emanated from the painting.

Gabriella saw something in the painting she'd never noticed before—the artist's hand extending to the woman on the bed wore a ruby set in gold on his first finger. There was a text scrolling around the stone that appeared indecipherable. Yet Gaby could hear her own voice reading the text in her head, in an ancient language she recognized. It was the language of Aranthur and Velia, the language she'd heard during her vision of a past life at the burial chamber in Populonia.

She could feel Velia, the Etruscan priestess, in her mind, and the voice rang pure as a bell.

"The gift of time is precious and should be spent well. There can be no reward for those who use and abuse our small allotment for selfish gain. Those that ignore the warning of the sacred trust will not find favor with the Holy One. Hold fast to the ring, for its power is great. The red stone bestows the breath of life or soaks the ground with the defiler's blood. Yours is the choice—do with it as you will, but know the consequences. Make no plea of ignorance, for none will find acceptance from the universal tribunal. The punishment will be the loss of time forever. Only the truth will prevail and bring peace and lasting love. Only love will bring enlightenment. It is not gold or gems that are the most precious things in the world, but love."

"I will see you in hell," screamed Catarina.

"Not this time, contessa," said Iris, who stepped closer to the painting. The red aura surrounding her grew brighter the nearer she got to the portal.

The contessa followed, her eyes gleaming wickedly. "Killing you will be the greatest pleasure I have ever known. Wolf Krämer, the Nazi who shot your parents, was a capable killer, but he let his lust cloud his judgment, destroying him in the end. He was sloppy, but I am not."

She inched nearer but was suddenly stopped. Colin, Xavier, Jack, and Beauford moved in front of her, forming a wall of solid muscle that blocked her from going farther.

But Catarina merely laughed, producing a rondel dagger. She held the thin, pointed knife over her head threateningly. "How many of you will I kill before I am stopped?"

In unison, Emily, Jenee, and Gaby cried out, "No!"

Meanwhile, Iris had reached the painting and, turning, faced her enemy. "You will not harm them. Thank you, my friends, but you must step away from her. This is between Catarina and me."

The men stepped to each side, forming a line of solid bodies that would force Catarina to run the gauntlet to reach Iris. Meanwhile, Gaby stood with Em and Jenee on one side of Iris, with Constance and Cynthia on the other.

"Iris, dear friend, be careful," Constance said.

"I am not afraid." Iris turned to Constance, whose eyes were swimming with tears. "We have already said our farewells, *ma chère amie*. But I want you to remember that I will never forget you, Constance."

"Nor I you, dearest Iris."

Behind Iris, the painting had begun to ripple as if waves washed its surface. The image of the candle on the table next to the bed started to flicker, casting light and shadow as the painting came to life.

Marco's head turned slowly, his gaze landing on Catarina. His charcoal eyes seemed lit with a blazing fire that made Gaby shudder.

"Marco," Catarina called, "you cannot save her. She will never leave through the portal without me. She is no match for me or my magic, and neither are you." She touched the emerald pendant around her neck, and a blinding beam of green light engulfed the room, swallowing the ruby glow.

The eerie green light was so overpowering that Gaby had to shield her eyes to adjust to the brightness. Peering through her fingers, she saw Marco point his finger ringed with the ruby toward Caterina. Like a laser, a beam of red light burst from his ring, driving Catarina backward. She was stunned at first, but then a hysterical laugh poured from her. The ear-piercing sound echoed around the room. But Marco and Iris stood calm, radiating strength.

Gaby could see that not even a bolt of lightning could have displaced their determination. They were fighting for their lives, and they were fighting for their love and future.

She glanced at Emily and couldn't understand the smile on her lips. Jenee was smiling too. They knew something Gaby did not—but then again, what they'd experienced in London and Paris could not have been that dissimilar to this. They believed in Marco and Iris, and she took their belief to heart. She needed to believe too. Gaby could feel a powerful energy from everyone in the room, uniting them as a force for good against Catarina's evil.

A formidable gust of wind lifted Gabriella's hair. It was eerie, and the same as what she'd felt when she'd time-traveled. The swirling, spinning vortex emerged from the painting. Every second, the decibel level of howling wind grew, and the lights in the library flickered.

Catarina arched like a cat ready to pounce, and her eyes looked as black as her heart. Her voice rose above the gusts, repeating an indecipherable incantation. It sounded like an ancient tongue.

Iris's eyes closed, and she threw her head back, opening her arms wide as if in supplication. Marco's hand wearing the ruby ring reached through the swirling vortex of the painting, and a beam of light shot from the gem that he pointed at Catarina.

His voice filled the silence. *"Il tuo regno di terrore finisce qui!"*

Gabriella shuddered at Marco's powerful vow: *Your reign of terror ends here!*

The contessa responded with an evil laugh. *"Ci vediamo in Inferno!"* *I will see you in hell!*

The ruby's light hit the emerald, and the contessa's high-pitched scream of *"no"* pierced the air. The energy from the ruby shattered the emerald. In a blinding flash of illumination, it broke into a thousand shimmering pieces that floated in a circle for an instant and then disappeared.

In that instant, Iris reached up, and Marco grabbed her hand, lifting her into the whirling maelstrom of the time-travel portal. For a moment, wrapped in each other's arms, they gazed out of the painting, which was already beginning to disappear.

Above the roar of the wind, Iris's words were heard. "Thank you, my friends. May peace and love be yours forever." And then she and Marco vanished.

The contessa ran for the painting. With her hand raised and the dagger poised to strike, she hurled herself into the portal that was shrinking with every second. The contessa screamed a bloodcurdling cry, and out from the painting, a sword thrust and impaled her. She writhed as the blade passed through her, emerging from her back.

The ruby-ringed hand that held the sword retracted as swiftly as it had wielded its deathblow, and the contessa fell to the floor in a crumpled heap. A last burst of ruby light lit the room until it slowly faded away.

Gabriella expelled a breath of relief, her hand pressed against her heart as she tried to calm its beating. Catarina was dead, Marco and Iris were together at last, and all that remained of the painting was an empty frame.

I'm still here. Tears poured down her cheeks, and she turned around, seeing Jack stride toward her. He lifted her and turned her around in a dizzying circle. But she didn't care because she was in Jack's arms.

"My beauty," he whispered in her ear.

"My love," she whispered back. "Jack, I'm still here. I didn't get whisked away like before."

"I am eternally grateful for that. But now, I'm afraid you're stuck with me for good." His lips curved in a crooked grin.

"Well, I guess we'll just have to make the best of it." She giggled. "I'm sure I'll figure out some way to pass the time. You can always help me in the kitchen."

"Oh, I'm sure we shall be cooking up a storm, my beauty," Jack said before claiming her lips in a fierce kiss.

EPILOGUE

Maremma, Italy
October 26, 1902

THE DAY DAWNED with blue skies and autumnal sunshine that was unique to the magnificent coast of Tuscany at this time of year. Overhead, a flock of *fennicotteri*, flamingos, flew on the last leg of their journey to the *Laguna di Orbetello*, a lake where they would wait out the winter.

Gazing at such natural beauty, Gabriella imagined the beautiful pink birds to be a harbinger of blessings to come. After all, today was her wedding day, and her heart raced with excitement that soon she would be Jack's wife and their life together would truly begin.

Banished were any thoughts of the evil woman who had nearly destroyed them all. After the smoke had cleared, they all gathered in the dining room for the evening meal. Jenee and Xavier had whipped up a delicious French dish of cassoulet, and Emily had enlisted Colin for cleanup duty. Even Cynthia and Beauford helped. Beauford had formally apologized to Aunt Kitty, who'd been informed of the contessa's blackmail and the desperation he'd felt upon his father's suicide. She cried at the tragic ending of her brother-in-law and prayed for his soul to be at peace.

After dinner, over a simple dessert of strawberries dipped in

Gaby's chocolate hazelnut spread, Jack got on his knees and took out his mother's engagement ring. It was a magnificent ruby encircled with diamonds that Aunt Kitty had kept safe, along with the rest of his mother's jewelry. He asked Gaby to marry him again. She burst into tears and told him she'd already said yes. He replied that he would keep asking her every day until their wedding day. He had. And that had filled her heart with joy.

Em and Jen had rushed into her bedroom at the crack of dawn. Gaby was staying in the room Iris had been in. She still found it hard to believe they would never see Iris again, or Marco. She knew in her heart that they were finally truly happy and together forever.

Just as I am with Jack.

After a delightful morning spent with her two besties, giggling and teasing each other, Em and Jen had finally returned to their rooms to get dressed. Gaby took the opportunity to sneak out for a breather before the nuptials began.

With her veil trailing behind her, she opened the door and peeked out. Seeing the coast was clear, she scooted down the hallway and took the back stairs to the only place where she could find peace and calm, where she felt most at home.

A few minutes later, she entered the kitchen. The staff was busy preparing the wedding supper based on the menu Gaby had created. Both she and Jack would begin their life together on a creative note. She, with a spectacular meal she'd orchestrated, and Jack, accompanied by Aunt Kitty, would entertain after the nuptials with a recital.

Gaby had asked Jack what he planned to play, but he refused to tell her.

"You, my love, will have to wait like everyone else," he'd said, kissing the tip of her nose. "I don't believe I asked *you* what menu you have planned for the wedding. Please, allow me to surprise you, my darling."

The kitchen staff greeted her with shouts of congratulations. She and Jack had already informed them a few days ago that they would all be getting raises, to loud cheers. Gaby's eyes blurred with tears as she thanked her staff for their good wishes and asked them for a few minutes of privacy. Her devoted team wiped their hands on their aprons and walked out to the garden, giving her a few precious moments to gather her thoughts.

She'd been so busy preparing for today that she hardly had a minute to think about her family. She'd kept her emotions tucked inside, but she couldn't hide from her sadness a minute longer as tears spilled down her face.

I AM THE luckiest man alive. The woman he loved beyond measure would soon become his bride and countess, and his life would truly begin.

It would be a small wedding attended by friends and a sprinkling of family. Then Jack would whisk his beloved Gaby away to his ancestral home of Singly Park. Beauford had, to his credit, delivered on his word—Jack had received a telegram yesterday that his estate and title had been restored to him. "More cause for celebration," he'd announced last night to everyone at the pre-wedding dinner. But he'd noticed a faraway look in Gaby's eyes and surmised why.

Em and Jen had insisted that he and Gaby spend the night apart, much to his frustration. And the three "besties," as they oddly called themselves, had been in Gaby's room since the crack of dawn. He knew because he'd nonchalantly strolled down the hall several times to sneak a private moment with Gaby and heard their giggles.

Impatient, he rechecked his watch and thought he'd try again. He strode down the hall and laid his ear to the door. Not hearing any giggles, he turned the knob and poked his head in. The room was empty. A moment of panic took hold, and he turned to run to Emily and Colin's room—and then he stopped and realized he knew precisely where Gaby would be.

Jack entered the kitchen quietly, noting the delectable aromas floating in the air. He scanned the room, his gaze finding her just like last time. And just like last time, he waited for her to speak.

Jack's heart constricted at the sight of her tears. He didn't doubt her love and knew she didn't regret her decision, but he understood the source of her tears very well.

"You're not supposed to see the bride in her wedding gown," she said, sniffling as she wiped her cheeks. "It's bad luck."

"My darling, an old wives' tale will not cast any shadows on our union. Please, may I sit down?"

She wagged her finger at him. "Do not even think about this ending like last time. Em and Jen worked feverishly on my hair, and I can't show up looking like a rumpled mess and sporting a bedhead. Promise me no funny business."

"I promise," Jack said, crossing his heart, his lips twitching at Gaby's words. The way she spoke never ceased to delight him. Despite his promise, Jack couldn't help but remember the romantic tryst on this bench and struggled to control his yearning for a repeat performance. He cleared his throat. "I have something for you."

She held up her hand, displaying the beautiful diamond-encircled ruby set in gold. "What else could you possibly have for me, Jack? I have everything I've ever wanted. I have you."

"You don't have this." He pulled something out of his pocket and handed it to her. She shook her head, smiling. Jack watched Gaby remove the book from the velvet pouch he'd wrapped it in.

"*The Time Traveler's Lover?*" She looked up at him with eyes wide and questioning.

"It is the contessa's copy."

Gaby shuddered. "I don't want it!"

"It's all right, my love—it's just the book—but you need to flip to the end, the author's note in particular."

Jack wrapped his arm around Gaby's shoulder as she flipped to the end of the book, her hands shaking. She gasped and her voice trembled with emotion as she read. "*I dedicate* The Time Traveler's Lover *to three incredible women: Emily Christie, Jenee*

Lazaar, and Gabriella D'Angelo, without whose help I would never have been reunited with my soul mate, Marco Allegretto. Friendship and love are two sides of a coin. Without them, the world would be a sadder place indeed. Be happy, my dearests, with the love you have found, and may your families find peace in knowing you are with your beloveds. Until we meet again, Iris Bellerose."

A sob escaped her, and Jack pulled her against his chest. "I believe your family knows and is happy for you," he whispered. "When we come back here to visit Aunt Kitty, I thought we could take a trip to the village where your family is from."

"Oh, Jack, that would be wonderful. Imagine, I might actually meet my grandparents as children! That would make me so happy."

"I would do anything to make you happy, my sweet Gaby." He leaned down and claimed her lips in a deep kiss. "Shall we get married, my love?"

"Yes."

"Then let our journey begin."

ABOUT THE AUTHOR

Belle Ami writes breathtaking international thrillers, compelling historical fiction, and riveting romantic suspense with a touch of sensual heat. A self-confessed news junkie, Belle loves to create cutting-edge stories, weaving world issues, espionage, fast-paced action, and of course, redemptive love. Belle's series and stand-alone novels include the following:

TIP OF THE SPEAR SERIES: A continuing, contemporary, international espionage, suspense-thriller series with romantic elements. TIP OF THE SPEAR includes the acclaimed *Escape*, *Vengeance*, *Ransom*, and *Exposed*.

OUT OF TIME SERIES: A continuing, time-travel, art-thriller series with romantic elements. OUT OF TIME INCLUDES includes the #1 Amazon bestsellers *The Girl Who Knew da Vinci* and *The Girl Who Loved Caravaggio,* and the new release, *The Girl Who Adored Rembrandt.*

THE BLUE COAT SAGA: A three-part serial, time-travel, suspense thriller with romantic elements set in the present-day and in World War II. THE BLUE COAT SAGA includes *The Rendezvous in Paris, The Lost Legacy of Time,* and *The Secret Book of Names.*

The Last Daughter is a compelling and heart-wrenching World War II historical fiction novel based on the life of Belle Ami's mother, Dina Frydman, and her incredible true story of surviving the Holocaust. The story begins at the dawn of World War II and follows the Nazi invasion and occupation of Poland, focusing on the Nazi's six-year reign of terror on the Jews of Poland, and the horrors of the death camps at Bergen-Belsen and Auschwitz, where more than six-million Jews along with other vulnerable innocents were slaughtered.

Belle is also the author of the romantic suspense series THE ONLY ONE, which includes *The One, The One & More*, and *One More Time is Not Enough*.

Recently, Belle was honored to be included in the RWA-LARA *Christmas Anthology Holiday Ever After*, featuring her short story, *The Christmas Encounter*.

A former Kathryn McBride scholar of Bryn Mawr College in Pennsylvania, Belle, is also thrilled to be a recipient of the RONE, RAVEN, Readers' Favorite Award, and the Book Excellence Award.

Belle's passions include hiking, boxing, skiing, cooking, travel, and of course, writing. She lives in Southern California with her husband, two children, a horse named Cindy Crawford, and her brilliant Chihuahua, Giorgio Armani.

Belle loves to hear from readers—
belle@belleamiauthor.com
Twitter: @BelleAmi5
Facebook: belleamiauthor
Instagram: belleamiauthor